To Sal
lots of

Lisa J Hobman
xx

MC #2

COMPANY OF SINNERS MC

SIX

LISA J HOBMAN

For my awesome readers.

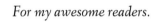

Your continued support means the world to me

CHAPTER ONE

CHLOE

"Nina, you're up."

The voice I dreaded hearing every Friday night sent the usual unwelcome chills down my spine and nausea swirling around the pit of my stomach. At twenty-one years old I should've been in college. I should've been mapping out my life and deciding where I wanted to be. *Who* I wanted to be. But instead there I was in *The Fox Hub* wearing a silver bikini top that left very little to the imagination and a matching lace edged thong as thin as cheese wire up my ass, virtually cutting me in two. Oh, in case you're not aware, body glitter is a *bitch*. No matter how many times I showered after my gigs, I could guarantee that I'd be finding the stuff in every crevice for days on end.

I checked my make-up one last time and smiled at my reflection in the mirror. "Come on, Chloe. You can do this. Just grit your teeth and think of something else. Anything else.

It's time to let Nina out to play." Giving my *real* self a firm talking to was a regular occurrence. The other girls would roll their eyes and snicker at me as I talked to myself in the mirror, but I didn't care. I *had* to switch into auto-pilot to have the guts to go out there—into the lion's den.

The other girls would do shots for Dutch courage, but I liked to have a clear head in case any of the clients got handsy. And I'd seen how ugly alcohol made people behave. Many of my so-called friends had wound up with unwanted pregnancies or STDs on account of the amount of alcohol they consumed, which lowered inhibitions *and* morals.

I wasn't prepared to go that way.

Not me.

I *had* been waitressing in town at a little round-the-clock coffee shop called *Hank's Place*, which was okay. It had contributed to the rent for a while but dancing—and I use that term loosely—was the thing that had brought in the tips and the big bucks. *And* it was the thing that meant I could stay in Utah. Going 'home' was simply *not* an option. So the coffee shop had been given up and replaced by more hours at *The Fox Hub*.

You're probably wondering why I couldn't just up and return to my 'real' home. Am I right? Well, let's just say that my upbringing was...*unhealthy* to say the least. I hadn't exactly had a great role model to look up to. My mom spent most of my childhood switching between two men. One who *could've* been considered father material—and who I presume *was* my real dad—and one had seen me as an inconvenience. Anyway, father material, Terry, died of a heart attack when I was twelve. *Inconvenience guy*, can't even remember his damn name, got sick of my mom and left when I was fifteen.

Unfortunately, when I was sixteen, a guy called Brett came into our lives. For a while everything was great. But, as with most things that appear too good to be true, Brett *was*.

Anyway, I digress.

Most of the patrons of *The Fox Hub* were great. There were always the ones who tried to cop a feel though. That made me feel physically sick. Especially when they were older guys who you could see had the shadow of a wedding band visible on their left hand. What the hell must their wives think they were up to while they were there drooling over scantily clad women? Having said all that, *I* was no one to judge. I wasn't exactly squeaky clean.

I stood and took a final long look in the mirror. Staring back at me was the almost unrecognizable woman I'd had to transform myself into. My naturally chocolate brown hair was mostly bleached blonde, except for a couple streaks in front. I wore thick make-up rather like a mask. I liked the fact that if Brett or my mom walked into the club they wouldn't recognize me easily. I didn't exactly blend into the background, but I looked *nothing* like the girl who had run away from home aged just eighteen.

I took a deep, calming breath and made my way out on to the stage. The opening bars to "I Appear Missing" by Queens of the Stone Age—the aptly titled song chosen for the night's dance—began to play and I slunk sexily out into the spotlight.

Gripping the pole and glancing out with a deliberate air of haughty nonchalance, I exuded an external confidence that hadn't quite reached my inner self. I wrapped one of my long, lean legs around the chrome pole. The chill of the metal startled me at first, as it always did, but I carried on regardless. It was fairly reminiscent of the chill seeping into my heart as I stared out at the nameless faces with their lascivious grins and beady eyes fixed on my barely-there bikini. The fact that Hogi —the club's owner—kept the air conditioning on freezing all the freaking time, meant that all the girls' nipples were forever poking through the minuscule slips of fabric they wore. *No* accident, believe me. Most girls just took their clothes off completely, but not me. I was clinging to my last shred of dignity.

No matter how small it was.

One guy in particular sat in the same spot every single week. He was one of the Company of Sinners bikers, that much I knew. But in spite of his gaze being fixed on me week after week, he never attempted to make any other type of contact with me. When I came off stage to collect empty glasses, he never once tried to touch me.

It was strange. It may sound pretty crazy, but the way he looked at me was somehow different. Okay, so there was a certain amount of lust in his eyes, but there was *more*. The way he periodically glanced around at the other men surrounding him, told of some misplaced desire to protect me from them. It was as though he was waiting for one of them to step out of line. Make a wrong move. I don't know. Whatever it was, I felt so much safer when he was there.

I'd never had a guy in my life who had wanted to protect me. Terry, father material guy, had *tried,* but Mom made it too difficult for him. She pushed him away so much that he never had the chance to really get to know me. But hey, I don't have daddy issues or anything like that so don't go feeling sorry for me. It was just nice to feel someone was looking out for me, you know?

The biker had this dirty-blonde, shaggy hair and a beard.

He was definitely older than me, but I couldn't figure out his age. Maybe twenty-six or so, I don't know. His eyes were dark, but then again the lighting in the club wouldn't let me see their color. He wore the CoSMiC leather cut and a T-shirt that showed off muscular tattooed biceps. The way his clothes fit to his body told me he was sculpted and worked out a hell of a lot. His hand rested on his thick, denim clad thigh while the other gripped a beer bottle that he would lift to his lips every so often. His eyes mostly remained fixed on me.

Every performance was for him. It was just a shame he didn't know it.

As I hung upside down, with my stilettos pointed to the ceiling and the pole between my ass cheeks, I fixed my gaze on him. My dirty-blonde biker. I wondered if I was imagining the protective edge to his stare.

I hoped not.

Josh Homme sang about the pain of loss and about disappearing, as the lyrics seeped into my psyche ringing a little too true. I glanced to my left and spotted another lecherous pair of eyes fixed on me. They belonged to a greasy looking, dark-haired man, and clearly in need of a shower. He undressed me with his seedy stare and I felt violated. It was a feeling I was too familiar with thanks to Brett, my mom's boyfriend.

A cold shiver traveled the full length of my spine and I had to look away when I realized where his hand was. The dirty bastard was playing with himself in full view of everyone, but he clearly didn't care. The CoSMiC guys were way over the other side of the stage and I was relieved about that. Imagining how my dirty-blonde haired biker would react if he saw this man getting off right there scared the shit out of me. Luckily, his gaze was still firmly trained on my body.

As the song finished, I lowered myself into the splits and arched my back, thrusting my breasts forward as a cheer and catcalls erupted from the CoSMiC biker's side of the stage. I felt heat rise in my cheeks and was thankful for the dim lighting as I snuck a glance at Dirty-Blonde. He was standing there banging his hands together like I'd just performed Beethoven's Fifth or something. Way to boost a shy girl's ego, biker man. I pulled my lips in to stifle a smile and rushed off stage.

CHAPTER TWO

Six

My beer bottle hovered just in front of my lips, but went no further as my eyes were transfixed on the curvaceous beauty before me.

My God she could fucking move.

And I don't just mean the incredible way she wrapped her toned legs around the pole and hung her lacy thong-covered ass upside down. There was something so *graceful* about the way she held herself. I mean that in the *general* sense of the word if you get me? Kind of like a butterfly...all beautiful and delicate. As poised as a ballerina. All long legs and tiny waist. Slender neck and delicate fingers.

Nina.

Even her name got me hard.

She couldn't have been a ballerina though. Nah...her gravity-defying tits would've stopped that career from the get go. Maybe that's what had happened? Who knew? All *I* knew was *she* was the main reason I came into *The Fox Hub* as it was. And yeah, okay I'm a hot blooded guy. Of course I get a kick out of watching pretty, half naked girls gyrate with their asses and tits on display, but there was more to it.

Much more.

She was amazing to watch.

Her long, wavy, bleached blonde hair with its darker streaks, cascaded down her lightly tanned, perfect skin as she tossed herself around with the most outstanding amount of strength for such a little thing. She wore too much make-up, but I could forgive that seeing as she was up there on stage. The triangles of fabric covering the peaks of her tits made my mouth water and I longed to see what was underneath. She was one of the only girls at the Hub who didn't go full frontal. She left a little to the imagination. And boy my imagination was good, but I was sure it was *nothing* compared to seeing her beautiful pink nipples in all their glory.

What I wouldn't give just to see...just to *taste*.

But that didn't change anything. I literally could—and did —watch her for hours both on and off stage. She was a real life, walking hard on. Fucking sexy as hell. Beautiful *and* graceful all tied up in one hell of a hard to reach, outta-my-league package that oozed a *don't-you-fucking-dare-touch-what-you-can't-afford* air of confidence.

I was becoming obsessed.

Who the fuck was I kidding? I was already there.

Friday nights at *The Fox Hub* were the main event for me. After the shit of the week, and the politics of the MC, it was good to let loose and chill with the guys in a place where we all fucking agreed for once. Our charter of Company of Sinners MC had been going through some major changes and we all agreed that the best way to spend the night was drinking ourselves sick and watching naked women dance.

Fuck *yeah*. We agreed all right.

This Friday was no different apart from the fact it was my birthday. Twenty-seven and I felt like an old man. Birthdays meant shit to me and it had been the same pretty much my whole life. The guys were planning something, I could just tell. But all I was bothered about was what was coming next.

Or should I say *who*.

I was sitting there, beer bottle in hand, waiting for Nina to make her first appearance of the night. She always came on at eleven. It was my favorite time of the whole damned week. Friday night...eleven p.m. My dick was already flinching in readiness.

Ever since I'd first laid eyes on her she'd played the focal part in my fantasies. Whether I was gripping my cock in the shower and imagining her on her knees before me, greedy and willing to suck me in between those ruby red lips, or whether I was laid in my bed picturing her straddling me—she was there. In my mind I visualized her perfectly rounded, pert tits bouncing when I lifted her, and slammed her down onto my dick as she screamed my name in sheer ecstasy.

Every. Single. Fantasy.

But of course the guys took great pleasure in poking fun at me. Fuck, I was always half expecting the "*Six and Nina sitting in a tree*" shit. Those fucking pricks were so goddamn immature. And of course the school-yard humor always kicked in when it came to our names.

Six and Nina.

You know how those celebrity couples get kinda merged when they get together? Brangelina, TomKat, etc? Yeah well the guys referred to us as *SixtyNiner*. Like I said...real fucking mature.

There wasn't even an 'us' to think about.

The other thing was, I knew that she didn't go by her real name.

Sadly, the same couldn't be said for me.

I'm gonna digress. Now this may become a pain in the ass, but I'll have to tell you things as they come to me. So if you wanna know my shit, then you'll just shut the fuck up and stick with me. Okay?

Okay.

So...I should probably explain my name, huh? I can warn you that it's not pretty. But I won't bore you with *all* the gory details. Let's face it, there are more exciting things I could talk about than my sorry-ass excuse for an upbringing.

My mom was an MC fuck buddy down in Florida where I was born. Oh boy, does it make me proud to say that. Note the fucking sarcasm *please*.

Anyways...she had six kids to six different guys. My siblings range in normality of name from Kyle...the oldest...to Star-Unicorn...my older sister who thankfully now goes by the name of Una. We were all taken into care at various stages as Sherry's—my mom's—drugs habit got the better of her.

By the time I came along I think Sherry had *totally* given up on thinking of *actual* names for her kids. That or she just couldn't be bothered. Either way I was named *Six*. Six Navarro if you want my Sunday name.

My father was the President of a motorcycle club in Florida—nothing to do with Company of Sinners—or CoSMiC as we're known—but I don't actually know much about the guy. Kind of difficult to remedy, seeing as I have no fuckin' clue where he is these days. And I don't have much memory of him. Well nothing positive anyways. He walked out of the club house after a charter meeting when I was four, left his bike and just fucked off. Never to be seen again. No one knows why. No one has heard from him since. Talk about a kid growing up with abandonment issues. Although I can't say I had an *actual* relationship with him as such. The memory that seems to stick with me—well more of a *sense* that I remember really—was that I was kind of an inconvenience when I was around him. I guess I cramped his style. It's hard to get pussy when you've got a little kid following you around and clinging to your leather cut.

I can't say I really know my mom all that well either. She's still alive. That much I'm pretty sure of. My brothers and sisters are scattered all over the country in the various places they were sent to get them away from our dear mother and I don't see *them* either. That kind of makes me sad. I guess when you've all been through the same crap it'd be nice to compare notes every now and again.

I had a shitty life going from foster home to foster home. Each family trying to convince me to cut my dirty-blonde shaggy hair and become *Steve* or *Simon*. But Six was both *what* and *who* I was. So I was determined that it would stay that way.

Unlike the other members of my dysfunctional family, I invariably ended up back with my mother at the club. Not that she noticed. It was the other women in the MC who did most of my caregiving. In fact, it was one such woman, Marla, who helped me find Colt and his crew up in Utah. I was eighteen and had already been in trouble with the cops for assault and theft. Marla told me she wanted me to get away from

Sherry in case I inherited her ability to make the worst decisions possible for any human being. I think she would've preferred for me to leave MC life all together but you tend to stick with what you know.

Okay...enough of my regression bullshit... I'll save it for my shrink. Ha! Fucking hilarious. I think I'd terrify the shit out of any fucking doctor. I kill myself sometimes I'm so funny. Sorry I'm digressing again.

So, there I was sitting in *The Fox Hub*. Front row. Waiting for Nina to make her main appearance of the night. My best buddy and *literal* partner in crime, Cain, was to my right with his lover in his lap. Why the fuck he wanted to bring Melody to this place I'll never know, but from the way they were sucking face I guessed that their surroundings were the last thing on their mind. That or it was doing their sex life a power of good. They should've just gotten a room. Cain's tongue was carrying out excavation work at the back of Mel's mouth from what I could see. It was weird to see him in a one on one relationship. Believe me when I say it was something of a rarity. You could say he was quite the ladies' man until she came along. Shit, who am I kidding? He was a man-whore! But Melody and her innocent ways reined him in.

Cain had always been the confident one. The girls just wet their panties as soon as he clocked them with his fucking blue eyes and gave them that half a smile thing he did. My hazel eyes didn't have the same impact. My beard pretty much hid half of my face, and I'm guessing that my unkempt dirty-blonde, in-need-of-a-serious-overhaul locks did nothing to add to my sex appeal, or *lack* thereof. Okay, I may be selling myself short a little. I've always worked out. I mean my fuckin' muscles have muscles. Add to that my abundance of tattoos and I think you get that I'm not the type of guy you take to church on Sunday.

Don't get me wrong. I got my fair share of attention. But the one woman that I *wanted* attention from didn't even know I existed. And that's why I sat there, every Friday night drinking my beer and hoping my dick wouldn't end up deformed on account of the way it strained at my jeans as soon as Nina wrapped her slender leg around the shiny chrome pole before me.

CHAPTER THREE

CHLOE

The darn glitter just wouldn't come off.

Once I was off stage, I sat there for what felt like forever, trying to get the sparkle off my crawling skin. I felt *anything* but sparkling on the inside. What I *really* wanted was a shower, but that wouldn't be happening for a while seeing as it was my turn to close up for the night. It was a shitty job, but we all had our slot and *this* was mine.

I walked back out and over to the bar to collect a tray. I hated that the patrons got so handsy when I walked around picking up the empty glasses. Unfortunately it was an occupational hazard and one that I couldn't seem to avoid. As I wandered around with the tray balanced on my hand, I wished I was somewhere warm. Somewhere cozy with someone who loved me. Okay, so I was twenty-one and I wasn't ready for *marriage* and all that crap, but just to *have* someone in my life who cared would've been good. It would've been enough. The one flaw in my dream was that I simply didn't trust men. Especially the ones that came into the club and let's face it, working the unsociable hours I did, it was the only place I was likely to come into contact with guys.

The boyfriends in my past had never stuck around long. I guess I bored them. They thought that they were dating some dirty nympho on account of my job and when they realized that in 'real life' I enjoyed lounging around in my PJs and watch romance movies, read or listen to music they lost interest. All I wanted was to be *loved*. My mom had loved me once.

Until Brett.

"Hey, Nina! C'mere, sweet cheeks." I turned, tray in hand to where Hogi had called me from. I rolled my eyes, thankful for the dim lighting in the club and made my way over to him.

"What's up Hogi?" The lack of enthusiasm in my voice was very evident, but I didn't care.

"Got a chance for you to make some extra cash tonight. You up for it?" He rubbed his chin as a sneaky smile lit up his rugged, aging features. He was a nice guy and he cared for his girls, but *everything* came down to cash.

Dread washed over me at what he was about to suggest. I placed my tray down on the bar and folded my arms across my chest. "Oh yeah? I'm not sleeping with anyone if that's what you're going to suggest."

His eyes widened and I regretted my words, knowing full well he would *never* ask one of his girls to do such a thing. "Fuck, Nina, I can't believe you would even *think* that. It was nothing like that. Jeez."

Sighing, I stepped closer, reached out and patted his tattooed forearm. "Sorry, Hogi. I know you would never ask that. Go ahead and tell me what you were going to say."

He smiled and held up his hands. "Okay, so, you don't *have* to say yes. No pressure. Just say the word and I'll tell them it's a no go."

"Tell *who* that *what's* a no go?" I just wanted him to get to the point so I could say no and get on with my job.

"The Sinners want to pay you for a special dance."

"The Sinners? You mean *Company of Sinners*? The *bikers*? They want *me* to do a special dance for *them*? Oh...I...I don't think...I mean I don't do—"

Hands rested on my shoulders from behind me and I turned my face to be greeted by one of the members of the MC. A really handsome guy, if you like the conventionally good looking types.

He squeezed my shoulders and smiled. "Hey, don't worry, it's not for *all* of us. Just one. My buddy has a birthday today and he *never* celebrates. We figured we'd treat him to something special. He watches you like a hawk and we reckon he'd love you to dance for him. I'll make it worth your while."

I swallowed and my heart began to pound. "I just don't usually *do* that kind of thing. You know the private dance stuff. I think I'd be too...I don't know...awkward and gawky. I'm fine with a pole but—"

The handsome guy placed a finger over my lips to silence me. "You're over thinking. He'll just be happy that you're *there*. And like I said, it'll be *worth* it."

Exhaling the breath from my lungs along with what felt like that last shred of dignity I was trying to hold on to and I shook my head. "I...I just don't know."

He turned me around and slipped his arm around my shoulder and pointed at his group of friends. "See that huge hulking, hairy bastard over there? It's *his* birthday. Now I totally understand if looking at him makes you wanna throw up." I gasped and turned to see handsome guy chuckling beside me. He continued. "But believe me, you would make his fucking *day*. No, his *year* if you said yes."

Oh. My. God. He was pointing directly at my dirty-blonde haired biker. My heart skipped. Here was an opportunity to actually *talk* to him. All I had to do was jiggle my tits in his face.

That thought halted me and I turned to face handsome guy again. "I'm sorry but I don't get naked. And I don't do 'extras'. Maybe you should get one of the others." I turned to make a hasty retreat as fear of humiliation niggled at me.

He stopped me. "Whoa. Look, I'm not asking you to *fuck* the guy. Just to *dance* for him. That's *all*." He held his hands out as if to express his innocence.

I looked back to Hogi who stood there, arms crossed over his chest and concern etched on his weather worn face. He shrugged at me and I took it to mean it was up to me.

Great.

Nervously, I returned my focus to handsome guy. "Okay. Just a *dance*. No hands. No nudity."

A wide smile spread across his face and he kind of fist bumped the air. "Yeah! Okay, you go get ready and I'll get him over there to wait." He pointed to the area off to the side of the stage that was sectioned off into a couple small rooms. I rarely ventured into there except to collect empty glasses. I had no clue what to expect from being in there for any other purpose. I nodded and he walked back over to his group looking rather pleased with himself. Nausea knotted my stomach and I turned to lean on the bar.

"You okay, sweet cheeks? You didn't *have* to agree to do it. You can still back out. No questions asked."

Taking a deep breath and hoping I would inhale some courage from the universe I shook my head. "No, it's fine. I'll be fine."

Once I was back in my dancing attire, minus any extra glitter, I made my way to the private dance rooms. They were small and kitted out with curved couches in red leather. Dim lighting was supposed to set the mood but all I was in the mood for was high tailing it out of Dodge. I knocked on the only door that was closed—an indication that it was in use—and a deep voice bid me to enter.

I stepped inside and there he sat. Blindfolded with a black and white bandana, his huge hands resting on thick denim clad thighs as they always were when he watched me. The fact that he was blindfolded gave me the opportunity to trail my assessing gaze over him and it irked me that my nipples stood to attention and a throb began between my legs. I had *never* had such a physical reaction at just the mere *sight* of a man. But something about him pulled at me. Turned me on. The heat of desire coiled deep within me and I wondered what it would feel like to have those long, fingers trailing over my skin.

Suddenly his deep, gravelly voice snatched me from my fantasy. "Um... I'm sorry about this. My so called friends are a bunch of immature bastards. And I'm sure you're a sweet lady and all but I like my women more...um...my *own* age if you get me and I don't mean that to be offensive or disrespectful. But can we just tell them that we *did* this and then we can both go about the rest of our evenings in relative peace."

Shit. He likes his women older than me. Okay now I feel

really stupid. I cleared my throat. "I'm...gosh I'm sorry, I'll just go."

I was about turn when he reached up and almost ripped the bandana from his face. "Whoa wait!"

His eyes were wide and he held his hand up to halt me. "Fucking *dick*-weeds," he chuntered under his breath.

Confusion washed over me and I folded my arms over my chest to cover my almost naked breasts. "W-what? I don't—"

"No, *I'm* sorry. They told me *Cynthia* was going to dance for me. I mean she's a sweet old gal and all but...well that's just it...she's *old*."

I burst out laughing. "Cynthia? The seventy-year-old cleaning lady? Oh my God!" By this time I was bent double and holding my stomach. "They got you good!"

When I glanced up at him he was laughing too and shaking his head. Caramel eyes sparkled and laughter lines appeared at their corners. He had the best smile I had ever seen. This was the first time I'd seen it, but my gosh it was beautiful and lit up his entire ruggedly handsome face.

Once we had both calmed down and the laughter had subsided I thought I'd better find out if he wanted me to continue. "So...should I go or do you want—"

"God *no*, don't go. I'd like to...to watch you dance if that's okay?"

I chewed on my lip trying to stifle a smile. For a huge man who was part of the motorcycle club that had a bad reputation around the place he was awfully sweet.

My cheeks heated to a temperature just below spontaneous combustion. "Sure. But...You should know...it may not be that *great*...I'm a...a virgin."

His eyes widened in horror. "Shit, okay, um I think maybe you *should* go...I don't want to be the one—"

Okay he's completely misunderstood me. Stupid girl. "Not *that* kind of virgin. I mean private dance virgin. I've never done..." I waved at the empty space between us. "*this* before."

He heaved a huge sigh and rubbed his hands over his face. "Fuck. I wish we could start this over."

I smiled and our eyes met briefly and that was it. I was lost. I had to close my eyes to break the weird spell that had been cast and so I turned to flick on some music. "Breathe You In" by Stabbing Westward filled the void in the room and I inhaled deeply to calm my shredded nerves.

As the singer began his sultry delivery of sensual lyrics I began to stalk toward the biker like a she-wolf to her prey.

———

Six

It was as if some kind of mask descended over her beautiful features as she walked slowly toward me, one shapely, lean leg in front of the other with each pulsating beat. Eventually, she was standing in the space between my parted thighs and I gazed up at her, dumbstruck and with bated breath in anticipation of her next move. She ran her slender fingers down her neck, over her luscious breasts to her stomach and I watched every single part of their journey, wishing it was *me* touching her.

But I wasn't allowed.

Slowly and with a sultry grace, she turned and swayed her hips in time with the music, her perfect ass only inches from my face. My dick was hard as a rock and straining at the denim, and the lyrics of the song seeped into my brain. Had she chosen this song for me? Because *fuck,* the guy could've been singing from my own damn thoughts. I adjusted myself as discreetly as possible because if she looked at my crotch right then she would've clearly seen how aroused I was.

Bending over with parted thighs she ran her delicate hands along her legs and gripped the heels of her stilettos. Fuck me she was supple. The fact only fuelled the fire that had been set alight deep in my groin. My eyelids were heavy with a level of lust that I had *never* experienced before and I was shit scared I'd blow my fucking load just watching her.

Her neat little pussy was so close with only a thin string of silver fabric hiding it away from my greedy eyes. But my mind was working overtime. *What I wouldn't give for a taste...or to inhale the smell of her.* To slide my fingers...or my cock into her tight body and watch her writhe on top of me as I returned the pleasure I know for sure she'd give me. I had to swallow a groan as she turned and rested her hands on my thighs, pushing her firm, round tits in my face. Her nipples were stiff under the barely-there bikini top she wore and I wondered if that was because of the air conditioning...or if it was because she was as turned on as I was. She moved her face so that her breath feathered over my ear and I had to clench my fists tight to stop them from moving of their own volition.

Arching her back she grabbed her tits and pushed them together as she raised her leg and rested it on my shoulder. My breathing quickened along with the pounding of my heart as I came face to face with her flat belly and minuscule bikini bottom again. It took all the physical restraint I had to stop from leaning forward and inhaling her intimate scent. Breathing her in, just like the song had said. But in a split second she moved and the song began to fade.

She crossed her arms over her chest and cleared her throat. "Umm...I think...I think we're done."

I took a deep breath and nodded my head unable to gather my thoughts. Well actually, I was gathering *plenty* of thoughts, but none of them were appropriate to speak out loud.

After rummaging around the lust filled fog of my brain for what seemed like hours I rubbed my hands over my face and then smiled up at her, hoping to be reassuring. "Well, wow...that was...that was..."

"Dumb. I know. God, why did they ask me to *do* this. I'm useless." Her voice wavered and she covered her face, turning her back on me.

I stood and stepped toward her. "Whoa, Nina, hey..." I placed my hands on her shoulders and she flinched.

She shrugged my hands off and turned to face me once more. Her eyes were glassy and I could feel the shame radiating from her body. "No touching, remember?"

Holding up my hands I smiled again. "Sorry. Sorry, you're *right*. But you're *wrong* about being useless. You certainly know how to move...and how to get a guy...you know...riled up and all."

"Yeah well you can blame your stupid friends. They could've gotten someone more experienced."

For a beautiful, sexy woman she had the self-esteem of a bucket. I stepped toward her carefully, still with my hands up. "Nina, *you*'re the one they knew I'd want to dance for me. That's why they chose *you*."

Before she could reply there was a knock on the door. "You done in there?" Hogi's harsh tone told me what I couldn't see in his expression. He was none too happy about letting this girl be alone with me. It was kinda sweet that he was so protective.

She called back, "Yeah, Hogi, we're done."

The door flung open and he thrust a robe into Nina's hands. "Go on and get changed, sweet cheeks. There's glasses to collect out there."

She grabbed the robe and scuttled off, wrapping it around her as she moved. But I caught one last glimpse of her gorgeous ass.

Hogi's voice once again ripped me from my fantasy when he growled. "Hey. Mind out of the gutter, kiddo. She ain't *like* that. And I don't care who the hell you think you are, you ain't getting what you want if I got any say in it."

Anger spiked within me. How the hell did he know what I *wanted*? And who the hell was he to judge me anyway? Okay, so I had a reputation. The whole Company of Sinners did. But he didn't know *me*. He didn't know my fucking mind.

I stepped toward him. "Oh, don't you worry old man. I know she's not one of your *usual* girls."

"Hey! What do you mean by—"

I stepped around him and walked away. I'd had enough judgment to last me a damn lifetime. And yes he was *right*. I *did* want her. Who *wouldn't*? But it wasn't *like* that with her. *She* was different.

Completely and utterly different.

CHAPTER FOUR

Chloe

Thankfully, the ladies room was empty. I stepped into a stall, closed the door, flipped down the lid on the toilet and sat on the closed seat. My heart was hammering at my ribs and my cheeks were on fire. I had never felt so humiliated in my whole life. I knew that I could dance but *that* kind of dance, up close and personal, for *him* of all people was just the most horrific thing I had *ever* done. *Why couldn't I have more confidence? Why was I such a klutz?* I almost fell over when I lifted my leg and rested it on his shoulder. *Why the hell did I do that anyway? Do lap dancers even do that?* I had no damn clue. Because I was a complete novice and they should have asked *anybody* but me to do that for the poor guy's *birthday.*

Shit I forgot to wish him a happy birthday. Urgh! Dumb bitch.

I had visions of him going back to his friends and laughing

about what a lame dance I'd given him. I imagined him telling them all about how I shoved my ass in his face as they laughed *their* asses off. *Oh shit, why did I shove my ass in his damn face? What must he have thought? I must have looked so fricking stupid! Not at all like his other women I bet.* I could have slapped myself I was so angry. The shitty thing was I knew I had to go back out there.

I had to face him again.

Could my night get any worse?

———

I despised the booths section. This was where the sleazes usually hung out and as much as I tried to avoid it I could guarantee that the other waitresses did the same and it would be left to *me* to clear them.

Tonight was no different.

The area seemed darker than usual and as I leaned in to lift some empty glasses from a table someone grabbed my wrist and pulled me down. I yelped and peered up at the dark figure whose sinister laugh and acrid breath sent a wave of nausea rolling through me. If I had believed in demons I would've guessed this guy was one.

"Hey sugar lips. Hows about you wrap those long legs of yours around me and I show you a good time?"

More nausea.

As he leaned forward and the club lights glinted in his eyes I recognized the sleazy pervert from the side of the stage earlier. I struggled against him but his grip was tight and my heart began to race as panic took over.

"Let. Go. Of. Me." I requested slowly and firmly through gritted teeth, desperate not to show fear. Creeps like him got off on that.

He pulled my hand to the bulge in his jeans and I think I threw up in my mouth a little as he pressed it there. "Awww come on, baby. I'm hard and ready for you. You know you want it."

Memories of Brett's advances rushed back to haunt me and I struggled to remove my hand from where it was trapped. "Believe me when I say this. There is *nothing* I would dislike more than wrapping *anything* around you, except my hands around your throat, you fucking pervert, now let GO!!" I shouted, and with all the strength I could muster I shoved him back.

He gripped me again and tried to push me back into the booth. "You're a fucking prick tease you little whore. If I wanna fuck you then I'll fuck you and you'll take what I got, you hear me?" As the slime bag used the same words as my mom's boyfriend Brett had, and *his* voice echoed through my mind, I cursed the ridiculously loud music and dark corner of the club. I cursed the fact that I'd run away from home and into a shitty life. I cursed my mother for believing her asshole of a boyfriend over me when I told her about his sexual advances.

I began to scream and slap the predator looming over me with the small amount of movement I was able to make; but his legs were wrapped around mine and my struggles were almost in vain. Tears stung at my eyes and I hated the fact that this bastard had no regard at all for me as a human being.

Thankfully he'd had a lot to drink and his coordination

wasn't great. As I struggled, I managed to pull myself to a sitting position and shove him back once again. He lurched forward to make another grab for me and caught my cheekbone with his knuckles. It hurt like a bitch and I whimpered trying in vain to free myself from his vice-like grip. His face was getting closer and in my brain he was like some rabid dog about to bite, but a huge fist flew over my shoulder and connected with his face with a loud crack that I heard even *over* the music.

My assailant fell backward, out cold.

With a pounding heart and tears in my eyes, I yelped again as two huge arms scooped me up and carried me toward the exit. I wanted to fight—to resist being carried away by yet *another* predator, but I was spent. Almost resigned to my fate. With my face buried in the hard chest of whomever it was that had pulled me from the booth, I crumpled into a sobbing mess, hoping he would take pity on me and let me go.

As we passed the bar I heard a deep, gruff voice shouting. "Hey, Hogi, you dumb bastard. So much for protecting her. I suggest you take better care of your damn girls before one of them gets into serious fucking trouble. Nina won't be back any time soon. Fucking ass-wipe."

"What the— Hey! Who the fuck do you think you are? Bring her back!" Hogi shouted in response.

My captor stopped in his tracks and I felt him turn around. "Who do *I* think I fucking am?" He growled. "Take a good look at my face, Hogi. You *know* who the fuck I am. I just saved this girl from being molested by an unwelcome guest. He's out cold in booth four. I suggest you contact Loki's Legion and get them to collect their fucking trash." The familiar voice vibrated through my head where it rested on the man's chest as he pushed through a door and a cold blast of air hit me.

We were outside.

I began to shiver and shudder, and the arms of the man who carried me tightened around my body. His heat seeped into my bones and relief flooded me. I knew I was safe with him. I felt myself being placed down on the hood of a car and I finally dared to lift my gaze. Slowly I began to raise my head. First, taking in the tight T-shirt and leather cut that was covered in patches depicting winged skulls. One of them held the words 'Vice President' and my foggy brain wondered *"Of what?"* As my chin tilted further upward I encountered tattooed biceps and the straggly ends of dirty-blonde hair, followed by a square but bearded chin and lips pulled into a tight line. Finally I locked eyes with the man who I had danced for only an hour earlier but who had rescued me from the clutches of the monster.

"Hey. Are you okay?" His voice was soft and his concerned gaze trailed over my face and body as if he was assessing me for damage.

"I'm...I'm...thank you...thank you so much. If you hadn't come, I don't know—"

He cupped my chin and delicately ran his thumb over my lips. "Shhh. Don't even think about that, okay? It's over now." He tucked a strand of hair behind my ear. "You look like you're freezing. Hang on." He stepped away and opened the car door. I watched as he rummaged around a while and then he came back with a hooded sweater. Without speaking, he pulled it down over my head and I slipped my arms into the ridiculously long sleeves.

He stepped back as I pulled the sleeves up my arms until

my hands poked out. I felt my cheeks heat again as I shyly smiled up at him.

He chuckled. "See, looks better on you for sure."

A combination of shyness and embarrassment tightened my stomach and I glanced down to take in the CoSMiC logo on the hoodie. Bringing my gaze back up to meet his I whispered, "Thank you." Now that the panic had subsided I could really look at the man before me. "And thank you again for what you did."

He shook his head. "No need to thank me, Nina. He shouldn't have been in there. He's on CoSMiC territory and that shit's not allowed. And you shouldn't be treated that way."

He had the most beautiful, kind, caramel eyes I had ever seen and his soft tone made me relax further. I hugged my arms around myself. "I...I didn't catch your name earlier on, you know, in the private room. Oh and happy birthday."

He rubbed the back of his neck and scrunched his face. "Thanks. Six. I'm Six."

Around a hundred silly retorts fought to get out about him looking a hell of a lot older than that, but after the guy had been so good to me I couldn't bear to set them free.

Instead I said, "That's...*unusual*. Is it a nickname?"

His eyebrows rose and he shook his head, turning away as if embarrassed or something. "Nope. It's the real deal." He must have taken my silence for a questioning pause and continued, "Long story. Don't wanna bore ya."

Who names their child 'Six'? From the way he wouldn't meet my gaze suddenly I guessed it wasn't an easy story to tell and so I didn't pry. "Well *Nina* isn't my real name."

He turned to meet my eyes once more and tilted his head

to one side as a half-smile tugged his mouth up at the corner. "Truth be told, you don't *look* like a Nina."

I was intrigued with the fact that he didn't enquire about *my* real name and so I offered it. "My name's Chloe."

His eyes widened and a huge grin appeared on his face. "No kidding? Chloe dancer, huh?" He wagged a finger at me as if something had just slotted into place in his mind. "There's a song by Mother Love Bone about you."

The handsome smile that had spread across his face was infectious and sent tingles down my spine. I was even more curious. "Really? I've never heard it. And it's Chloe Meyer actually."

He held his hand out and I took it. "Six Navarro. Good to meet you...officially that is. You should check the song out. Every time I listen to it from now it'll remind me of you."

God, could he get any sweeter?

He cleared his throat and ran his hands through his scruffy hair and I guessed if the lights in the parking lot were brighter I would have seen him blushing.

He gestured to the car I was sitting on. "Anyway, can I give you a ride home?"

I turned around and glanced at the sleek black car and then back to him with raised brows. "*This* is you? I thought you guys rode motorcycles."

"Yeah we do. But I like cars too. Sue me." He shrugged. "This old Camaro here is my pride and joy aside from the Harley of course. Don't worry, I don't drive drunk. Only had one beer the whole night."

I scrunched my brow. "*One* beer? Seriously? On your *birthday*?"

He laughed and from the way he stepped from foot to foot

I could tell he was embarrassed by his admission. "Yeah...kind of had my attention elsewhere I guess."

Realizing he meant he had been watching *me* rather than drinking excessively, my heart did a funny flutter in my chest. "Look, I think I'm okay to go back in there. I feel okay now and—" The vehement shake of his head and his wide eyes told me he had other plans.

He held his hands up. "Uh-uh. No way, Chloe dancer. Once that bastard wakes up he'll be looking for you and he'll he baying for blood. Best thing you can do is go home. Those guys don't take no for an answer. If I'm completely honest, I probably didn't help. I'm guessing he saw us coming out of the same private room. He'll think you're mine now and that'll make the challenge all the more exciting. There's some serious shit between the clubs right now. Maybe you should lay low. Maybe take off for a few days."

I laughed incredulously. Little did he know that there was nowhere I *could* go. "Hey, I'm a big girl, Six. I think I can look after myself. And besides *this* is my livelihood. Without this place I have no rent money, no food money..."

He stepped into my space again and tenderly cupped my face in his shovel of a palm. The sweet gesture took me by surprise and I inhaled sharply as his eyes bore into me.

He grazed his thumb over my cheek. "I get that you're independent okay? I really do. But...you don't mess with these guys. With...with the likes of *us*, I mean. I'm telling you this for your own good. We're not..." He inhaled deeply and his nostrils flared. "We're not the most understanding people. And the last thing I want to hear is that he *hurt* you again, okay? Please...for me?"

The intensity in his warm eyes caught me by the heart

and once again it skipped and began to pound at my chest. "O-okay."

Relief washed over his features and his furrowed brow relaxed. "So how about that ride home, huh?"

"Sure, thanks. It's not far."

CHAPTER FIVE

Chloe

He held his arms out to help me down from the hood of the car and I slipped my hands into his where they were swallowed up. Once I was back on terra firma he opened the passenger door for me and I climbed in just as a commotion began to kick off over at the club. Six slammed the car door and hit the lock on the key fob. My heart began to race once more as I saw him running toward a crowd of people all wearing leather cuts. Fists were flying and the sounds of shouted insults and expletives filled the air.

I leaned forward to get a closer look and it appeared that there were two separate groups of people engaged in the ruckus. Some I recognized as Six's crew and some I knew were not. The guy who had tried to molest me was there and I watched in horror as I saw his balled fist connect with Six's cheek. A yelp left my chest and I frantically tried to unlock the car door. I wasn't sure how he had managed it but the door was stuck fast and I had no escape. Although I wasn't sure what I would've done if I'd been *able* to get out. I just wanted to go protect him as he had me.

The piercing sound of sirens began to get louder and suddenly the crowds began to scatter. Six and another one of his crew jogged toward me and I heard the door unlock.

As he reached the driver side door and opened it he bent to look at me and my hands sprang to my face. "Oh my gosh, Six, are you okay?" Blood oozed from a deep cut on his cheek.

He reached up and touched his face and then glanced down at his blood covered fingers. "Yeah. I'm fine. It's just a scratch. Sorry you had to see that. Oh...this here is Cain, my buddy."

A face appeared beside him and I immediately recognized the blue eyed chick magnet from the bar. Girls were usually all over him but lately he only had eyes for the auburn-haired beauty that seemed to have pride of place on the back of his bike *and* in his lap these days. The way they looked at each other made me jealous. To have someone so into you must be the best feeling. And he was quite a handsome guy...like I said if you liked *obviously* handsome men. He had those bright, piercing irises that would draw most girls under his spell. But not me. I only had eyes for *one* bad ass biker.

I smiled politely. "Hi, Cain. I'm—"

"Cain you know *Nina* from the club right?" Six's voice startled me.

I turned to find his gaze fixed on my face and confusion washed over me. Why didn't he introduce me as Chloe? He climbed into the driver's seat and turned the keys in the ignition. The engine purred to life.

Cain chuckled. "Yeah we've met. Hi, Nina." He shook his head as he muttered something about the number sixty-nine that I guessed was some crude sexual reference connected to our names. It didn't surprise me. Those biker types were known around here for their promiscuity and bad manners. Although some charters were worse than others. From what I had heard CoSMiC were kind of the *good* guys. If that was even possible.

"Come on, I'll get you home." Six shoved his friend out of the way and he almost fell backward laughing hysterically.

He bent double with laughter. "Six, dude, don't be so sensitive."

I had to pull my lips in to stop my own giggle from escaping.

Six was not impressed, however. "Fuck off, Cain. Go sober up and take Melody home okay? She doesn't deserve to see you in such a fucking state, man.

Cain threw his head back and guffawed. "Whatever, *Dad*. Bye, Nina. You kids behave yourselves now!" He winked at me and once again I tried not to giggle as he wobbled around the parking lot in the direction of his girlfriend.

A couple of police cars pulled into the lot and before I had a chance to speak, Six slammed the door. I watched Cain flip him the bird with a cheesy grin on his face just before he grabbed his girl and dodged into the alley by the club and out of sight. So the player had a girlfriend huh? Poor woman. Did she realize what she was getting herself into?

Six pulled the car out of the lot with a screech of tires and he headed in the direction of my block. "I...I didn't tell you where I live."

He cringed and I watched his jaw working under his skin as his eyes remained fixed on the road. "I already know."

Although alarm bells should have been ringing something about him told me he was trustworthy and there would be a reasonable explanation. "Oh? How?"

He flicked his gaze to mine briefly and then focused on the road again. "Look, don't take this the wrong way, okay? But... I tend to follow you home when it's your turn to close up."

Suddenly the enclosed space felt too small and claustrophobia began to overtake me. I couldn't breathe as my life seemed to flash before my eyes. *Frick he's some kind of crazy, stalker maniac. I'm done for. He'll probably cut me into little pieces.*

I needed to get out. "Okay, that's *really* creepy," I said with a wavering voice and a pounding heart as I tried to process what he had just admitted to me. I reached for the door handle and pulled at it but my now clammy hands just slipped off and the door wouldn't budge which was probably good, as we were moving at speed. "*Please*...pull over and let me out of the car," I pleaded as fear needled at my skin.

He flicked his gaze between me and the road again. His brow crumpled and I couldn't tell if it was through anger or concern. "Chloe, you don't understand. I'm...I'm not some fucking crazy stalker." *Oh fricky-frick, he reads minds too?* He slammed his hand onto the steering wheel.

Not helping your case here buddy. "Really?" My raised voice surprised me. "Because you sure *sound* like one. I have enough creeps to deal with at the club I sure as hell don't need to be taking rides with them. Pull over and let me out of the fricking car!"

He heaved a deep, forceful sigh and did as I asked. The car jerked to a halt at the side of the road. He cut the engine and his knuckles turned white as he gripped the wheel. I felt my lip began to tremble. This was it. *Oh my gosh please let me escape. Please.* We were in the middle of an area surrounded by industrial buildings that were empty thanks to the time of night. Anxiety gripped my chest and my breathing rate increased. I was beginning to think I had jumped out of the frying pan and into the fire. He had warned me that he wasn't a guy to be messed with after all.

I had to try and make amends. To try and appease him somehow. "Look, I'm sorry for shouting at you. I didn't mean to call you a creep. Please...please don't hurt me."

He turned slowly to face me and shook his head. "Chloe dancer, sweetheart, I would *never* hurt you. *Ever*. I want to explain something to you. Can I just explain? *Please?*"

Tears spilled over from my eyes and I nodded. What choice did I have? I was trapped in this car with someone who had confessed to following me. *Stalking me.* Someone who never took his gaze off of me when he came into the club.

A sob left my chest.

He reached out and wiped the moisture from my face. "Oh fuck, I'm sorry, darlin', I didn't mean to scare you. I'm such a fucking idiot." His voice was tender and I began to hope that maybe I had misunderstood. "Look...I follow you home to make sure you get there safely. I stay out of sight because I don't *want* to freak you out." He gestured to our external surroundings. "This neighborhood is a scary ass place at night and I know who's out there. You have to know that I would *never* have approached you. I would *never* have tried to even *talk* to you. I...I just wanted to keep you *safe*. Nothing else. I promise you that. *Nothing* else." Pain was evident in his hazel eyes and I felt like such a fool. The poor guy had been looking out for me and I had almost accused him of being as bad as the bastard from the club.

Racked with guilt I covered my face with both hands and began to sob again. "Oh God, I'm so, so sorry. You must think—"

He reached out and pulled my hands away. "I think you're a girl who's been through a hell of a night. Don't cry, CD. I didn't mean to scare you. Of course the fact that a complete stranger knows where you live and has admitted to *following* you is going to scare the shit out of you. I'm an ass-hat. Feel free to slap me." His mouth widened in a heart stopping smile and I think my insides may have melted a little.

I laughed through my tears and scrunched my brow at what he'd called me. "CD?"

He shrugged. "Yeah. *Chloe dancer*, I shortened your name. Kinda cute huh?"

His smile was infectious and I responded with one. "Kinda... And thank you for caring."

His smile faded and he began to reach toward me but stopped. "Anytime. I care more than you know. Now come on, let's get you home."

Leaving those words hanging in the air he pulled away from the curb once more and we rode in silence until he turned into my apartment block lot and stopped.

Without making eye contact he dropped his gaze to his hands. "Is it... Should I ask? Aw hell...is it okay if I walk you up?"

I didn't need to think about it. "Sure it is. Thank you."

He turned to me and smiled that same delicious smile. "Great. Come on, Chloe dancer."

His pet name for me made me grin like an idiot. He came around, opened my door and held out his hand. "Oh and I'm sorry about earlier. The passenger door sticks shut and I need to get it looked at. I didn't mean to trap you in here. I swear."

I slipped my small hand into his and watched as his fingers closed around mine, engulfing them once more. A strange sense of belonging came over me and I tilted my head up toward him. He smoothed his thumb over my knuckles and I climbed out of the car.

Once the door was closed we began to walk toward my building but he didn't let go of my hand until we reached my door.

He turned to face me. "I'll wait until I hear the door lock before I leave. But... I meant what I said about laying low. The Legion and the Company are not the best of friends and after tonight I'm guessing there may be more shit hitting the fan. I don't want you caught up in it."

I began to protest. "I'm fine, honestly—"

Before I could get any more words out, his mouth was on mine and I staggered back. His thick arm came around my waist to steady me and he pulled me flush to his body. The thick ridge of his cock pressed into my belly and I inhaled sharply. His other hand slipped into my hair and cradled my head as I reached up and gripped the soft, worn leather of his cut.

The kiss was meant to shut me up and oh boy it worked. His lips were soft but demanding at the same time and his beard tickled my skin sending shivers down my spine. A number of irrational and inappropriate thoughts rambled around my head considering the night I'd had. But now I was sure he would never hurt me I wanted to feel his lips on every part of my body. What the hell was wrong with me? This was *so* not me.

Suddenly he pulled away and let go of me. He stepped back and rubbed his hands over his face. "Fuck, I'm sorry, Chloe. I had no right. Not after everything you've been through tonight. I've just...I've wanted to do that for the longest time. *Fuck*, my timing is shitty though huh? I didn't mean... I mean I—" His rambling was endearing.

I held up my hands. "No, no it's fine. Really." The truth was that, in-spite of the fucked up night I'd had, I hadn't *wanted* him to stop. Yes, it had been traumatic but *he* had saved me. And despite the earlier misunderstanding there was something about him that pulled me in. "Look, your face needs cleaning up. Why don't you come on in and let me look at it for you?"

He reached up and touched his cheek where a trail of blood had trickled. When he glanced down at the red smear on his fingers he cringed. "Aww shit, it's still bleeding."

I laughed at his response as the color drained from his face. "Huge guy like you scared of a little blood, huh?" I turned and unlocked the door. "After you. Although we may not fit in here at the same time." It was no joke. My apartment was *very* small and he was quite the opposite.

He followed me in and glanced around the living room. "Cute. *Tiny*...but cute." He laughed.

"Have a seat and I'll get some gauze and water." I walked through to my bathroom and collected what I needed from the cabinet. After closing the door, I stood there staring at my flushed reflection. I was still drowning in his oversized sweater and specks of glitter still glinted on my cheeks. I wondered absently if any had transferred onto Six. *A sparkly beard. Now that would look ridiculous*. I chuckled at the thought of him having to explain it to the rest of his MC.

CHAPTER SIX

Six

She disappeared through a door to my left and I could hear her rattling around. Her apartment was so fucking small. But then again so was she...well compared to *me* anyways. As I took in my unfamiliar surroundings, I noticed that there were lots of pictures on the walls, but none of them seemed to be photos. I couldn't see any indication that she had a family and my heart ached for her. I knew what *that* was like and it made me sad to think that someone as sweet as her may be the same.

She reappeared and placed a bowl of water on her coffee table along with some squares of gauze. She bent and dipped a square into the water.

Gazing up at her as she hovered over me I told her, "You don't have to do this you know. I can clean up when I get home."

She shrugged and carried on preparing the gauze. "It's the *least* I can do."

As she reached toward me, I grabbed her wrist. "Chloe, you owe me *nothing*, okay? I did what needed to be done. Any decent human being would've done the same." As she glanced down at her wrist and frowned I realized the irony of my words. *Decent? Me?* I realized that I sounded a little too aggressive which probably totally iced the shit cake and I released her arm. "Fuck, I'm sorry. I just... I don't want you thinking you *owe* me." Why couldn't I behave *better* around her?

I doubted that her responding smile was supposed to be sexy, but fuck if it was. My cock wanted in on the action and I felt my blood rushing south.

She reached toward me and dabbed gently at my face with a damp piece of gauze. "I *don't* feel that I owe you. But you got this nasty cut from protecting me so I'd like to take care of it for you."

Fuck me. She really was perfect.

And *I* wasn't.

Why the hell was she being so sweet? I'd scared her half to death, dragged her away from some molesting bastard who she then witnessed me punching, and then after all that I'd confessed to pretty much *stalking* her.

As she touched my face I closed my eyes. What I wouldn't give to make her mine. I'd wanted her since the moment I first laid eyes on her months ago, but I always thought she was out of my league. Maybe I was wrong.

Nah...who was I fucking kidding?

I was *damn* right.

I suddenly felt her soft lips press to my cheek where the bruising was and for a moment I didn't respond. I sat there, like a statue. Frozen and unable to move. Her breath warmed my skin and my dick strained at my jeans. I had *never* shown so much self-restraint. I told myself I deserved a pat on the back later.

Her feather light touch wiped the strands of hair from my forehead. "All done," she whispered and I blinked my eyes open. Her gaze was fixed on me and I wished that I could read her thoughts.

I swallowed hard and reached for her hand. I smoothed my thumb over the silky skin there. "Thank you. I really appreciate that, CD." My eyes were drawn to her full pink lips and I wanted nothing more than to kiss her again. To taste her lips once more. But after what she'd been through she didn't need another greasy fucking biker pawing at her. I stood quickly and stepped away from her running my hands through my hair just to keep from touching her. Being so close was messing with my head *and* other parts of my anatomy.

"I-I should go," I stuttered. "I'll check on you in a couple days. Just for my own peace of mind."

She stepped toward me and stopped as if unsure, her hands twisting in front of her. "You...you should stay for a drink."

I smiled sadly and slowly shook my head. "No...no I really *shouldn't*."

I knew that if I stayed I'd want *more* of her. I'd want to take her to bed. I'd want to find out what her skin felt like under my fingers. What her pussy would taste like and how it would clench around my cock as I made her come. But in the back of my mind was the worry that she would let those things happen out of some misplaced *gratitude*.

She was a nice girl and I would be damned if I was the one to change that—to corrupt her in any way. She wasn't like the other girls at the club. They threw themselves at guys on a regular basis but not Chloe. There was something pure about her. Regardless of the fact that she took her clothes off and danced around a shiny pole for money. I just knew that wasn't *who* she was. She was the only girl who didn't go full frontal. She was holding onto her dignity. But all it did to me was make me imagine what she would look like in all her naked glory. Pink nipples beading and neatly trimmed pussy displayed just for me.

What I wouldn't give.

She shrugged and dropped her gaze. "Oh...okay."

I lifted her chin and placed a kiss on her forehead. "Hey, don't misunderstand me, Chloe dancer. I have a voice in my head that's screaming at me to stay but... you've had a very rough night. You need some rest and I...well I need to go home and take a cold shower."

A blush spread from her chest to her cheeks and she chewed on her lip. "Okay. Well...thanks for bringing me home."

"Thanks for *letting* me." I turned and walked toward the door. "It was great to finally meet you."

She smiled widely and nodded. "Likewise." She glanced down at the sweater that swamped her curvy but slender frame and went to grab the hem. "I should give you this back."

I held up my hands. "Like I said, it looks better on you. Keep it." She folded her arms around her body and nodded and I had that urge to kiss her again. "Stay safe, CD...*please.*" And with that final comment I opened the door and left her, making sure I heard the door lock before I walked away.

———

I left Chloe's apartment and made straight for the MC. When I arrived I found Cain sitting in a corner kissing and cuddling with Melody and I wondered if he'd genuinely changed his player ways. Melody was a great girl and she deserved a guy who would treat her right. Unlike the skanks he used to end up in bed with who had a different guy every night. She was different and she deserved better. Much like Chloe dancer. Perhaps they were that rare type of girl who actually wanted to be *loved* not just *fucked*.

Delilah, one of the club's...what do I call her? Friends? Fuck buddies? Anyway, you get the idea. She was cleaning up behind the bar and I made my way over. Her longing gaze was fixed on Cain and Melody where they sat huddled together. Pity tugged at my insides for the poor girl. She'd always loved him. And he was like her walking piece of artwork. Almost every tattoo on his skin had been put there by Delilah. She was one bad-fucking-ass tattoo artist that's for sure. Cain was probably the finest walking example of her work.

I chucked my chin at her. "Hey, Dee. What's up?" I knew the answer but she looked like she needed someone to ask.

She smiled but her eyes didn't light up. In fact, they reflected such sadness that I almost vaulted the bar to hug the poor bitch.

She sighed dejectedly. "What does *she* have, Six? What's so amazing about *her*? Is it her fucking long, girly auburn hair? Is it her innocent green eyes? It sure as hell ain't her rack. And she has hardly any fucking ink. Jeez I just don't *get* it. Why was I not *good* enough for him?"

Her envious stare remained fixed on the loved up couple and so I stepped in to block her view. I glanced around behind me to observe the woman who had apparently stolen my best friend's heart. You could say that Delilah was the complete antithesis of all that was Melody, from the cropped blonde hair to the multitude of piercings and tats that adorned her curvy figure. Obviously I couldn't say all that out loud. I'm not a fucking *cruel* douche-bag.

So I settled for, "Aww Dee, it's not that at all, babe. He's a jerk. You're worth ten of that jackass."

She laughed and poured me a straight up Jack. "He's your best friend, Six, so I know you're lying. And flattery will get you nowhere. You know my heart belongs to another. But thanks for the vote of confidence."

I chuckled and downed my drink in one. "Anyone using the end room?"

"Nah, although Colt was saying we may be on lockdown if Loki's Legion decide to try and kick some CoSMiC ass. So it may not be free for long."

I rubbed my tired eyes. "Yeah...I'm surprised Colt hasn't kicked *my* ass over the whole deal."

She whacked me lightly with a towel. "Hey, from what I heard you're the hero. Saved one of the Foxes from one of the Legion bastards."

"Yeah. It was Nina."

Her mouth formed a knowing O and she widened her eyes. Everyone knew my thoughts about the dancer. Even the MC girls. I stood from the bar. "I'm gonna go take a shower."

Delilah winked at me. "Want me to send someone up to wash your back?"

I rolled my eyes and shook my head. She knew the answer. The MC girls did nothing for me. Not these days. I only had eyes...and other body parts...for one girl and much to my gut wrenching disappointment she wasn't there.

CHAPTER SEVEN

Six

The end room smelled fresh, which was a novelty. There was nothing nicer than climbing in between clean sheets. Unless you were climbing into clean sheets with a sexy naked body beside you.

And of course I wasn't.

I shrugged off my cut and pulled my blood splattered T-shirt over my head. Before I discarded it on the floor, I held it to my nose. In spite of the stains from the fight at *The Fox Hub*, I could still smell *her*. Her sexy perfume had clung to the fabric where she had nuzzled into me as I carried her. Fuck, I didn't want to wash that smell out but the blood needed to go. And so did the fucking specks of glitter she'd left there like the damn tooth fairy. The guys would rip the shit out of me if I wore a glittery fucking T-shirt. The blood on the other hand wouldn't even get a second glance. Sad but true.

Once the rest of my clothes were in a pile, I walked into

the adjacent bathroom and switched the shower dial round to the hottest setting I knew I could stand and waited for the room to fill with steam.

I'd had no intention of taking a *cold* shower regardless of the joke I'd made to Chloe. The hard on I'd carried since being in her presence had only softened slightly and that was about to change. Once I had stepped under the scorching cascade I closed my eyes and thought back to the kiss I'd shared with her. Okay, so I maybe *forced* a kiss on her but thankfully she didn't slap me or kick me in the balls so it was all good.

And I'd do it again in a heartbeat.

I blindly reached for whatever soap had been left in the shower and squirted a generous amount into my hand. I took a firm grip of my cock and squeezed. *Fuck.* What would it be like to have her pussy tightening around me? To feel my length slide into her tight body. I began to slip my hand up and down my soapy dick and groaned as pleasure radiated through my groin. I slid my other hand down my chest and flicked the bar piercing at my nipple as my imagination played images of Chloe's mouth... her tongue teasing me there.

As my hand moved to the tip of my dick I saw Chloe as Nina wrapping her long, slender leg around the chrome pole—and in this fantasy I was her only audience; only this time she was naked. Her firm breasts displayed for *my* eyes only, perfect rosy nipples and all. She stalked toward me in her silver stilettos—just like she had in my real life encounter—and stood over me. Her neatly trimmed pussy hovering just in front of my nose. My mind conjured up the smell of her arousal and I wished *so much* that she was really with me. I wanted to touch her skin. Slide my fingers into her wetness and suck her pebbled nipple into my mouth.

I let my hand travel down my stomach and cupped my balls as my strokes became faster, more urgent. Every muscle in my body began to tighten as I imagined lifting her against the shower wall and fucking her hard and fast. Taking what I needed. She deserved slow and sensual but this was *my* fantasy. And I'd have her *my* way...for now. My breathing accelerated as my slippery grip on my rigid cock did what I so desperately wanted *her* to do.

My heart pounded in my chest and a growl erupted as I came. "Fuuuck...Chloe...awww fuck. Awww fuck, Chloe." I repeated her name over and over as orgasmic waves rolled over me, the tension left my body and I sailed back down to earth.

I crumpled against the wall and rested my head on the cool surface of the tile as my breathing slowed. I doubted that my fantasy in *any* way resembled what it *could* be like with Chloe but she was out of my league and regardless of how much I wanted her I couldn't drag her into club life. It wouldn't be fair. Hell, I was waiting for shit to go wrong for Cain and Melody as I was sure it would. It was inevitable and so I'd have to get the dancer out of my system *somehow*.

And if shower gel and my imagination helped then so be it.

————

CHLOE

I didn't really sleep. And when I did I was plagued with nightmares about ugly, menacing men trying to hold me down. I awoke on several occasions crying out into my lonely bedroom and each time it happened I wished that I'd asked Six to stay. Even if he'd slept on the couch, I would have felt better. *Safer.* I was angry at myself for initially misunderstanding his motives for following me home. I feared that I would never get a chance to make things up to him. Or to thank him properly for what he'd done for me.

I climbed out of bed and rubbed my tired, stinging eyes before making my way into the bathroom. The water in my shower never got hot enough. No matter how many times I talked to the Super nothing was ever done. Thanks to the lukewarm temperature, my shower was over in record time. Once I was dry I slipped on a tatty old T-shirt and a pair of panties before going through to the kitchen to make coffee. Once the coffee was done I poured a mug full, relishing the earthy, soothing aroma. I figured I had better go check the lock on the front door seeing as Six had made me promise to stay safe and I was trying to do as I was asked for once in my life. As I headed for the door, I spotted an envelope on my door mat.

Intrigued, I picked it up and took it with me until I could set my coffee down and open it. Inside was a disc and a note that simply said "Chloe Dancer" and I knew that Six had been by. Excitement set the butterflies fluttering around inside me and I chewed on my lip as a dumb wide smile spread across my face. This guy was an enigma. Curiosity got the better of me as I remembered Six telling me about the Mother Love Bone track. After flicking on a lamp I slipped the disc into my sound system and hit play. I flopped onto the couch, hugged my knees up to my chest and closed my eyes letting the music and lyrics wash over me.

There was a hint of sadness and melancholy to the song that my biker said would remind him of me and I wondered if he knew more about me than he let on. As rain spattered the windows of my compact apartment, I wondered what he was doing. Was he thinking about me? What did he really *want* from me—if anything? And would he ever kiss me again? Or did he see me as some kind of breakable, fragile little doll that he simply needed to protect?

My mind drifted back to the intense urgency of his kiss and—despite my intention to try and keep my lustful feelings for the dangerous stranger in check—the muscles low in my belly tightened and my nipples peaked. I raised my fingers and touched my lips where they tingled at the memory of our fervent exchange. How could I *want* him? All I knew about him was that he had some kind of possessive intent for me. Maybe that was it? Maybe it was the fact that he wanted to protect me that attracted me.

I'd never experienced that before. Someone who wanted to look after me. Since Brett, my mom's boyfriend had come onto me when I was just eighteen, I had found it hard to trust *any* man. And so the easiest thing had been to just steer clear of relationships. After all, the guy who is supposed to love your mother should be trustworthy, right?

Wrong.

Well in my case it was. He could do *no* wrong in my mom's eyes, however. When I told her what he'd done, and the inappropriate suggestions he'd made while she was out at the bar working, she didn't believe me. She even said I was jealous of their happiness.

So I left.

I took five hundred bucks from a tin in the kitchen that Brett was saving for who the hell knows what, cleared out my college fund and I got as far away as my meager cash stash would allow. It was distressing enough that my mom chose to believe that bastard over me. But the fact that he threatened to come find me *because* I told her was something that had stuck with me. *Terrified* me. Utah had been my savior. My safe haven. And I didn't want anything to change that.

But here I was fantasizing about a guy who oozed dominance and danger from every pore whilst simultaneously radiating sex appeal. How the hell did he *do* that? I sat there watching the droplets of water drizzle down my window pane and I pictured him. All six feet four—at a guess—of rock hard muscle, tattoos and hair. He wasn't what you could call conventionally attractive. No sir. But there was definitely *something* about him. Something that had pulled me in from the first time I had spotted him at *The Fox Hub*.

The Mother Love Bone track was long and deeply emotive. How could such a fearsome looking wall of muscle have such a tender heart? It didn't correlate at all in my mind. Perhaps there was something deeper to his need to protect me. I wondered if he'd had sadness in his life too. If he'd been betrayed by those who were supposed to love him the most.

As I listened to the lyrics the thought sprang to mind that perhaps he saw me as some kind of kindred spirit. You can't judge a book by its cover and the tough exterior could have been hiding a multitude of painful memories that made him who he was. Was I reading too much into the lyrics? I really didn't know for sure but most of the time a song sticks with someone because it connects them to a memory or feeling;

whether good *or* bad. And as I absorbed the emotion of *this* song I could understand how it could have that effect on someone.

It was affecting me deeply on the first listen.

As the track ended I realized that tears had escaped and left damp trails down my cheeks. They mirrored the rainy weather outside my window and for some reason I was drawn to it. I peered through the glass, down at the soaked street below and inhaled sharply. Six stood across the street staring up at my window. He swiped his drenched hair back from his face and as our eyes connected. I felt a jolt of electricity that made me gasp.

He was *here*.

I should've been completely freaked out by the fact but instead and for some inexplicable reason I felt pulled toward him all over again. As if he read my mind he began to jog toward my building keeping his eyes trained on my window until I could no longer see him. Without thinking I spun around, ran for the door and yanked it open, leaving my apartment without giving its security a second thought. My bare feet slapped against the cold tile floor in the hallway and I ran down the stairs as quickly as I could, my heart racing in anticipation of seeing him again.

I pushed through the outer door and was immediately scooped up by strong, familiar arms. One hand held me at my bottom and the other slipped into my hair and pulled me forward until our lips collided. I gripped the wet strands of his hair urgently as his tongue entered my mouth. The rain hammered down on us where we stood and we were no doubt putting on quite a display for the neighborhood but I didn't care.

All I cared about was kissing him.

A lust-filled growl erupted from his chest and the door to the building slammed open. I hadn't realized his boot had stopped it from closing but I was grateful as I probably wouldn't have remembered the door release code at that precise moment. Without letting me down he carried me through the door into the stairwell and began to climb the stairs his mouth still on mine. My legs wrapped around his body and our tongues tangling together as if we were long lost lovers only just reunited.

We reached my door and once he realized it was open he pulled away from me and peered into my eyes.

His jaw clenched. "Chloe dancer. Don't *ever* leave your door open like that. *Fuck* you scare the crap out of me, do you know that? I don't want anyone *hurting* you. And why the fuck did you come outside with hardly any damn clothes on? You're gonna get yourself sick."

My chest heaved as I pulled much needed air into my lungs. "I'm sorry, Six. I just...I needed to get to you."

My words did something to him and in a split second his mouth was on me once more. He was devouring me and I couldn't get enough. Once inside my apartment he kicked the door closed, carried me into the living room and laid me down on the couch hovering just inches above me. His wet clothing clung to his sculpted body and his hooded gaze was firmly fixed on me.

CHAPTER EIGHT

Six

She lay there beneath me on her tatty old couch. Mine for the taking. And fuck did I want to take. The rain soaked white T-shirt she wore clung to her tits and shit it was the most beautiful sight I'd *ever* seen. Her dark nipples were visible through the transparent, wet fabric and her chest heaved from our passionate exchange. My cock strained to reach her and all I wanted was to be naked and inside of her.

But I couldn't do it.

Don't get me wrong I had a fucking hard on like a rod of steel. I could *perform*, but I couldn't take advantage like that. I *wouldn't*. I had a war raging in my head. Two opposing sides—one urging me forward and the other, a side of myself I was only just becoming acquainted with, was urging me to leave before I did something that *she'd* regret.

Not *me*.

Her.

"Chloe...I...I..." Typical that my brain should be lacking in blood supply thanks to the massive rush of the damn stuff that had headed south. I couldn't put into words what I wanted. She'd think I was a fucking pervert. I thought better of it and stood quickly. I stepped back and almost toppled as a head rush swamped my brain. I turned away from her to gather my thoughts.

My perverted, *dirty* thoughts.

Was her pussy as wet as her T-shirt? How tight would she feel around my cock? What would she taste like if I went down on her and fuck the consequences?

Oh yeah I was gathering my thoughts all right.

Fuck. Dumb-ass move, Six.

"Six?" Her sweet voice dragged me back to the surface of the earth from whatever depths of depravity I'd been lurking in.

I ran my hands through my straggly wet hair and turned to gaze at her once more. She was still laying there. *Waiting.* Her long legs stretched out and parted slightly. Her perfect tits begging for my touch. My head was screaming at me to just fuck her. Get her out of my system. To just take what I wanted but as I trailed my gaze down at her transparent T-shirt something tugged inside of me—I guess it was my conscience, I hadn't heard from it in a while—and I swallowed hard. She was too sweet. I couldn't just maul her on her couch. That'd make me no better than the fucking asshole that I'd rescued her from at the club.

I cleared my throat as my mind raced back to the urgent kiss we'd shared...or should I say the one I'd *taken*. "I'm... I'm sorry about that Chloe, I keep acting like an ass and I shouldn't have done it." My voice cracked like a teenage boy and I felt stupid.

She pulled herself up to a sitting position. "The kiss? But I wanted it too."

I closed my eyes and pinched the bridge of my nose. *What the hell do I say? How do I let her down gently?* When I opened my eyes again she had dropped her head forward.

When I opened my eyes again she had dropped her head forward. "It's okay...I get it. You don't want me. I guess *Chloe* isn't as enticing in her ratty old T-shirt as *Nina* is in a silver thong." Her voice held a kind of desolation that told me someone had made her feel that way before.

What the ever-loving fuck?

I crouched before her and tilted her chin up with my finger. "Hey, you're so damn *wrong* it's ridiculous. Don't *ever* think that. I just... aww, forget it. No matter what I say it'll come out wrong. I'm thinking with my dick. But just know this. I *do* want you. I've wanted you for so long and you've made me so damn hard dressed like that...or *un*dressed like that." I chuckled. "I think my junk might be deformed down there." I gestured at my jeans, trying to lighten her mood.

She giggled and glanced up at me. "So why... why didn't you want to have sex with me?"

I sighed heavily. "Chloe, you're a sweet girl. *Way* too sweet for me. You don't deserve to be *treated* like that. To *just* be fucked. And that's all I could offer you, but you're worth so much more. You should have better. Better than *me* anyway."

She didn't reply but the line between her brows told me that what I'd just said had gone in one ear and right out the other. Why didn't she believe me? Why would I lie? But then I remembered she didn't really *know* me and what bit she *did* know wasn't exactly *good* shit. I was a violent man in a motor-cycle club who had stalked her, pretty much kidnapped her and then to frost the fucking cake, I'd forced myself on her. What was there *not* to love?

I lowered my voice and spoke softly. "Look, I think I'd better go. I just stopped by your block to make sure you were safe. I see that you are so... so I should leave."

She nodded and wrapped her arms around her legs, resting her chin on her knees. Disappointment graced her pretty features and embarrassment colored her cheeks. I felt like a fucking prize ass. She'd done *nothing* wrong.

I stood slowly this time and reached down to squeeze her shoulder. "Like I said before stay away from *The Fox Hub* for a while okay? Just until the dust settles."

She raised her chin and locked eyes with me as an air of defiance stiffened her spine. "I'm an *adult*, Six and I *need* to work. I'll be fine. I'm not your responsibility and now I think you're right. You *should* go."

I clenched my jaw. For some stupid reason I was ready to argue. To shout if necessary to get my point across but the look on her face told me that I'd be wasting my time.

Stubborn-ass woman.

With a resigned sigh I told her, "I'm only trying to protect you from the shit that goes on in my life, Chloe. I just want you to be—"

"Safe, yeah you mentioned that. Look, I have to be some-where so you should leave now."

I shook my head as I trailed my gaze over her once more. Mentally kicking myself for making her think I didn't want her. And for being so damned sensible for once. What the hell was *wrong* with me?

I left the apartment and she followed to slam the door behind me.

Yep, I'd really fucked up.

Again.

————

Chloe

Maybe Brett—my mom's handsy, pervert, asshole of a boyfriend—was right. *No* man would want me. I watched Six leave the building after I had unceremoniously slammed the door on him like a moody, errant teenager. I could see him out of my window as he climbed onto his bike and ran his hands roughly through his straggly hair. He glanced up at my window and I jumped back. I didn't need him to see me spying on him that's for sure.

Brett's words rang around my head as Six pulled away into the evening. *"Take it from me, no one will want you, Chloe. You're an awkward little thing. Eighteen and all tits and legs but your face...well...let's just say you'd maybe be good for a fuck if the guy keeps his eyes closed. Face it, honey, you have a face for radio. No one will want to look at you. I'm trying to take pity on you here. Trying to show you what sex can be like. Because to be honest, no one is going to want a relationship with you."* He squeezed my breasts and pressed his erection into my denim clad ass as fear made my heart pound. Thank goodness I wasn't wearing a skirt. I'd been warned not to scream or to tell my mom as he had already said he would deny everything and make it out that I had come on to him.

The thought of his hands on me made me want to vomit.

Maybe he had a point. Maybe all Six *saw* was tits and legs. Okay, when I was made up for my performances, maybe I looked *marginally* good from the neck up *and* at a distance. But when Six saw me that morning, without the layer of face paint he was used to, my appearance had clearly put him off. He couldn't even bring himself to have *sex* with me. I had wanted to repay him for caring in the only way that men seemed to appreciate but I was obviously too gross and he was just being nice.

Yeah, as much as I hated to admit it and as much as I hated the man himself, Brett was right.

CHAPTER NINE

Six

When I left Chloe's apartment I took a long ride to clear my head. By the time I got back it was getting dark and I'd had several missed calls from guys in the MC. I arrived back at the club house to find that all hell had broken loose in my absence. I wasn't sure what the fuck had gone down but what I *did* know was that there were some pretty pissed off bikers hurling abuse at each other in the bar. Delilah was standing there watching the whole thing unfold as she twisted her hands in front of her. Now if you knew Dee like I did you'd have been shocked too. *Nothing* spooked her. She was a tough cookie.

I made my way over to where she stood. "What the hell happened, Dee?"

"Oh God, Six, where the hell have you *been*? The shit has really hit the fan. I've tried to call you like a billion times."

"Hey, I've told you a *trillion* times not to exaggerate." I chuckled at my own joke but she just rolled her eyes and whacked my arm.

"Six, it's *not* funny. Loki's Legion are making a play for the land out by the freeway. They want to build a warehouse. Colt says it's some kind of retaliation for what happened with you and that moron who tried to maul the Fox you like."

"Her name is Chl...*Nina*."

"What-the-fuck-ever, Six. Shit has gotten serious."

I didn't really get what the fuss was about. "So, Colt tells them to take a hike. It's all good."

"God, Six don't you *get* it? It's not that straight forward. That area is no man's land. If Loki's crew take over it imagine what the hell *that* will be like. It's too close, man."

She had a point. Colt, our club Prez, had been guardian over that land for around ten years after he struck a deal with the former President of Loki's Legion. But since the guy had retired and Deak had taken over things had changed. And *not* for the better.

Colt spied me standing there and began to walk toward me. His almost black hair was tied back in its usual band to expose the Company of Sinners tattoo around the front of his neck. He matched me for height but was a little leaner. To anyone else he'd be an intimidating bastard but not to me. I'd seen him at his lowest when his old lady had died of cancer four years earlier. The man almost followed her to the fucking grave and I swore at *that* point that love just wasn't worth the pain.

I glanced around the room looking for Cain but he was nowhere to be seen. *Shit*. Where was my partner in crime when I needed him?

Colt stepped up to me with a menacing glare and jabbed a

thick finger in my face. "Where the *fuck* have you been?" *Oh great. An ear bashing from Colt. My favorite thing to pass the time.*

I shrugged. "Went for a ride to clear my head. Why?"

His jaw was clenched and his eyes kind of wild and staring. Dude was real pissed. "I'm guessing Dee has told you what's gone down tonight while you were off sightseeing and fucking your whores."

I wasn't in the mood for his shit and I rolled my eyes feeling like a teenager being chastised by his Pa. "I wasn't *fucking whores.* Like I said, I needed to clear my head."

"Yeah? I don't see how you needed to, seeing as it's empty up there. You're supposed to be the fucking VP of this club, Six. And thanks to you and your little fuck buddy Fox we have a situation here. It seems Loki's Legion are laying claim to the land by the freeway. We need to make moves to stop them."

I suddenly felt drained and just wanted to go upstairs and shut out the noise. But the way he had spoken about Chloe made anger draw to the surface.

I gritted my teeth. "She's *not* my fuck buddy. I *haven't* fucked her."

Colt lifted his bulky arms and dropped them with a slap by his sides in an exasperated shrug. "Well I'm so sorry for getting *that* little snippet wrong. *Please* won't you accept my sincere apology and pass one onto the *stripper* while you're at it. Now get to fucking chapel *ass-hat!*" He turned and stomped up the stairs.

I fucking hated sarcasm. *Hated* it. And Colt used it a whole *lot.* Who the *fuck* did he think he was anyway? He was only around twelve years my senior but *still* acted like he owned my ass.

I finally caught sight of Cain over by the door and it appeared he had just arrived too. He waved me over, a look of worry on his face. I decided Colt could wait and went to talk to my buddy.

"Hey, Cain. S'up?" I embraced him and slapped his back.

"Fuck, Six. You're never going to believe what the hell happened, dude."

"Loki's crew and the land?"

He scrunched his brow. "Oh...so you heard? Shit, man I've been out looking for you. Colt wants you in chapel right now."

I couldn't help laughing. "Yeah I figured that from the way he just hollered at me in front of everyone."

I flung my arm around Cain's shoulder and we made our way up the stairs to try and figure a way out of this shitty situation. The thought of a rival club being so close to our land and our business made me uncomfortable to say the least. But I didn't want to show my concern.

———

Chloe

Phoning in sick wasn't something that sat easily with me. But regardless of the fact that Six apparently thought of me as some sad sack pity case, he had made the whole situation with the rival MC sound serious. And the last thing I needed was to get caught up in the middle of that shit. So I faked the flu and stayed home. My girlfriend, Ellie Cassidy, from the coffee shop I used to work at had heard on the grapevine that I was sick and she came to visit.

I hadn't seen her in a while, but she was the closest thing to a best friend that I had in the area and in true best buddy style she came armed with lots of nice things which I presumed were to make me feel better.

After looking through my peep hole I opened the door to her and was greeted with a loud squeal and her red, curled locks bouncing like a giddy puppy dog. "Hey girl!" Which was rapidly followed by a knowing glare and pursed lips. "Um...You don't *look* sick."

I stood there in the doorway chewing my lip and cringing as guilt washed over me. "No... I guess you should come in and I should explain, huh?"

"Damn *right*, girl."

I stepped aside and she walked past me shaking her head. She placed the shopping bags full of goodies on the floor and at a glance I could see Oreo cookies, chips and a Magic Mike DVD poking out the top of one of them.

I sighed, wondering where the hell to begin to explain the shit storm that had rained down on me lately. "Okay...so it's a long story."

"I've got all evening, babe. Fire away." She flopped down onto the couch, tucked her hair behind her ears and smiled up at me. "Oh and seeing as you're not stacked up on meds go grab some glasses. I have wine."

I walked over to the kitchen and returned to her a few moments later clutching two glasses and a corkscrew. She pulled a bottle of merlot from one of the bags and grabbed the corkscrew from me with a grin.

As she opened and poured the wine I began to explain

what had happened at *The Fox Hub* with the sleazy bastard who had attacked me. She sat open mouthed and wide eyed clutching her wine glass and transfixed on me as I revisited the disturbing drama of that awful night.

She gasped and a look of horror set in place on her pretty features. "Oh my God, Chloe that's *terrible*. You see I *told* you that leaving the coffee shop was a mistake. Things like that just don't *happen* at Hank's. You need to leave that damn place and come back. Hank would take you back in a heartbeat. I *know* he would."

Her concern for me was touching but the money I made at Hank's was nowhere *near* to what I made at *The Fox Hub*. Ellie was okay, her parents subsidized her income and she lived over their garage in a little converted apartment just large enough for her. She had her parents on her doorstep to look out for her, but I had no one to help me in that way. And there was nowhere else for me to live. Unless I wanted to live in a hovel surrounded by drug dealers. And I sure as hell did *not*.

"You know I can't do that, Ellie. I just can't afford to."

She sighed deeply and then took a large gulp of her wine. "Yeah... I know. It's just... I would hate to have to work somewhere like that. And you're so much better than that place and *those* people."

"Honestly, it's *good* there. Most of the time anyway. This was just a one off stupid incident." I was aware, thanks to the edge of anxiety to my voice that I sounded as though I was trying to convince *myself* as well as my friend.

She nodded but the crease between her brows told me she wasn't exactly convinced. "So...this biker guy... The number guy... He's not creeping is he?"

I smiled as I thought back to the misunderstanding I'd had with Six. "No...nothing like that."

"Umm, okay why have you gone beet red? Is there something you're not telling me here?"

Shaking my head, the heat in my cheeks intensified. A total giveaway. "No...nothing at all. He's just... I just..."

She placed her glass down with a jerk onto the coffee table, slopping some of the contents out. "Oh my God! You *like* him! The hairy ass biker!"

I frowned at her choice of words as I reached for some tissues to wipe up the spillage and was compelled to defend him. "Hey, he's not a *hairy ass biker*."

If I thought her mouth and eyes couldn't widen any further, I was *wrong*. "You've *seen* his ass?"

I scrunched my face hoping to show every ounce of the incredulity I felt at her *almost* accusation. "No! I have *not* seen his ass. Shit, Ellie, what do you take me for?"

She leaned over and grabbed the wine bottle, proceeded to top up my glass and replace the contents of her own and then stared at me with eagle eyes. "Spill it woman. I need details. You're holding out on me and you clearly have the hots for this guy. Although from what you've said about him I'm at a loss as to why the hell he'd even register on your radar. How old is he anyway?"

I pursed my lips as I pondered her question. "He's maybe around twenty six...twenty seven...I don't know. It was his birthday on Friday."

"Twenties, huh? Oh...well that's better than what I was expecting. I figured he was like forty or something."

I snorted, almost choking on my mouthful of wine. "Ellie, you've never met him and forty isn't *old*."

She giggled and I was thankful she was relaxing. "Too old for *you*. So come on. Describe him."

"Well...he's tall—"

"Kinda figured that too. Gimme the good stuff."

"He's..." I felt heart rate increase as an image of Six formed in my mind. "He's kind of like a bear." I giggled at my own choice of description but it fit him well.

Her nose crinkled as if assaulted by a pungent odor. "A bear? Oh my *gosh* is he like *really hairy*?"

I burst out laughing and had to place my wine glass down for fear of another spill. "What is it with you and the hairy thing? No, he has a beard and long shaggy hair. And oh *boy* is he built. You know...*muscular*. His biceps...they're...I mean *huge*." I gestured the thickness with my hands. "And his thighs too. But he's ripped. You can just tell he works out. He has those pecs that clothing just moulds itself to. And he has tattoos. *Lots* of tattoos. His eyes are a kind of caramel colour with little flecks of gold. Oh and his hair is a dirty-blonde color. And I know it's crazy but... he makes me feel safe in a way that I haven't since I was a kid."

Realizing I had been vomiting my inner thoughts and feelings on my friend I turned to make eye contact with her again and she had a wide grin on her face. "Oh fuck. You *seriously* have it bad, girl."

I shrugged off her comment and shifted my gaze to my wine glass. "What? *No*. No it's not like that. I mean...I mean he *kissed* me but then he stopped and apologized and things felt kinda awkward so I think he doesn't see me that way."

The snort that came from Ellie right then reminded me of the pigs on my Grampies farm when I was tiny and I turned to face her again.

Oh yeah she was laughing at me alright. "Are you *kidding* me? He rescued you from an attacker, brought you home *and* kissed you. Oh yeah...I can see why you'd think he wasn't interested." She rolled her eyes and shook her head.

Heat rose in my cheeks along with my embarrassment. "Well, when you put it like that... Oh and...he calls me *Chloe dancer.*"

Her hand came up to cover her mouth and her eyes misted over. "Like the *song?*"

I raised my eyebrows in shock. "You *know* that song?"

She nodded. "My brother used to love Mother Love Bone in the nineties. The singer died. So sad. But that's kinda sweet. It's a sad song, you should listen to it."

I pulled my lips in between my teeth for a moment as she peered at me questioningly. I took a deep breath. "He brought me a CD with it on. Just that one track."

"Oh yeah. He's sooo not into you."

CHAPTER TEN

Six

Shit was about to get ten times worse. Not only was there a major issue with Loki's Legion but something was going on with Cain too and he was choosing not to confide in me which got me worried. He usually told me *every*thing. But not this time. Whatever the hell was going on he was keeping his cards so damn close to his chest that I just couldn't figure it out. I'd seen him on his phone looking at this cute little house in Rose Acres, but when I asked him about it he swiped the screen and made some dumb-ass joke about casing the joint.

Yeah right.

I could smell fucking bullshit a mile away and I knew there was more going on with him and that house than he was letting on.

More threats had been made by Loki's Legion about the land they'd set their sights on and rumor had it that all fucking bets were off. We were seconds away from a lockdown and I was living on a knife edge just waiting for the order. Colt was trying his best to play the whole thing down but when I heard on the grapevine about some of the rival MC hanging around *The Fox Hub*, it got personal. I knew what they had in mind and I didn't like it one fucking bit.

I'd been watching Chloe's apartment from a distance and I was relieved to see that she'd taken my advice to stay away from *The Fox Hub* until things calmed down. The only visitor she'd had had been some pretty red haired girl carrying groceries. I figured she was another dancer although I didn't recognize her and presumed she must have been one of the ones who wore a wig when they danced. She'd left Chloe's place in a cab around two in the morning and once the apartment was in darkness I'd gone home.

The day after the redhead visited I decided to stop by and check up on CD. It was ten o'clock on the Thursday morning and I'd hardly slept, so I knew I must have looked like death on a fucking stick. As someone left the building I managed to wedge my boot in the door as it was about to close and I sneaked in to make my way up to her apartment.

I wasn't really sure what to expect when I knocked on her door, so I stood there with a clenched jaw, waiting for her to respond. I could hear music coming from inside. When it registered what the music was my heart did this funny tripping over itself thing. *What the fuck*? So she liked the song I sent her enough to listen to it more than once. So what? Jeez what was *wrong* with me.

When she opened the door I stood there with a dumb-ass fucking grin on my face. Like a kid on prom night.

She scrunched her face as she stared up at me. "What's wrong with you? You're grinning like an idiot."

Try as I might I could straighten my face. "Oh...nothing. Just thinking I like your taste in music is all."

A pink tinge spread from the rise of her tits and rose up her neck until it reached her cheeks. I could've warmed my hands on the glow and I couldn't help chuckling.

She rolled her eyes and turned away from me mumbling something about me being a prize a-hole. But it only made me laugh more. I watched her little round ass as she walked into the apartment. She was wearing those cut off jean shorts that showed off her shape and my dick sure was appreciative of the fine sight.

"You coming in or are you going to stand in the doorway all day?" she called out to me. I realized I'd been blatantly staring at her behind and had to adjust myself in my boxers before I could walk.

Fuck, what she *did* to me.

Her bleached blonde hair with its brown streaks was piled up on the top of her head in a knot and she wore a black tank top that showed off her slender neck to perfection. Her flawless skin was free of make-up and she looked fresh and innocent. Immediately I wanted to slide my hand around the back of that neck and kiss a trail from just below her ear down to her nipples.

Yeah I wasn't helping myself *at all*.

I made my way over to the couch and sat down, following her every elegant move with my gaze fixed on her.

"Hey, it's rude to stare." Her harsh words dragged me from my trance and I made eye contact with her. Her cheeks were still bright pink.

So fucking cute.

I cleared my throat and tried to calm the wood in my

pants. "Huh? Sorry. Sorry I guess I'm tired. Been a long night."

She crossed her arms over her chest and her tits pushed upward. "So do you want a drink or not?"

Her reception to me was less than cordial and I couldn't figure out why. I lifted my hands and rubbed my face roughly. "Umm... yeah sure. Coffee would be good thanks."

She disappeared into the kitchen. I stood and made my way over to lean on the door frame. Fuck me if she didn't make preparing coffee look sexy as hell. "So, how've you been?"

Without turning around, she huffed. "Oh I think you already know that, *Stalky Stalkerson.*"

Busted. I sighed heavily and shrugged. "Hey, I'm just looking out for you, Chloe dancer. Wouldn't want the big bad wolf to find you and get in here, now would we?"

She turned to face me and I watched as she swallowed hard and twisted a spoon around between her fingers. "I... I think it's a little too late for that, don't you?" she whispered.

Suddenly I was unable to speak, caught up in those damned beautiful brown eyes of hers. Sucked into a speechless trance all over again. And for a couple seconds I stood there trying to figure out what to make of the fact that she had insinuated *I* was the big bad wolf.

I stepped toward her, heart pounding, cock straining at my jeans, mouth dry. My gaze never strayed from her and when I was only inches away I lowered my face so our lips were almost touching. She was panting and her warm breath mingled with mine. On the verge of closing the remaining gap I heard her sharp intake of breath and thankfully it dragged me back from the edge of an abyss I *swore* I wouldn't fall into.

I couldn't and *wouldn't* do that to her. The mantra played over and over in my head, she deserves better, *she deserves better, she deserves way better*.

I stepped back and ran my hands through my straggly hair as my heart hit my ribs with such force that I feared a blackout. When I turned to look at Chloe again her head was down. Fuck she had actually been expecting me to kiss her again and I'd pulled away like it was the worst thing that could happen.

Way to go asshole. "Hey, look I'm sorry. Like I said, I'm tired. And I only came to check up on you. You...you seem fine so I think should probably go. I've got tons of shit to do, you know?" Jeez it was like I only had one set of damn words to say. Like I was a broken fucking record.

She lifted her head until her eyes locked on mine once more. "Oh yeah. I can imagine. *Tons* of shit," she repeated with an edge of disappointment *and* sarcasm to her voice. She leaned over, flicked the kettle switch off and began to gather up the mugs.

Fuck. What the hell is wrong with me? I stepped forward and reached out but my next action took *me* by surprise just as much as it did her.

I ruffled her fucking hair. "Well, kiddo, I'll see ya later. Be good now."

She opened and closed her mouth like a goldfish and I felt so, so stupid.

She eventually frowned and shook her head. "S...see you later."

Before I could apologize, try to take the action back or say *any*thing else, I turned and made for the door. I *had* to leave. I'd just treated her like Cain treated his kid sister Rosa. Why the fuck had I *done* that? But I figured maybe it was for the best. Maybe this was the way I *needed* to act around her. She needed my protection from the Legion bastards. She didn't need me trying to get into her panties.

I left the apartment without looking back and as I made my way to the bike I resolved that even though the hair ruffling shit was dumb as fuck it was the right way to go. If I treated her like a kid, then maybe eventually I'd start seeing her that way and my dick would co-operate.

A guy could fucking hope, right?

————

Chloe

After calling in sick all week, in some stupid misplaced loyalty to a guy who now thought of me as a kid—he *ruffled* my fricking hair for goodness sake—I was so pissed. Not only at *him* but at myself too for being so easy to manipulate. I needed to get my damned head on straight and more to the point get *him* out of there. So when Friday came around again I figured I couldn't stay away from the club any longer. And why the hell should I anyway?

I needed the cash and dance night was always the money spinner.

I'd been torturing myself by listening to the disc Six had dropped though my door and each time I had, my heart had ached for something but I wasn't really sure what. He had made it quite clear that he wasn't about to cross the arbitrary line he had made for himself in the imaginary sand.

So my resolve was firm.

This Friday night I *would* be *Nina* once again.

As I blow dried my hair and plastered on my first layer of make-up, I wondered if Six would be there to watch. My stomach fluttered with what seemed to be a thousand butterflies all taking flight at once and in spite of myself I hoped desperately that he *would* be. Partly because I felt so much safer when he was there and partly because I wanted to remind him why he had wanted me in the first place. That I wasn't some little fragile kid in need of a big brother. And if wearing make-up and hardly any clothes got his attention then so be it. Maybe that was all I was good for and I'd have to get used to it.

———

As always *The Fox Hub* was super busy when I arrived. I scanned the room looking for my dirty-blonde haired biker but he was nowhere to be seen and my heart sank. Maybe now that he had seen the *real* me more than once he wouldn't show up any more. I went backstage to drop off my bag, change and add the finishing touches to my thickly plastered on make-up.

A short while later there was a rap of knuckles on the dressing room door. "Nina, you're up."

As usual the dreaded words sent shivers down my spine. I took a deep breath and checked my appearance in the mirror to see that I was once again unrecognisable as quiet, unsure little Chloe. *Mission accomplished.* I stood and slipped my feet into the six-inch silver stilettos that made my toes hurt like hell. Tonight's nipple covers were black lace with a matching thong. The black was a stark contrast to the fake blonde of my hair and my ruby red, glitter lipstick made me look like a hooker or a porn star. I laughed humorlessly as I remembered the guy who had offered me a contract around six months earlier to star in his porn movies. I had turned him down even though the wages had been so high they would have solved *all* my money worries. But the romantic in me still wanted to find someone to love. And starring in porn films would no doubt make it even *harder* to meet my elusive Mister Right.

The eerie piano of the night's song rang out around the buzzing room. Nine Inch Nails' "Right Where It Belongs" was the track I had chosen. After my usual pep talk to the mirror I stepped out onto the stage, once again scanning for the man who could make me feel safe.

But this time he was nowhere to be seen.

CHAPTER ELEVEN

Six

Hearing that Loki's Legion were up on our piece of land, and that they were trying to stake some kind of claim over it, wasn't the news any of us wanted to hear. Of course, Colt wanted us to go right on up there and make sure they left under the correct assumption that they'd got things totally wrong. They *had* to know that the land was not—and was *never* going to be—*theirs*. Colt had overseen the land for so long now he—and the rest of our MC—considered it CoSMiC land.

This wasn't how I was hoping to spend my evening. There was a certain sexy little bleached blonde dancer that I wanted to check on, but sadly there was no way I could be in two places at once. She appealed to me a hell of a lot more than a brawl in a field, but I had to join my crew in trying to resolve this latest war game. When we arrived up at the land, however, things were not as we had expected.

The Loki's Legion bastards had been drinking and they were armed.

But the worst part was they weren't alone.

How the *hell* things descended into such carnage so damn quickly, I really don't know. No one had expected a young *girl* to be there. What the hell had Deak been thinking of letting her follow the drunken idiots out into the middle of nowhere when they were clearly intent on raising hell? In fact, I wondered if he had even known she was there. I hoped not, or he was even more of an asshole than I thought.

And what the hell had Weasel, from our crew, been doing with my buddy Cain's gun? Come to think of it, where the fuck had Cain even *been*? Weasel and Cain were of a similar height and it was as if Weasel were trying to *be* Cain or maybe he was trying to deliberately frame him. Like it was some kind of a set up. Weasel's beanie hat was pulled far down and thanks to the darkness it wouldn't have been possible for the Legion to see that it actually *wasn't* Cain. Add that to the fact that Cain's gun was *very* distinctive—even from a distance— with its engraving and there was just enough light to glint on the surface and make the markings visible, and I knew that if any of Loki's Legion had seen it they would presume that *Cain* was the one who had fired the shot that killed the girl.

Fuck!

I had no damned idea what the hell was happening with the MC but it felt like everything was crumbling around me and the uneasy knot in my stomach was growing with every second that passed since the gunfight.

Images of the girl crumpling to the ground after the shot rang out, rampaged around my head and turned my guts to the point where I almost lost the meager amount of food I'd consumed during the day. The blood-curdling scream of agony that rent the night air as it ripped from her throat would live in my brain forever; and I wasn't sure how the hell to *deal* with that. I mean, I'd seen death before. Shit, I'd *killed* before. But *this* was different. *She* was an innocent. Fuck. She was *eighteen*.

Eighteen.

No fucking age to die. Again I wondered why the hell they had even *been* there. Why had any of them been there? Nothing had been decided about the land and so the Loki's Legion crew had no damn right to stake a claim. And why take a young girl out there? Jeez.

I gripped the handles of the bike until my fingers were almost numb. I needed a drink. The rest of the MC had gone back to the clubhouse and Colt was eager for me to go back too. He wanted us to lock down and figure out how the hell we were going to sort this whole mess of crap out. There was a good chance that Loki's Legion would go for the 'an eye for an eye' approach. And what Cain failed to realize was that there was a good chance that Rosa, his kid sister and the youngest female connected to our crew, was in grave danger for that very reason.

I also had other things on my mind. I needed to check on Chloe. Knowing how fucking stubborn she was turning out to be, I imagined she was probably at the club seeing as Friday was her main night to dance. I wondered if she had expected me to be there. I wished I *had* been. At least that way I wouldn't have witnessed the hell that went down over at no-man's land.

There were so many unanswered questions but I wanted to forget the harrowing scenes I had witnessed. Alcohol would be the best way to do that but with the situation as it was I needed my wits about me. I needed to know that if Loki's Legion decided to retaliate—which there was no real doubt about—that I'd be in a fit state to fight. Or at least to *defend* myself and Chloe. I cursed the night that the Legion bastard had stepped into *The Fox Hub* and laid his hands on her. If only he hadn't stepped out of line like that and caused me to intervene, maybe we could have dealt with the whole land situation like the adults we claimed to be.

I pulled up outside *The Fox Hub* with a pounding heart, hoping and praying that my dancer was unharmed. Only problem was it was almost closing time. I questioned myself as to whether I should go ahead in and check on her but I figured I'd wait. I knew the sleaze who had tried to molest her before wasn't around seeing as he'd been out with the crew when all hell broke loose up at the piece of land that everyone was so desperate to get their grubby hands on.

After toying with the idea of going inside to her—if she was there—I decided to wait outside on the bike. I reasoned with myself that she wouldn't take kindly to my over-posses-sive nature only a day after I showed up at her apartment. Although why I expected staying outside would be more acceptable I don't really know.

Sure enough around a half hour later she left the club. Relief flooded my veins at the mere sight of her. Her black hooded sweater was zipped up tight and her head was down. But I'd know that figure and that walk anywhere. As always when she left the club she looked nothing like the made up, scantily clad bimbo she portrayed on stage. Old sneakers and yoga pants were her outfit of choice for her walk home. That way she would blend into the background like she wanted. Like she preferred. But regardless of what she wore she still stood out to *me*.

I climbed off the bike and removed my helmet. "Chloe! Hey!" I called out to her as I jogged over in the hope I didn't scare her half to death. Although jumping out on her unannounced would have, so I was hedging my bets.

She stopped and pulled down her hood. "What are *you* doing here?" Her tone was anything but welcoming.

"I just came to check on you. Make sure you're okay."

"Yeah? Well you did that yesterday remember, *Stalky*? So now you see I'm fine *again* you can go home. Like I said I don't need a big brother." She began to walk away from me and I reached out and grabbed her arm. She jerked her head around and her sharp intake of breath and wide eyes made me let go immediately. I didn't mean to scare her but it didn't seem to stop me from continually doing so.

"Shit, I'm sorry, CD. I just... I want to protect you. That's all. You think of me as the big bad wolf but really I'm *not*. And if you think about it...I guess you're like a wolf too. You're independent as hell and stubborn as fuck and you've got a fierce bite but... like all wolves we work better in a pack...more protection. Safety in numbers you know?"

She snorted derisively and shook her head. "I'm *not* an animal, Six. I'm just capable of looking after myself. And tell me this, why is it that men are continually trying to do *me* favors when *they're* the ones who'll benefit and *not* me?"

Huh? I scrunched my brow and shook my head. "I...I don't know what you mean."

"Seriously? Well lucky for you I *do* know what I mean.

And what I mean is just go *home*, Six." She began to walk again and I followed after her.

I had to come up with something. "Wanna go to Hank's all night café and grab a coffee?" It was a lame ass suggestion but it was all I had.

She stopped again and swung around to face me. "For the love of *all* that's holy would you just *stop* feeling sorry for me? I'm *fine*. Okay? So some jerk tried to force himself on me. So what? I'm over it, okay? I appreciate you stepping in but you can just leave it now. I don't need your God damn pity."

She really wasn't going to make things easy on me and fuck if I wasn't getting pissed at her. "Whoa, hang on, pitying and feeling *sorry* for you? How the *fuck* am I feeling sorry for you by wanting to spend *time* with you?"

She sighed and let her head fall back so she was gazing up at the stars. "Six, I *threw* myself at you. You turned me down. Then yesterday you *almost* kissed me but changed your mind at the last second and made me feel foolish. You can *stop* trying to make me feel better now. *Stop* trying to let me down gently okay? Message received loud and clear. I *get* it." She connected with my eyes once again but the pain I saw in hers made me angry.

I stepped in front of her—but not too close—reached out, placed my hands on her shoulders and squeezed gently. "Get *what*? And why the fuck would you think I was trying to make you feel better?"

Her lip began to tremble and she lowered her gaze again. "Because I'm only attractive to you when I'm half naked and have all my make-up on. When I'm thrusting my tits in your face or wrapped around a pole. Look, I'm just being realistic, okay? You've seen me up close more than once now when I've just been *plain old me* and it's turned you off." She shrugged. "Brett was right."

Who the fuck is Brett?

I tentatively stepped closer once more and tilted her chin up with my finger. "Hey, now hang on there, woman." I tried not to sound pissed but failed miserably. The thought that some dick had made her feel insecure made my blood boil. "I have no idea who this *Brett* douche is, but if he told you that you're *ugly* or something then he's one dumb-ass fucking prick. I don't *care* if you have make-up on or none at all; you're the most beautiful girl I've ever laid eyes on." *Well fuck that's out there now.* "So don't *ever* say that I feel *sorry* for you, okay? Or that I'm not fucking interested 'coz you couldn't be any fucking farther from the truth." My voice was getting louder and I was aware that I was swearing a hell of a lot but I couldn't seem to control my mouth as my hate for the shit-head Brett guy in her life dug at my insides and I continued with my barrage. "You don't live in my head, okay? So you have no damn *clue* how I feel about you or what you *do* to me with or without your face paint on. You drive me nuts and you're the stubbornest and most frustrating little bitch I've ever met but I happen to *like* that for some stupid reason." *Okay, Six now you're babbling all kinds of shit. Just quit it.* I stopped talking for a second and she opened her mouth to retaliate so I held up my hand and stopped her. "Now before you butt in with your own snide little sarcastic comments you should know that I'm taking you home. And before you argue I'm doing it for *me*, so I know you're safe and I've had the fucking night from hell so *you* better *not* argue about this 'coz if you do I swear I'll take you over my shoulder and fucking carry you home if I have to and I may even spank your ass. So go get on the fucking bike, Chloe. *Now!*" My chest was heaving and I was waiting for her to slap me, scream, or kick me in the balls.

She'd have had every right.

CHAPTER TWELVE

CHLOE

I stood there open mouthed as he verbally lashed out at me. Shouting and swearing right in my face. For a split second I wondered why his night had been so bad and I guess I should have been pissed off or at least *angry* at him for the way he was behaving. But his words were somehow the most romantic thing I had ever heard and so I quickly refocused on them. *He thinks I'm beautiful? With or without make-up? Is this a joke? Is he for real?* His shoulders and jaw were tensed and his whole demeanor screamed rage as he turned and stalked toward the bike across the lot.

I was shocked to my core but touched by his concern at the same time. And his threat of spanking my ass had an even stranger effect on me. The fire in his eyes wasn't one of rage at that point but *lust*. And my God it turned me on. That was a definite first for me.

I wasn't afraid, but the dichotomy of his words and actions had me frozen to the spot.

He turned once again and glared at me. "You comin' or do I *have* to carry you? 'Coz you fucking *know* I'll do it."

As if I was being pulled toward him by some invisible force my feet began to move. Once I was up close he thrust a helmet into my hands. "Put this on."

I stared at it with confusion and shook my head. "Wh-where's yours?"

"Only got one. And *you're* wearing it. *No* arguments." His pouty-faced response made me smile and I pulled my lips in to try and stop it. "Are you *laughing* at me Chloe dancer?"

I didn't put the helmet on and when I lifted my gaze to his he was smiling. I nodded. "Maybe a little."

He scrunched his brow but his smile remained in place. "Oh you are, huh? What's so funny?"

"You, when you're angry. You look cute...kind of like a sulky teenager."

He stepped toward me and slipped his hand around my waist and the heat of arousal began to creep up my skin.

Leaning in close he whispered into my ear, "Oh *do* I really?"

I nervously chewed on my lip and nodded again as the butterflies took flight once more.

He leaned in closer still and ran his nose down mine before pulling away and locking his eyes on mine. "Hmm, I can't have you thinking of me as a *teenager*, now can I? I need you thinking of me as a *man*." He reached his other hand up and rubbed at his beard and I desperately wanted to feel it scratching against my skin...preferably the skin of my inner thighs. I watched as his mouth turned up at one side mischievously. "Now how could I possibly do *that* I wonder?"

Before I knew what was happening he pulled me to him and crushed his lips to mine. Desire coiled deep in my belly and my muscles clenched as his tongue slipped and slid with mine in a passionate duel that he was winning without a doubt. With one hand I limply held on to the helmet he had given me and with the other I gripped the stiff leather of his biker jacket. The hand that he had slipped around my waist slowly moved down to my behind and he squeezed me there, unabashedly pressing me against the rigid erection in the front of his jeans as we kissed. My heart pounded in perfect rhythm with his and I was ready to give him *anything*, right there in the parking lot of *The Fox Hub*.

When he ended the kiss abruptly and pulled away he raised his eyebrows questioningly. Once my lust filled fog has dissipated I swallowed hard. "O-okay...the t-teenager has *definitely* gone."

Satisfied that he had proved his point, he flung his leg over the fuel tank and sat on the bike. I tugged the helmet on and fastened the chin strap, suddenly shaking at the prospect of being pillion passenger to such a perfect and *huge* specimen of masculinity. He held out his hand and I gripped it as I too straddled the hunk of shining metal with legs that had turned to jelly.

He fired up and revved the engine before pulling away in the direction of my apartment. A shiver of excitement traveled the full length of my spine as we took off. Being on the back of his bike was exhilarating and not at all what I expected. The most surprising thing was that I wasn't scared like I'd thought I'd be. The cool night air took my breath away and my nipples stood to attention under my clothing. I wasn't sure if it was the thrill or the chill but nevertheless I was very much aware of the tingling sensation around my breasts. As the minimal street lighting flashed past us at speed I found myself wishing I lived farther away so the ride could last longer.

The dingy town took on a whole new appearance from the back of the bike to the point where it was almost beautiful. Buildings that were usually menacing and foreboding through the day time—and just plain eerie on my regular journey home—had a kind of homely orange glow late at night that they never seemed to have when I was walking.

Strands of my hair, that were poking out from under the helmet, flapped and whipped around my neck issuing a mixture of scratches and tickles that were kind of distracting. But nevertheless, I clung onto Six, my arms only just circling his broad body. The vibration of the bike coupled with being pressed so close up against him was sending thrills through my core and in a bizarre way I was so turned on I felt sure I'd hyperventilate or *come*.

Eventually we came to a halt outside my apartment and with shaking limbs I extricated myself from the bike and pulled off the helmet making sure to drag my fingers through the rats tails that were tangled together as a poor excuse for my hair.

I was very much aware of the dampness in my panties and knew for a fact I was blushing like a teenager. "W-would you like to come up for a drink?" I asked Six as he watched me from the bike.

His sexy smile spoke volumes but I was determined not to get my hopes up.

Not again.

He nodded slowly. "Only if you're sure. I mean... I fucked things up last time... I don't want to fuck things up again."

His hesitancy surprised me but I shook my head and handed back his helmet. "You won't. Come on." I turned and headed for my apartment as my heart pounded at my ribs. *Don't throw yourself at him this time you ho. Just breathe...just frickin' breathe.* My internal voice was scathing but I was desperately trying to ignore it as his heavy footsteps crunched on the gravel behind me. Desire mingled and combined with the excitement and nervousness in my stomach and caused a familiar fluttering to begin.

Once we reached my door and I had unlocked it I turned to gaze up at my dirty-blonde biker. Although he wasn't technically *mine*. I wished at that point that I could read his mind as he stood there, jaw clenching and hands firmly wedged in his pockets as if he thought he could control them better there. Something inside me melted yet again. Another reaction I was becoming familiar with around him.

I stepped inside and held my hand out gesturing for him to do the same. He tentatively followed me into the apartment but kept his hands in his pockets.

As I placed my keys on the coffee table, Six walked over to the little wooden bookcase that housed my romance novels and I watched with increasing embarrassment as he picked one up and thumbed through it. "Hmm. I didn't even know there *was* a bridge over the Atlantic. Or maybe it's some kind of metaphor, huh?" he murmured as he glanced over the back cover of the book, his lips moving as he read the blurb. I smiled, wondering whether he was really *that* interested. He turned his head toward me and held the book up. "So, you like romance novels, huh?"

A nervous giggle escaped me and I immediately felt my cheeks heat. *Idiot.* "Well, I figure it's the only way I'll get to meet the man of my dreams." He frowned at my response and I suddenly wanted to change the subject. "W-would you like that drink now?" I inwardly cursed the stuttering mess I'd become around him. Another thing I promised myself I wouldn't do again.

He shrugged. "Um...yeah...coffee would be good."

Oh? "I have beer, if you prefer."

He shook his head vehemently and held up a hand. "Nah. Bike. I don't drink and ride."

This guy never ceased to amaze me. He had broken the law by riding without a helmet just so I was safe, yet he wouldn't drink and ride.

He was a true enigma. And my respect for him was growing, along with other feelings I was trying *very hard* to ignore. It was far too soon.

"Okay, well make yourself comfortable and I'll make you a coffee." I scurried off to the kitchen, but as I was pouring the grounds into the filter I felt his presence behind me. His hands lightly rested on my shoulders and a tingle traveled down my spine. Long thick fingers engulfed my collarbone and I turned slightly to see just how small he made me appear by the presence of his huge frame.

He squeezed, massaging the tensed muscles in my neck as he asked, "So...how were things at the club tonight? Any more ass-hats trying to grope you?"

His gravelly voice was tender and filled with genuine concern and his magical fingers were making it hard for me to concentrate on what I was supposed to be doing. With as much will as I could muster I carried on with my task trying not to turn into a puddle of mush at his soothing touch. "No, everything's been fine. No problems. None at all. Not a single one."

He chuckled and I felt his breath on my ear as he leaned forward. "Do I make you nervous, CD?"

He removed his hands from my body and I turned around to find him dangerously near. His broad, hard chest so close to my nose that I could inhale his delicious, masculine scent.

I gazed up at him. "Honestly? A...a little *yes*."

He stroked a thick, calloused finger down my cheek. "I don't *mean* to scare you."

His gruff but soft voice vibrated through my bones and I swallowed. "No...no...you don't *scare* me as such. I just... I kind of feel...*helpless* around you."

I watched as a line appeared between his brows. "But I would *never* hurt you, Chloe. That's not the kind of guy I am with women. Well not any more anyway." His eyes widened as he seemed to realize what he had just admitted to. "I mean I never *physically* hurt a woman. I maybe broke a heart or two..." I got a secret kick out of watching him flounder. It was exactly how he made *me* feel. He sighed and rolled his eyes, clearly exasperated with himself. "The point I'm *trying* to make is...I would *never* try to pressure you to do anything you didn't *want* to do. I'd never *force* myself on you. I'm not *that* guy."

"I...I didn't mean *that* kind of helpless." My voice was small and weak.

His confusion appeared to grow and the furrow in his brow deepened. "So in what way *do* I make you feel helpless?"

"Because..." I felt heat rise in my face again until my cheeks could have spontaneously combusted.

He stroked my cheek again. "Come on...you can tell me."

"Because... Because I've never been so attracted to a man before and it scares me to want you so badly when I've only just met you. I shouldn't feel this way so quickly. It doesn't seem right. I don't do this. I don't..."

A sweet, sexy smile stretched his luscious mouth, showing perfect white teeth and he lowered his face to meet mine. "Chloe dancer, you just brightened my day and I'm gonna kiss you now," he said just before his lips touched mine gently.

It started as a chaste, sweet kiss, his soft lips gliding effortlessly and sensually over mine but as I slipped my hands up his toned arms and around his shoulders he grasped my hair and tilted my head back. His tongue entered my mouth and his other hand snaked down my body until he gripped my behind, kneading and squeezing as the kiss gained urgency. He inhaled a deep, long breath through his nose and a growl emanated from the back of his throat. It was the most erotic sound I had *ever* encountered and I fought for control over myself but I was desperate for more of him.

He pulled away and fixed his gaze on mine. "I don't think I want coffee anymore." He effortlessly lifted me and carried me back through to the living room, placing me gently down on my couch. As he stood over me where I lay, he ran his hands through his hair and I watched as he bent to slowly unzip my hooded jacket. I fumbled out of it and threw it over the back of the couch. My chest heaved and my heart thrummed at my ribs.

From the throbbing between my thighs that had begun on the bike I knew I was already wet. He tugged the jacket from his body and dropped it the floor, gripped the hem of his T-shirt and dragged that free from his skin too. Next to go were his heavy biker boots that hit the far wall with a resounding thud as he kicked them away.

The sight of him looming over me, bare chested, ripped and tattooed was one of the sexiest things my eyes had ever beheld. He was even sexier in the flesh than I had imagined. And I had imagined him a *lot*. All six foot plus of man toned and ready to take me. The ridges of his abdomen expanded and contracted as he breathed heavily. His lust-filled, hooded gaze locked on me as I slowly removed my T-shirt and yoga pants. I was almost naked apart from my plain underwear. I watched him taking in the sight of me and wished that I'd had the sense to wear something more alluring.

"Fuck...Chloe...I..." His apparent reticence began to worry me again and I waited with bated breath for him to bolt once more.

CHAPTER THIRTEEN

Six

I wanted her.

There was *no* doubt in mind about it. But part of me was still playing over the awful scene I had witnessed earlier in the evening. I needed to forget. I needed to think about something *good*. To lose myself in nothing but sensation.

Her gaze lowered and she closed her eyes for a moment. "It's okay, Six. Just say it."

I ran my hands over my hair and licked my lips as I tried to memorize the sight of her in case God struck me down there and then for being such a selfish bastard for what I was thinking. She was offering herself to me willingly and I was on the verge of taking what I wanted from her body.

My cock was desperate for release from its confines and I wanted nothing more than to grant that wish. I took a deep breath in through my nose and pulled her scent into my lungs. She smelled so clean and fresh and...*innocent*.

But why was she acting like I was about to leave?

I dropped to my knees and before I could stop them my lewd thoughts spewed out in spite of my tightly clenched jaw. "I think you misunderstand me, Chloe. I need... I need to be inside you. I wanna be fucking *balls deep*, baby. I *need* to fuck you so much right now."

At the second the words left my mouth I hated myself. Why the hell couldn't I be more romantic like the guys in those books lining her shelves? Why did I say *fuck* so fucking much? My subconscious was right, she deserved *much* better than me. And I expected her to immediately kick me out of the apartment for how crudely I'd spoken to her.

She closed her eyes briefly again and I really thought I'd overstepped the mark. But when she opened them she sat up, reached forward and released the button and zipper on my jeans, allowing her eyes to follow the trail of her fingers downwards.

I inhaled sharply and her fingers lightly grazed the base of my straining cock. Once my zipper was open she reached around her back and unhooked her bra, letting it slip down her slender arms and fall to the floor. And there she was, bared to me from the waist up. Just a pair of black girl boxers covering her pussy. She had the most amazing tits I had *ever* seen. All natural. None of this fake, inflated silicone shit. They were perfect, firm and round with little pink buds that stood to attention just begging to be tasted. They were just the right size for my hands and I clenched my fists at my side to stop from reaching out to touch them.

"Fucking beautiful," I whispered as I devoured her naked breasts with my lustful gaze. My fists were still balled hovering near my hips.

"Six...it's okay, you *can* touch me. I *want* you to." Her voice was a breathy whisper and I couldn't help groaning and letting my head roll back. I stared at the ceiling for a moment and wondered what the hell I'd done right for God to grant me *this* and *not* strike me with a lightning bolt...whatever the hell *this* was.

I felt her moving and I returned my focus to her just as she kicked her panties off the end of her toe. She maneuvered up to a kneeling position and locked eyes with me. Reaching for my hand she opened my up my tensed fingers and placed my hand over her left breast. My cock flinched and the ache in my groin intensified. I squeezed lightly and tried not to blow my fucking load. I rolled my thumb over her pebbled nipple and licked my lips. Fuck I wanted her but... What if I went too fast? Took things too far? *Hurt* her? I mean she was so fucking petite and I sure as hell wasn't.

She pulled her lower lip in between her teeth as she fixed me with a determined gaze. My attention was drawn to the plump pink flesh as it popped out again.

Her voice snapped my focus back to her eyes. "I know you think I'm fragile, Six. Innocent even. And that you're scared of taking advantage of me. It's written all over your face. And even though I'm *not* a virgin I know you probably usually fuck girls who are a lot more experienced than me. And I want you to know that I've *never* thrown myself at a guy before...apart from you that is. It's just not *me*. But I want you, Six. I can't explain this intense need inside of me but something tells me you're the only one who can sate it. I need to feel you inside me."

The intense, deep caramel of her eyes pulled me in and I leaned down until our lips were almost touching. I could feel her rapid breath on my mouth and I fought the need to taste her. She was right. I *was* scared to touch her.

Scared that I'd somehow lose control.

She reached up and grasped the waistband of my jeans and pushed them down my thighs along with my fitted boxers. She shoved them toward the floor until I could bend and yank them over my feet along with my socks. I discarded them and turned to watch her again. When I was fully exposed to her she sighed as she raked her eyes over my tattooed chest. She reached up and delicately touched my ink and grazed her finger nails down my pecs over to my nipple piercing. I hissed in through my teeth as she flicked the metal bar. It sent sparks of desire through my body and felt so fucking good.

"Six, don't make me beg you."

Hearing her say my name again was all the encouragement I needed. I stooped and reached into my jacket pocket to retrieve a condom from my wallet and then with my eyes locked on hers I opened it and stretched it over my rigid flesh. It flinched toward her and she gripped it with both hands. Once again I let my head roll back as I got lost in the intensity of sensation just like I'd wanted. I clenched my jaw and scrunched my eyes tight as I absorbed the immense pleasure radiating through my veins and relaxing me.

She released my erection and took my hands pulling me down onto the couch beside her. I opened my eyes and watched as she slipped my hand down her slender body to the junction of her thighs. *What* the fuck was *wrong with me*? It was like I fucking froze. Like I needed *guidance*. I cupped her silken skin and dragged my thumb through the fine line of hairs over her pussy until I could feel how wet she was.

It was like an awakening.

My heart rate picked up and I *had* to have her. I just had to take what she was offering and what I so desperately wanted. *Needed.* I slipped two fingers into her slick opening and she gasped and clung to me with her free hand. Her other hand covered mine where I was sliding my fingers in and out of her body. She pushed me deeper and moaned my name. No woman had ever moaned my name in such unabashed pleasure before. I fucking loved it.

I needed *more*.

I removed my fingers from her entrance and her eyes snapped open. Sucking her arousal into my mouth, I groaned at the taste of her and her cheeks colored the sexiest pink. I leaned down and slipped my arms around her slender body.

"Can I take you to bed, Chloe dancer?"

She nodded and wrapped her legs around my waist. Her pussy hovering dangerously close to my stiff cock. I carried her toward the door that I remembered led to her bathroom. At the end of a short hallway I spotted a door that was ajar and nudged it open with my toe. Sure enough it was her bedroom. All pale blue flowers and fresh linen smell.

I laid her down on the soft billowing duvet that covered the bed and gazed at her. Her flawless skin was such a beautiful sight—such a contrast to mine—and I stood there just admiring the view. She parted her thighs and I took in the erotic vision before me of her naked and aroused body. Her pussy was glistening, wet and ready for me. I heard a sharp gasp and realized it had come from *my* body. Fuck, she was *stunning.* I'm talking portrait-worthy stunning. But not seedy and porn-like. Just beautiful. I climbed onto the bed and it dipped under my weight.

CHAPTER FOURTEEN

CHLOE

He crawled slowly up my body trailing kisses along the sensitive skin of my thighs and over my stomach. I shivered and gasped at the sensual torture and the delicious, delicate scratching of his beard against me. *Never* had I been so desperate for a man to be inside me as I was right then. I began to rock my pelvis in the hope he'd get the hint but instead he kissed his way back down again toward my pussy.

He nuzzled the thin, trimmed line of hair and inhaled. Dread washed over me. I'd been dancing at the club and hadn't showered yet.

Ohmygodohmygodohmygod.

I tensed but the vibration of his voice over my clit broke through my haze of panic. "Fuck, Chloe, I could get addicted to your pussy. You smell so fucking good. And I bet you taste even better." And with that his tongue slipped across my tingling flesh and he lapped at me with long sweeps that made my muscles clench with need.

I groaned and writhed as his skilled tongue circled me with precision. But just as I was on the verge of ecstasy he moved away and I wanted to scream.

I opened my eyes to find him smiling down at me and licking his lips. "I was right. Not that I doubted it for a second but you do taste amazing. And I'm going to want to taste you over and over, Chloe so you'd better get used to it." There was no way I would ever 'get used' to the way he made my body react. He leaned forward so that he was hovering over me again and he began to tease my nipples in turn, his eyes focused firmly on my face as he appeared to revel in the way I gasped and circled my hips.

I was desperate to close my eyes and let myself succumb to the sensations of pleasure radiating throughout my body, but his hooded gaze was mesmerising. No one had *ever* looked at me with such carnal longing and salacious need. I wanted to memorize the way his pupils dilated and his tongue flicked along his bottom lip.

He trailed his fingers down my tingling skin until he was cupping my pussy and slipping two thick fingers inside of me. A loud, wanton groan left my body and I realized my eyes had drifted closed. I immediately snapped them open and gasped up at him, filled with embarrassment at my involuntary expression of lust but it just seemed to spur him on.

"God, Chloe I love to hear you. It turns me on so much that I can bring that side out of you. Don't be embarrassed, baby. Just let go, okay?"

I had little choice but to obey him as his fingers slipped

and slid within my clenching body once again bringing me to the verge of ecstasy. But all too soon I was empty of him again.

In a split second a gravel filled croak informed me, "I've gotta fuck you now. I can't wait any longer." He maneuvered so that his whole body was between my thighs and my eyes trailed down his abdomen to where his cock flinched toward me. I held my breath. With one urgent thrust his thick, rigid length slammed into my wet and waiting body. *Finally*. I was so desperate for him and almost immediately exploded into a mind blowing orgasm. My pelvis circled and his thrusts became harder as I panted and scratched my nails down his muscular back.

He held himself aloft over me allowing me to peer down between us and observe the delicious way our bodies joined so intimately; like a perfectly carved jigsaw puzzle. He fit me. And I somehow fit *him* in spite of his size. I never wanted this connection to end. Fear began to clutch to at me as to what the hell would happen when this was over.

Thankfully I was pulled back from the darkness by his deep, voice as it resonated through my body. "Aw fuck Chloe...you make me wanna come so fucking hard."

His strained voice and words, regardless of how crude they seemed, sent me over the edge once more and I cried out, repeating his name over and over as I soared. A few seconds later Six gripped my behind with one hand and lifted me half off the bed so my legs automatically circled his waist. With a deep, lust filled groan from within his chest he thrust one last time and collapsed on top of me.

Oh. My. God.

Six

As my breathing calmed once more, I removed the condom and after knotting it, I discarded it in the little trash can by the bed. Then I moved to lay beside Chloe and pulled her naked body close to mine. A possessiveness overtook me and I didn't want to let her out of my sight *or* my arms.

Kissing her tenderly I huffed the air from my lungs. "Wow...just...fucking *wow*."

She giggled and my heart swelled in my chest. Her arm slipped around my waist and she gazed up at me, a hint of just-fucked pink flushed her cheeks. "Thank you."

I scrunched my brow not quite sure how to take her apparent *gratitude*. "For *what*?"

She broke my gaze and nuzzled my chest. "For saying 'wow' like you meant it."

Huh? I moved so that I could look down at her where she lay. The most beautiful post orgasmic glow tinged her skin. "But I *did* mean it."

She moved her face again so that she was staring at the ink on my chest, reluctant to look me in the eye and something she had said before niggled at me. Someone had made her feel unworthy of genuine attraction. Someone had killed her self-confidence. And I was beginning to put two and two together. My only hope was that I was going to come up with four. I needed to find out what the hell this douche had said to make her feel so inadequate. Ultimately I wanted to know who the bastard was so I could deal with him and make sure he learned a lesson about respect.

I had avoided asking her earlier but after this reaction I needed to know. "Chloe, who is Brett?"

She didn't look up. "Oh...no one."

Nuh-uh...not accepting that response. "Look, I know I'm a big hairy, bad-ass biker guy but I'm not dumb. This Brett asshole has made you insecure. And I want to know why."

She sighed heavily and pulled away from me to roll onto her back, turning her face farther away from me in the process. "He's...just someone from my past."

"No shit." I clamped my mouth shut and inwardly cursed myself for my sarcastic response. She didn't move and so I continued, "Well, if he makes you feel like shit I'm *glad* he's in your past. But whatever he did to you is still in your mind and that bothers me." I turned her face around so that she looked at me again. "Tell me. Come on. What did he say to you? Who the fuck is he?"

She pulled her lips in between her teeth and closed her eyes. Tears escaped and trailed downward into her blonde hair. "My mom's boyfriend."

Oh. "So you didn't get along with him?"

She laughed with a humorless venom. "Not in the way *he* wanted, no."

Okay. I'm gonna fucking rip him apart. With a measured calmness to my voice I clenched my jaw and asked, "Chloe, what did the bastard do to you?"

"Nothing." She kept her eyes firmly closed.

"Chloe, you've tensed up and won't look at me. I know that means you're lying. I just want to put your mind at rest and I can't do that unless I know what he said and did."

She pulled herself to a sitting position and pulled the blanket from the end of the bed to cover her nakedness as if she was suddenly ashamed of what we had done. Her knees came up to her chest—a sign I now recognized as defensive—and she rested her chin on them.

Still without looking at me she began to speak. "It started just after I turned eighteen... Brett was always flirting with me when my mom was at work. It was harmless at first and I just used to ignore him but... then he'd touch me but claim it was an accident. You know...like he'd reach past me and graze my breast with his arm...or he'd stand too close behind me and reach around me for something so that he was pressed up against me. I...I started to avoid being around him."

My blood began to boil and my heart was trying to escape through my ribcage. I wanted to rip the bastard limb from limb.

Making an effort to keep my breathing calm I listened intently as she continued, "But he made sure to find ways to be alone with me." She gave a humorless laugh. "And when we *were* alone, he'd full on grope me and tell me that it was *my* fault for teasing him. But when I wouldn't give in to him and have sex with him he started telling me I was ugly..." She swiped tears away from her cheeks and turned again so I couldn't see her face. "He said I was all tits and legs and all I was good for was *fucking*. That no one would *ever* love someone as ugly as me." She gave a snide huff. "He kept offering to fuck me so that I'd *at least* know what it was like to be with a man. And he threatened me with violence if I dared to tell my mom. I... I wanted to prove him *wrong*. I needed to prove to myself that I wasn't as hideous as he made out. So I went out and slept with some random guy just to prove to myself that I *could* find someone. But really he was right about everything. I saw the guy for a few weeks but then he dumped me. Said I was too clingy and needy. So once again I felt worthless. I slept around a little believing that *one* of the guys would eventually fall in love with me and *then* Brett would see he was wrong but... well *that* didn't happen."

My fists and jaw clenched simultaneously. I wanted to find this ass-wipe and pummel him into the fucking ground. But seeing how hard it was for her tell me all this I fought my instincts and remained as stoic as I could on the surface whilst a tumult raged beneath my skin.

"All the while he was being proved right and I started to believe him. That I *was* ugly. That I *was* worthless and even that I *was* a tease. At eighteen I should've been able to wear what I wanted but I found myself zipping everything up tight and covering my body so that he couldn't say those things. I began to wear baggy, oversized things because he said that when I wore T-shirts I was showing my breasts off to him to tease him on purpose with what I wouldn't let him have."

She took a deep shaking breath. "I snapped one day and slapped him after he'd groped my breasts and tried to stick his hand in my pants. I told him I was going to tell my mom everything but he pinned me to the wall and was on the verge of attacking me like he'd warned me he would. I honestly daren't think about what he had in mind back then. But he kept saying he'd just deny everything." She exhaled a shaking breath and her hands knotted in front of her. "My mom arrived home and so thankfully he let me go. Later that night I plucked up the courage and told my mom about what had happened and I expected her to kick him out..." A sob escaped her and I sat up to face her and place my hand on her shoulder. "But she believed *him*. Can you believe that? He told her

I'd been coming on to him for *months*. That I was trying to break them up because I was jealous. And she was so fucking blind with stupid love for the bastard that she *believed* him." She covered her face with her hands and I was desperate to just hold her but I was frozen to the spot trying to absorb all the shit she'd just told me. I closed my eyes and lowered my head searching my mind for the right words. She sniffed and I glanced over at her again. She had straightened up and stiffened her spine. "She told me I should leave. And so I stole a box from the kitchen that had some money and small pieces of jewelry in it and I left. I hated Brett so much for treating me that way. For causing my relationship with my mom to fall apart. I hated him for potentially ruining my future too. Until he started coming on to me I was doing great in school. That all changed. But when I left I was determined that I *would* make something of myself. Initially anyway. I came here and managed to finish off high school after explaining to the Principal what had happened. He was very understanding and after lots of discussions and meetings I was accepted onto the roll. They wanted to get the authorities involved but I just wanted to move on. Forget. I refused to press charges. Got my high school diploma, made a few friends. Then it all fell apart again. I couldn't afford college. Lived on couches, you know? Worked at the café to make some cash. The rest...well...you know..."

No sooner had the determination to go on taken over her, than it disappeared and her head dropped forward into her hands, her body was racked with shudders as she poured her heart out again. Mine was pounding so hard in my goddamn chest, I thought I was going to have a fucking heart attack and anger had knotted my guts so tight I felt nauseated. My jaw ached from being clenched so damn hard and a lump of emotion had tightened my throat.

She hadn't deserved *any* of that bullshit. *None* of it. I grabbed her petite body and pulled her into my lap, holding her against my chest as she cried. Warm tears trailed down my exposed skin and pooled in the lines of my abs as I held her and let her vent her sadness and despair on me. I pulled the blanket around us both and we sat there together for what seemed like hours.

Eventually she calmed and lifted her head. Her eyes were puffy and her nose was tinged pink to match her cheeks. "Shit, I'm sorry, Six. I...I shouldn't have regurgitated all my shit onto you. You didn't ask for that."

I smiled in what I hoped was a reassuring way and wiped some errant tears from her cheeks. "Hey, if you remember I *did* ask." She smiled too and I relaxed a little. "But I want you to know Chloe, that he was so wrong about you. You are beautiful. And sexy...and fucking hot as hell. Whatever the bastard said to you was an out and out fucking lie. And what he *did* to you was beyond wrong. A betrayal of your mom's *and* your trust. You deserved *none* of that. No woman deserves to be treated like that but especially not a kid. You were a *kid,* Chloe. Okay so eighteen is supposedly adult but...you'd only *just* turned eighteen. And *he* was an adult in a position of trust. The dirty bastard should've known better..." She stared blankly at me as I spoke. As if the words were just not sinking in. "Is that... Is that why you ended up dancing at *The Fox Hub*? Because of what he put you through?"

She shrugged. "Yeah... I figured no one would employ an ugly bitch like me unless I was showing off my body. It seemed to be all I had going for me."

I shook my head and took her face between my palms. "Oh God, Chloe. You are *so* wrong, sweetheart. You're bright and funny. You're so beautiful and you dance like...like a fucking professional dancer in one of those Broadway shows. But you are so *not* worthless. You're worth more than a *million* of him, baby." I smoothed my thumbs over her cheeks and placed a gentle kiss on her forehead.

Suddenly she flung her arms around me and kissed me with an urgency that stole my breath away. One of her hands snaked down my body until she had a firm grip on my cock.

What the hell? "Whoa...whoa...Chloe stop. Stop, baby." She pulled away and stared at me.

Her cheeks colored red and she clambered off my lap. "Oh great. Now you're *pitying* me again. Dammit, Six I don't *need* your pity."

I held up my hands. "That's not it at all. I *don't* pity you. You're getting me all wrong. I just...I don't want you to feel you have to be *grateful* to me or...or pay me in sex every time I compliment you. I'm gonna compliment you. A *whole lot*." I hoped my voice exuded tenderness. The last thing I wanted was to add to her embarrassment. "So you don't have to *do* that. I meant what I said. Every single word. But I think he's colored the way you see yourself. And I want you to know that I don't see you that way. And some day I hope *you* see you just how *I* do."

Tentatively I leaned toward her and kissed her lips gently. And fuck me if my dick didn't want in on the action.

She pulled away and glanced down at my groin. With a giggle she kissed my cheek. "Should I go make some coffee maybe?"

I smiled as heat rose in my own face and I tried in vain to

hide my raging wood. "Yeah. Coffee would be good. And while you're at it get me your phone. I'm gonna put my number in there...you know...just in case you need it and I'll take yours too." She narrowed her eyes at me and I shrugged. "What can I say? I guess my stalking habits are ingrained."

She smiled, shook her head and left the room.

CHAPTER FIFTEEN

CHLOE

After we had swapped phone numbers under the guise that my sexy stalker wanted to be "contactable in an emergency," we sat cross legged on my rug eating toasted bagels with cream cheese as Queens of the Stone Age played in the background. It was around four in the morning and we'd both gotten the munchies after we'd had sex and drunk coffee. Six sat there in just his boxers and I was being swamped by his black T-shirt which fell sexily off one shoulder and I made no attempt to change that. It was hard to concentrate on eating when the sculpted, tattooed Adonis was so close that I could feel his body heat warming my skin.

Trying to think of anything else but the delicious sensation of him filling me and his weight on top of me, I cocked my head to one side inquisitively. "So, what happened earlier tonight that got you so pissed off?"

He stopped chewing and placed his bagel back on the

plate. He sucked the cream cheese from his thumb and dropped his gaze to the floor. "I'd rather not talk about it. Don't want to spoil the mood, you know?"

I nudged him. "Oh come on. I shared my shitty baggage with you. It's only fair." I was trying to be playful but I had watched as the smile vanished from his face and was immediately filled with regret.

Me and my big mouth.

He sighed a heavy, weight filled breath and turned to face me. "There are things going on at the club. Politics and shit. A rival club is trying to get their hands on our land." He shrugged as if that explanation was sufficient.

I wasn't buying it. Remembering how he had pushed me to confess all my deepest darkest secrets I continued. "So... what got you all riled up about that tonight?"

He reached out, grasped his coffee mug and took a long gulp. "I said I'd rather not talk about it." He didn't look me in the eyes and a shiver of dread traveled my spine. There was clearly something he wasn't telling me and I was affronted at the fact that he had encouraged me to tell him about Brett yet *he* was unwilling to divulge anything further.

"Six, you *can* talk to me. You *can* trust me."

He slammed his coffee cup down and the loud bang made me almost jump out of my skin. "Just fucking *leave* it, Chloe. I said I won't fucking *talk* about it. So just *drop* it, okay?" He pushed himself up from the rug and stomped through to the bedroom. My heart skipped but my interest was piqued and all sorts of scenarios began to run around my mind. I tried to ignore them but failed miserably.

When he returned to the living room he was fully dressed apart from the T-shirt which I was still wearing. And oh my

God if he didn't look hot as hell in his jeans with his bare, tattooed chest on display.

But his next words were *not* what I wanted to hear. "Look, I should go. I need to be back at the club house. I've got like ten missed fucking calls." He ran his hands through his hair but didn't look me in the eye.

I nodded despite the fact that his eyes were focused anywhere but on me. "Okay, sure. I get it."

His head snapped in my direction. "No. No, Chloe you *don't* get it at all. You have no fucking *clue* what you're trying to get mixed up in here." His voice was raised and his eyes glowed with a caramel fire that scared and thrilled me all at once.

I stood carefully and began to slowly approach him. "Then *explain* it to me, Six."

A long exasperated exhale left his body and the sexy, care-free smile from earlier had completely vanished.

His jaw clenched and unclenched a few times before he answered. "Look, my life is a shit storm mixed up in a fucking tornado of guns and death. You don't need to be involved in that shit."

I forced a smile. "Is this you letting me down gently again? Because it's not very gentle."

"Yes...*no*...awww fuck I don't know, CD. I honestly have no *idea* what's going to happen next. Shit is so messed up right now. I can't...I won't *drag* you into that."

The fact that he still used my cute pet name gave me a glimmer of hope that maybe things were not over between us. At least I hoped that was the case. I nodded, keeping my eyes on him and digging my nails into my palms to stop me from crying. The last thing I wanted to do was cry in front of him *again*. If I *did* he would *definitely* think I was a fragile, weak little girl. And I couldn't *be* that to him. Not after the night we'd shared. And not with the life he led.

I *wouldn't* be that to him.

I shrugged. "Okay. Well, if and when things change I'll maybe see you at *The Fox Hub*."

His brow crumpled in confusion. I guessed that he had expected more of an argument. "Yeah...*maybe*. Look, tonight was... You were..." He stepped closer and slipped his hand around the back of my head and tangled it into my hair. "You. Are. Fucking. Beautiful. Don't *ever* let Brett or any other bastard tell you otherwise." He kissed my forehead and inhaled the scent of my hair before letting go of me, turning and leaving my apartment in a hurry.

Once the door had slammed shut my lip began to tremble as a mixture of sadness, humiliation and confusion washed over me. I dashed to the window just in time to watch him take off on his bike at speed down the road, his leather jacket open and his chest exposed to the cool early morning air.

———

I was awoken by someone knocking on my door. Glancing at the clock the time registered in my brain. *Shit I must have been tired*. It was gone ten in the morning and I was still wearing Six's T-shirt. It smelled of him and an air of sadness washed over me. I was beginning to acquire a collection of his clothing and while that should have made me smile it only served to lower my frame of mind further. I rubbed my eyes and then glanced over to the side of the bed where he had laid as he held me only hours before. I wondered if he was okay and then remembered that someone was knocking at my door. *Shit! It could be him!* I scrambled out of my bed and grabbed my yoga pants, hopping on each leg in turn as I pulled them on.

I smoothed my hair down and opened the door.

"Oh my God, thank goodness you're okay! I was so worried." I was enveloped in a bear hug from a very pale faced Ellie.

I hugged her back and laughed lightly. "*Why* were you worried? How long were you knocking?"

"Oh not long. But I came as soon as I heard."

My sleep fogged brain failed to grasp what she was talking about and so I pulled away and looked her in the eyes. "Heard about *what*?"

Ellie's voice wavered. "The girl. She's...she's *dead*."

I felt the color drain from my face and dizziness caused a ringing in my ears. "*Who's* dead?"

"Look, let me come in and I can explain the parts you don't already know." She pushed past me and walked over to the couch. She flopped down onto it and peered up at me with a worried expression.

I walked to the opposite side of the coffee table and peered down at her with my hands on my hips. "Okay, now you're totally freaking me out. *Who* is dead and what parts should I already know?"

Her eyes widened. "Shit. You don't know at *all* do you?"

I flung my hands into the air becoming increasingly agitated at her cryptic clues. "Know *what*? Shit, Ellie, can you just *start* making fricking sense?"

She nodded slowly and held her hand out toward me. "I think...I think you'd better sit down, sweetie."

I walked slowly around the table and sat beside my friend. The concerned frown on her face did nothing to relax me. "What the hell is going on? Just *tell* me already."

"Okay... But... I want you to know that I heard this from a *very* reliable source. I'm not *trying* to cause problems here. I'm telling you this as a friend. I hope you understand that."

I huffed. "Yeah, yeah, whatever. Don't shoot the messenger and all that shit. What *is* it?" I could hear the annoyance in my own voice and my stomach twisted with a combination of guilt and panic.

"There was a major incident last night. Up at the old farm land on the outskirts of town." She took a deep breath and something niggled at the back of my mind. Six had mentioned something about some land. "There...there was a... a shooting..."

My stomach plummeted and took my heart along for the ride. "And?"

"A girl... a *young* girl I went to school with...couple years younger than me...than *us*...one of the biker gang kids...was... was *killed*."

I felt the blood drain from my face. "Shit...that's *awful*." I clutched my chest where my heart was still thundering. "H-hang on...did I *know* her? Is that why you're acting all weird?"

Although I had met Ellie after I had finished up high school locally, I knew of at least *one* girl related to a nearby biker gang, but then Ellie and I had gone to different high schools...

"No sweetie. She was one of the Loki's Legion kids. Went to *my* school. I didn't know her that well. But...the thing is..."

Frustration got the better of me. "Come *on* Ellie! What's the thing? What is it?"

"Your...your biker guy was apparently involved."

The room began to spin again and a wave of nausea washed over me forcing me to cover my mouth. From that moment Ellie's words ceased to make any sense to me. Her voice appeared to be a distant mumble and all I *could* hear was the pounding of my heart, loud like it was throbbing in my ears.

"Chloe...Chloe are you okay? Do you need to lie down? Oh gosh I'm so sorry to just blurt it out like that. I just wanted to protect you from *him*. You need to be careful, honey. You don't know what he's capable of. *None* of us do. These bikers are volatile characters. *Violent* men and women. We don't *need* them around here but there doesn't seem to be a thing we can do about that. But what we *can* do is keep away from them. Are you listening to me?"

I snapped my eyes up to her and rage boiled beneath my skin. "I think you should leave."

"What? No, Chloe, you don't get it. I'm trying to keep you *safe*."

"By coming here and telling me that the man who saved *me* from being raped has killed a young girl?" The incredulity in my voice was clearly audible.

But she was persistent. "Chloe, you maybe need to get away for a while. Just until this whole situation calms down. The cops are going to try and get involved but from what I've seen before that just turns ugly. You don't want to be dragged into this shit."

I watched her mouth moving and tried to listen but all I could think about was how Six had been strange. Tense. Unwilling to talk. But he wouldn't *do* such a thing. *Surely* he wouldn't? I needed to speak to him.

She *had* to leave.

Snapped back to reality I placed my hands firmly on her arms. "Ellie, I understand. And I'm grateful for your concern. But right now I need to speak to Six. I need to hear *his* side. He...he wouldn't do anything to hurt a young girl. I just *know* he wouldn't. He's a gentle giant. I... I feel like I know him well enough to hear him out."

"No!" She gripped my arms in return. "No, *please* keep away from him, Chloe. I know you really like the guy but he's not worth getting yourself *killed* for. You don't understand. These things usually go all biblical. An eye for an eye. Loki's Legion, they could come after *you*. You need to disassociate yourself from the Company of Sinners. *Please*."

I stood and encouraged Ellie to stand too. "Yes...yes I'll do that," I lied and I'm pretty sure she knew it. "I'll call you later okay? I need to shower and get dressed."

She nodded and then pulled me into another hug. "Please, be careful. *Please*."

I walked her to the door and said goodbye. Once the door was closed behind her I dashed to the bathroom. I needed answers and I planned on getting them sooner rather than later.

CHAPTER SIXTEEN

Six

When I'd arrived home in the early hours Colt had been hell bent on tearing me a new asshole. I'd had enough of his shit and I'd walked away as he hurled a torrent of verbal abuse at me. Apparently my actions and my lack of concern for the club were what was *causing* all the mess. The annoying part about the whole thing was that he wasn't *actually* pissed at *me*. Just as I'd gotten back, Cain had announced that he wanted out of the club and I didn't know what the fuck was going on with everyone. He'd told us that Melody was pregnant with his kid and he figured that 'club life' wasn't good enough for him anymore. It wasn't, and I quote 'any place to bring up a child.'

On reflection, he had a damn good point.

There was too much fucking carnage going on around me and I couldn't take anything else going wrong. Apart from Colt and his tongue lashing, I'd ignored everyone, including the club fuck buddy who'd almost humped my leg as I tried to walk away. Oh the things she was offering to do to me to ease my stress. *Not fucking interested.* But she clearly got off on anger and I almost had to amputate my arm and leg to get rid of the horny bitch.

I made my way upstairs and barged into the end room without knocking, much to the annoyance of Weasel who had his dick in the mouth of another girl, a brunette who'd been hanging around the place for a while. After extricating Weasel and his piece of trash from the room, I'd undressed and thrown what clothes I'd removed into a pile on the floor. Chloe still had my T-shirt and so after taking off my jeans and jacket I ended up lying there in the dark in just my boxers.

I hadn't been asleep long. Or at least it didn't *seem* like I had when someone started hammering at the door, but I initially ignored it. The thudding came again and I heard Delilah calling out to me.

"Yeah, what the fuck do you *want?*" My anger wasn't really aimed at her but she was a moving target and so she got hit.

The door swung open. "Six, it's after ten a.m. and you got a visitor."

After ten? And who the hell's coming to bother me now? Another club fuck buddy no doubt hoping to relieve me of my shitty mood. "Awww fuck. Just tell them I don't fucking *need* a blow job, Dee." I glared over at her.

She cringed and stepped to one side. "Ummm...it's not *that* kind of visitor. Well I don't *think* so at least."

I sat up and was met with the beautiful brown eyes of my dancer. *Fuck! Why did I have to mention blow jobs?*

I scrambled up from the bed and walked over to the door

as I ran my hands over my mussed up hair. I must have looked like a total waster. "Shit, Chloe, what are you doing here? How did you find me?"

She stepped toward me but the blank expression on her face told me it wasn't much of a *social* visit.

Her arms folded defensively across her body. "I asked around about where the club house was. I was directed here. I guessed it was where you'd be."

How the hell had she even been *let in*? We were supposed to be on fucking lock down for Chrissake. "Yeah...well you found me so I guess you'd better come on in."

I stepped aside and nodded to Delilah who mouthed the words "good luck" to me before she went back to the main bar downstairs.

I heaved a sigh. "So...to what do I owe the ple—"

"Cut the bullshit, Six. I want to know what happened up at that piece of land you mentioned to me last night. And don't try to brush me off with lies this time."

I clamped my mouth shut and raised my eyebrows. My VP side sprang to life. "Who the *fuck* do you think you're talking to?"

She stepped toward me, tenacious little bitch—fuck she gave me a hard on—and sneered up at me. "That's what *I'd* like to fucking know you lying bastard."

I gritted my teeth and closed the remaining gap between us. "Watch your mouth, Chloe. Cussing doesn't suit you," I growled down at her.

"Yeah? Well lying to my face doesn't suit *you*. And I know that something went down because the people downstairs are talking about a shooting. Now tell me the goddamn truth or I walk out of here and you *never* see me again."

This was my opportunity to extract her from my life and save her from the mess that it was no doubt about to become. To save her from even more heartache that she didn't deserve.

She really didn't need to be dragged into my B.S.

I laughed darkly. "And you think *that's* some kind of a *threat* to me? Like not seeing you again would somehow hurt me?"

She gasped and I felt like a prize bastard.

Her nostrils flared and she nodded slowly as her eyes became glassy. "Fair enough. If that's how it is then I'd better go. I clearly don't mean as much to you as I'd hoped." As she spoke her voice wavered. It *had* been a low blow considering the stuff she'd told me about her mom's boyfriend, Brett and how he'd treated her. She turned slowly and began to walk away from me but before I knew what the hell I was doing I reached out for her and pulled her back toward me.

"Why do you have to be so fucking beautiful and so damned stubborn?" It was a dumb question I know. But it was the *one thing* stopping me from letting her walk out of my room *and* my life for good.

She stood there all cute in a short little floaty skirt that showed off those smooth, silky legs. Tattered old cowboy boots with a heel gave her a little more height than I was used to, and her low cut tank top showed just enough cleavage to remind me how good her firm tits felt against my bare chest.

But her next words struck me like an electric shock straight to my heart. "And why do *you* have to be so damned cruel?"

Without thinking I scooped her up into my arms and crushed my mouth to hers. She fought against me for about ten seconds and I was thinking maybe I should let her go seeing as I'd promised her I wasn't *'that guy'*. But then her hands came about my shoulders and she gripped my hair and tugged desperately at the strands just enough to sting, kissing me back with as much urgency and need. Little whimpering noises vibrated from her body into mine and all I could think about was her tight pussy around my cock.

Maybe it was a distraction technique. Maybe I just couldn't get enough of her. Maybe it was a combination of those things but I threw her down on the bed and landed almost on top of her. My hand trailed roughly up her thigh as she moaned into my mouth. When I reached the junction of her thighs I found she was already wet and I slipped two fingers past her panties and into her pussy. She clenched as I thrust them in and out of her tight body and the urge to taste her was overwhelming.

I pushed her thighs apart and moved myself between them. Removing my damp fingers and sucking them clean, I tugged at the flimsy fabric of her thong until it tore and was no longer causing a barrier to me and I dove in. Tongue first. She grasped at my hair as my tongue slipped and slid in and out of her slick flesh. She tasted as amazing as I remembered and I needed more. I plunged my tongue as deep as I could go and lapped at her as she exploded around me. Her muscles spasming, her breaths ragged and loud as she cried out in ecstasy.

Hearing the incoherent noises as they left her body somehow got me harder. As she was coming down from her orgasm I leaned down to my pile of clothes and rummaged around my pockets for my wallet.

One condom left. Thank fuck.

I yanked my boxers free of my body, tore open the condom wrapper and dragged the latex down my cock as quickly as I could. I growled through my gritted teeth, "I'm gonna fuck you now unless you're planning on leaving."

Her eyes half opened and she peered up at me slowly shaking her head.

I clenched my jaw again unsure of the meaning of her gesture. "Is that *no* you're *not* leaving or *no I can't* fuck you? 'Coz I told you I'm not *that* guy, Chloe."

"I'm not leaving," she panted breathlessly. It was all the encouragement I needed and I slammed my cock into her making her cry out again, tightening around me and sending shock waves of pleasure shooting around my whole body like shafts of light. I reached up and shoved her tank top up over the mounds of her tits and pulled the bra cups down to expose the erect peaks to my hands. I sucked each nipple into my mouth in turn to prolong the orgasmic wave that seemed to be continuing to roll over her body. She keened and rocked into me causing an intense friction and making every single one of my nerve endings come to life as she repeated my name over and over like a fucking oath.

Hearing my name fall from her lips again drove me over the edge and I thrust into her once more with a guttural cry as I came hard. "Fuuuuck!"

I collapsed on top of her and she turned her face toward me. Her hot breath tickled at my ear and I lifted my gaze to meet hers but her eyes were closed and I was suddenly terrified of what I'd just done.

"You okay?" I asked nervously.

She nodded. "That was intense. I've never had angry sex before."

I chuckled and stroked her cheek with my thumb. "Well, I guess there's a first time for everything, huh?"

She opened her eyes and her bright chocolate irises penetrated me. "Not *every*thing." She raised her eyebrows.

The emphasis she had placed on the word made me grin. "Is that your way of telling me your ass is out of bounds?"

She gasped and a horrified, wide eyed expression took over her features. "Hell *yes* it's out of bounds!"

I reached around and squeezed her butt to emphasize my point. "Hey, don't knock it 'til you've tried it, babe."

I loved to wind her up and she was so easy to rile. She lightly slapped my bare chest and I pushed her back to kiss her again.

CHAPTER SEVENTEEN

Chloe

I was under the distinct impression that Six had just used sex to stop me asking questions. And while I had enjoyed it more than I cared to admit, I wasn't about to let him win the battle. He already *thought* I was stubborn but he was just about to learn it as a damned *fact*.

He sat there opposite me on the king sized bed in just his black fitted boxers as I assessed him with my gaze. Each tattoo no doubt had a story, from the Company of Sinners winged skull on his back to the phoenix on his chest and the Celtic sleeve that ran the whole way down his arm. I was trying hard not to let his physical attributes distract me from gleaning the truth. But it was ridiculously hard when he was almost naked in front of me.

Dragging my attention away from his fascinating ink and rock hard body, I tried again to get some answers. "So...are you going to tell me what's been going on?" I asked as I adjusted my bra and tank top.

He sighed and bent his knees up so that he could rest his forearms on them. "Don't you ever just give up and let things go?" His brow crinkled into a frown.

I crossed my arms over my chest. "Nope."

He rubbed his hands roughly over his face and back through his hair. "Look, Chloe, it's hard for me to talk about. And if I'm honest, I shouldn't be telling you anyway."

"Because I'm not part of your '*club*'?" I made inverted commas in the air which resulted in a disgruntled, unappreciative sneer from Six. "I've already told you that I'm trustworthy, Six. Whatever you tell me goes no further."

He let his head fall back for a moment. "Fuck, you drive me *crazy* you know that?"

I grinned. "Yup."

He shook his head, defeated. "Okay... But I'm warning you, once you know what's going on you may want to tell me to fuck off out of your life."

Nope, not a chance. "I'll risk it."

He laid back on the bed again and folded his hands behind his head, breaking eye contact. "There's a piece of land right next some land that *we* own. We call it no-man's land but really it's been more *ours* than anybody's over the years. But...Loki's Legion have decided *they* want it. They have no real claim over it but they're just stirring the shit pot. And after the stuff with the bastard who tried to rape you, and me stepping in, they've taken things a step further. Apparently they don't take too kindly to having their perverted plans fucked with. There were rumblings going on between the clubs anyway. But...well everything that goes on now is a battle of wills.

"They were on the land last night and we heard about it so we went up to see what was going on. We had no intention of starting anything, least of all a gun fight. But... one of the Legion guys pulled out a .45 and started firing. Fucking asshole had been drinking and so he missed with every shot...*thankfully*. But Weasel... he's one of our guys unfortunately...a bit of a loose cannon if you ask me...he began to fire back and..."

"And?" My heart began to thump at my ribs again as I knew what was coming.

I watched his throat working. He inhaled a shaking breath and closed his eyes. "There was a girl there... Deak's daughter —he's the Prez of Loki's Legion—anyway, she got caught in the crossfire and was hit." He cleared his throat and swallowed hard as his voice broke. "There was...there was a lot of screaming...and blood...I've never...it was... Anyway... she...um...she died before anyone could get help. Turns out she was hit right in the fucking heart. She was *eighteen*." His voice cracked and his eyes remained closed. The disbelief and emotion in his voice made my own throat tighten.

I gasped and clutched my own chest where my heart skipped and tripped over itself. "Oh my God, Six, that's awful."

Still without looking at me he nodded. "Yeah. It *was*. No one knew why the hell she was even *there*. She *shouldn't* have been there."

Suddenly a shiver traveled my spine and nausea rolled over me. Guilt hit me like a ton of bricks and I covered my mouth in case my stomach rejected its meager contents. Realization of what had happened began to sink in. This whole thing had gotten worse because of *me*. Because Six had stepped in to help *me*. That young girl was *dead* because of *me*. Before I knew what was happening a sob ripped from my throat and I crumpled forward onto the bed retching and gasping. I could hardly breathe and I began to see stars in front of my eyes as my lungs desperately tried to pull in air.

I was on the verge of blacking out when Six grabbed me and dragged me into his lap. I hadn't even seen him move.

"Don't you fucking *dare* blame yourself, Chloe. I *know* that's what you're doing and you're *wrong*. This is *not* your fault. Do you *hear* me?" He placed a hand on each side of my face and forced me to look at him. "This shit was going on *years* before I even knew you existed, baby. Just breathe. Okay? Just breathe. You didn't cause *any* of this. And if I had to stop that bastard from attacking you all over I'd do it in a heartbeat. You hearing me? In a fucking *heart*beat."

Six breathed along with me and I eventually managed to calm down. My hands gripped onto his where they rested on my face. His eyes locked on mine now as he repeated over and over, "In through your nose and out through your mouth, nice and slow..."

Once I was no longer in the midst of a panic attack he placed me back on the bed and disappeared into the adjacent bathroom. A few moments later he returned and began to wipe my face with a cloth he had soaked in warm water. His smile was reassuring but my heart was still refusing to co-operate.

He tucked my hair behind my ears. "That's much better. You okay?"

I nodded, not yet daring to speak in case the whole thing began again.

"I'm gonna go downstairs and get us a drink okay? You stay here. I'll be back soon." He rose from the bed and kissed the top of my head before walking out the door, still only in his boxers.

I sat there on the bed taking in the sparse surroundings of the room. I knew that he didn't actually *live* here and guessed that the room was used by others too. I wondered what MC life was really like and if *I* could fit into it. Did I *want* to fit into it? And more to the point did *Six* want me to fit into it with *him*? Or was I just a fling? It was a moot point if all he was after was a fuck buddy. I couldn't be that. Not even for him. It just wasn't me.

Ten minutes later he reappeared holding two glasses of amber liquid. He handed one to me and I took it tentatively sniffing at the contents. *Whiskey*. Not my drink of choice but I guessed this was his way of helping me to be calm. I took a small sip and almost choked as the liquid burned a path to my stomach.

CHAPTER EIGHTEEN

Six

As I held Chloe in my arms and tried to calm her down I inwardly cursed myself for spilling everything out on her like that. The last thing she should have felt was guilt for the crap going on in *my* life. And this was what I'd wanted to avoid. Dragging her into my mess was *not* something I had intended to do. But I'd tried to keep my distance and failed miserably.

Selfish bastard.

She was too pure. Too sweet to be tainted by the shit I was involved in. Okay she *had* lived and experienced stuff that had already marked her soul in *some* ways but I didn't want to exacerbate that. And here I was doing the exact opposite of what I'd wanted. I'd set out with the best of intentions. I'd wanted to *protect* her and instead I was ruining her fucking life. *I should just push her out. Force her to leave before it's too late.* My head had the sense to think it, but the selfish bastard inside of me wanted her. *Needed* her. It was like she was somehow the antidote to all the darkness I'd seen. It scared me that I might grow to depend on her ability to make me feel good.

To feel *worthy*.

I'd already been to the bar and gotten us a drink, but Chloe had almost choked on it. She was even too fucking innocent for whiskey.

That spoke volumes.

I didn't touch mine as I sat surreptitiously watching her. We sat there in an uneasy silence for a while until I could stand it no longer. "So...I guess I should take you home, huh?"

She shook her head. "It's okay. Just call me a cab if you want me to go."

A cab? No fucking way. "Uh-uh. I want to make sure you get home safe. This is no place for you to be."

She slammed her glass down on the night stand, sloshing the contents out and I jumped like a little girl. I'd pissed her off again.

"Six, would you just *stop* treating me like a child, *please*. I *chose* to be here. I don't actually *want* to go home. I came here to be with *you*." Suddenly she closed her eyes and dropped her head forward. "Unless you *want* me to leave?"

I *didn't* want her to leave. At *all*. But her being here was confusing the hell out of me. I needed a break.

"Look, I don't know about you but I'm starving. I'll go down to the kitchen and see if I can't rustle up something to eat." It was a blatant change of subject and I knew she had me pegged. But before I could see that in her eyes, I stood and left the room to make my way down to the bar. Delilah was sitting there watching Cain and Melody kissing in the corner, his hand flat on her belly. Why the fuck Dee continued to torture herself was beyond me.

She glanced up as I approached. "Hey. Don't you have any clothes? I don't wanna see your junk, man. You're like my bro and it's wrong on so many frickin' levels."

Aw shit. There had been no one to take notice earlier seeing as they were all occupied elsewhere but now, I suddenly remembered I was in only my boxers and I cringed. "Sorry, Dee. I just came down for a couple more drinks and some food. Things have gotten intense up there."

"She know what went down up at no-man's land yet?" I nodded and pulled my lips between my teeth. Delilah shook her head and jumped down from the bar stool she was sitting on. "Oh shit. She's still here though right? That's a *good* thing."

I snorted. "*Is* it?"

Her brow scrunched in confusion. "Well *isn't* it?"

"Shit. I really like her, Dee. And that's *not* a fucking good thing. She shouldn't *be* here."

"Hey come on. Like I just said, you're like a brother to me and I can honestly say that in all the years I've known you she is the *first* girl who has *really* caught your attention. You get those fucking doe eyes when you look at her. And she's a feisty one. I like her. She's a keeper."

I shook my head. I didn't *want* the club to like her. That'd only make it worse when I kicked her ass out for her own good. "She can't stick around. It's not safe. She needs out of my life."

Another frown. "She *said* that?" She handed me a couple large glasses of single malt.

"No. *I'm* saying it."

Delilah laughed like she knew something I didn't. "Oh, Six. You just don't get it do you?"

"Get what? Why you laughing at me?"

"She's *into* you, honey. It's too late. You're done for. Ain't no way you're getting rid of her unless you do something real bad. And I mean *real* bad."

What the fuck? "Worse than killing an eighteen-year-old girl?"

Suddenly Dee got pissed and slammed her hands on the bar. "You did *not* pull that fucking trigger, Six. *Weasel* is the one in the shit for that. *He's* the one who should pay." She was right.

But I had been there too and I hadn't stopped him. "Say what you want, Dee, but I know that having her here isn't helping me. I want her gone but I don't know how to tell her without hurting her."

Someone cleared their throat behind me and my stomach dropped to the floor. I spun around and was greeted by the beautiful, glistening, brown eyes of my Chloe dancer.

A deep sadness had settled on her features. "It's okay. Heard you loud and clear. I'll be going now."

Awww shit. Hello mouth here's my size thirteen foot. "Chloe, no, I—"

She shook her head to stop me. "Don't. I've said all along I don't need your protection *or* your pity. Just do me one last decent thing and call a cab for me...please?"

I heaved a defeated sigh. "I'll take you home. Just let me get dressed, okay?"

"You've been drinking. I can get a cab."

I held up my hands. "I only had a sip. I'm good. Wait here."

Realizing I had inadvertently solved my own problem I jogged up the stairs to the end room and pulled on my clothes as quickly as I could. I caught sight of my reflection and shook my head at the bearded idiot staring back at me. "Asshole."

When I arrived at the main bar area, Chloe was sitting on a bar stool chatting to Delilah who was patting her arm, I'm guessing trying to comfort her. She glanced up at me and I smiled. She didn't smile back and I don't really know why but my stomach knotted at the fact.

I pulled on my leather jacket and cut and sheepishly walked over to Chloe. "Come on. I'll take you home now." I handed her my helmet and then—remembering her look of disapproval the last time I had ridden with her without my own helmet—I grabbed Cain's off the bar, put it on and fastened the strap under my chin.

Once outside, I straddled the bike and held out my hand for her but being the stubborn, frustrating woman that she is. She ignored my offer of help and clambered on behind me...*pantiless*.

"Hold on tight." I called as I turned on and revved the engine. I felt her hands come about my waist and link in front of me. As I glanced down I got that knot in my guts again. Was this it? Was this the last time? I had to face the fact that I'd *wanted* her out of my life and she had heard me say so. The only problem was she had gotten the whole situation wrong. This was for *her* own good. It wasn't what *I* wanted for me. It was what I wanted for *her*.

I spotted Cain over by the open gates and nodded at him as I passed by and began to pull out into the road. The gates were closed and locked behind me and I checked around to make sure there were no unwelcome watchers hanging around. Thankfully the coast was clear and we set off at speed toward Chloe's apartment.

Eventually I pulled the bike to a halt in the parking lot and removed my helmet quickly so I could speak to her before she inevitably stormed off out of my life for good. Just as I expected she slipped off the bike and removed the helmet before thrusting it into my arms without speaking and almost winding me in the process.

I grasped her arm as anger at myself boiled beneath my skin. "Chloe, what you heard back there—"

She struggled trying to get her arm free. "Let go of me you bastard!"

"Whoa, hey, don't cuss at me woman. You know I *hate* that."

She sneered at me. "Yeah? Well I don't *fucking* care what you *fucking* hate. Now let go and *fuck* off!"

I gritted my teeth and yanked her toward me so that her face was only inches from mine. "You're gonna listen to me first."

With an edge of bitter calm to her voice she leaned in closer until her nose was almost touching mine her eyes wide and wild. "I don't have to do what *you* say. Now let me go or I swear I'll scream."

Seriously, I think I have a major mental problem or something because seeing her angry like that just made me want her more. I loved the strength she showed even when she was scared or emotional. She was sexy as hell and where most girls would have cowered away from a guy like me when I was angry *she* didn't. She had balls if you know what I mean.

I flared my nostrils and spoke through clenched teeth.

"No. You're *right*. You don't *have* to do what I say because you're not mine. But if you were..."

She snorted in my face. "You'd *what?* Beat me into submission? What a big, big man you are, Six. So *very* tough. I'm sure you'd make your momma proud."

Fucking ouch! "You bitch," I growled.

She seemed taken aback by my words and her expression suddenly changed. She knew it had been a low blow. But she carried on trying to put up a front. "Damn *right* I'm a bitch. And don't you forget it."

I released her arm and turned away as she stepped back. "Just go. I need to get out of here before..."

"Before what?" Why the hell was she still standing there? And why the hell did she sound so fucking mousy all of a sudden?

I glanced over at her and sighed. "All I have *ever* done is try to protect you. What you heard back there...that was *me* trying to save *you* a truck load of heartache. You didn't hear what I said before that, Chloe."

She stepped toward me again. "W-what *did* you say before?"

"Just go home, okay? You're better off letting me leave now before you get attached to me and I fucking break your heart like I break everyone's heart."

"I hate to drop this bombshell on you but... I'm kinda *already* attached to you."

Oh. Fuck.

CHAPTER NINETEEN

CHLOE

I *hated* myself for talking about him 'making his momma proud' in such a cruel way. I *hated* how I had a tendency to speak before thinking. And I *hated* the way I had clearly hurt him with my words.

He hung both helmets over the handlebars and scrubbed a hand over his face. "Don't say you're attached to me, Chloe, okay? Just don't. You know nothing about me or about my past for that matter. You don't know the shit I've done or the way I've behaved. You know this fucking weedy ass character that I've become since that night at *The Fox Hub*. That's *not* the real me. I'm not some whiny fucking pussy. Jeez I've been acting like a fucking doe-eyed teenager. But it's not real. None of that's me. I'm an evil bastard. And you'd do well to remember that. What you think you know is all bullshit."

"You're *not* evil, Six. Okay, so you've done things that were necessary at the time. But you're not alone in regretting things in your past. But it doesn't mean you have to let history repeat itself. No one *has* to allow that to happen. We can stop it because it's about how we change *ourselves* for the future. I can tell you don't like certain things about yourself and...if that's the case then *do* something about it. And just so you know, I happen to like the guy I've known since that night at *The Fox Hub*. I don't consider him a whiny pussy. Far from it. I consider him a hero actually. Just because a man shows he cares doesn't make him weak."

I stepped forward again and stroked my hand delicately down his gorgeous, bearded face. "If you don't want me then just *say* you don't want me. But don't push me away out of some misplaced desire to protect me from *you* and your life."

He turned his face into my hand and locked his gaze on me. "I just don't want you getting hurt because of *me*." His voice was a gravelly whisper.

"See...if you *were* evil you wouldn't care about any of that." I smiled trying to lighten the dark cloud that had descended over us.

He clambered off his bike and held out his hand. "Come on. I'll walk you to the main entrance."

I took his hand and we made our way to the door in silence. I turned to face him in the hope of kissing him good-night, but he gripped me and lifted me from the ground crushing his mouth into mine with a passionate ferocity that stole my breath and I wrapped my legs around him. Whatever the hell this was between us was so easy to spark.

He groaned as he rocked his pelvis into my naked flesh and the friction made me gasp. I'd completely forgotten that he'd ruined my underwear in his desperation to be inside me and here we were outside the main entrance to my building, making out in a *very* public place, but I really didn't care. All that I cared about was making him see that I didn't want to eject him from my life, regardless of the fact that it would probably have been the most *sensible* thing to do. But I was *done* being sensible. I *wanted* him so desperately that I was willing to risk *anything* to be with him.

After all, I had wanted him from the first moment I laid eyes on him as he watched me at the club all those months ago. And he had wanted me just as badly. Surely that was *something* worth fighting for? Something worth pursuing?

His hand slipped down to my naked behind and his fingers slowly glided toward the front of my body. Once again he found my pussy wet and wanting. He stroked at my clit and my breathing rate increased as his fingers masterfully played my body.

"Fuck, Chloe, all I want to do is make you happy. To *please* you. I love to watch you come for me. It's like an addiction to me."

His words and the desperation in his voice sent me into free-fall and his mouth stifled my cries of ecstasy as I came over and over, each intense orgasmic thrall made me surrender more of myself to him. I was completely undone.

Eventually my breathing began to settle and my body calmed as he kissed my neck, cheeks and collarbone all the while whispering how beautiful I was and how he loved to watch me.

I quickly remembered we were, in fact, outside in the early evening light in an only *slightly* sheltered entrance way where anyone could have caught us. He let my legs slide down his and my feet touched the ground just as one of my neighbors was returning home. He nodded his head and smiled as he passed us by, punched in the door code and entered the building.

I gasped and covered my mouth as my eyes stared widely up at Six. He pulled his bottom lip between his teeth and a laugh rumbled up from his belly.

Leaning forward he whispered, "Remember how I was saying that there's a first time for everything?"

I straightened my skirt suddenly realising that I could quite easily have been accused of indecent exposure. "You're *incorrigible*, Six."

He clutched his chest and feigned shock. "Who *me*? Ummm...pardon me for pointing out the obvious but *I* didn't just come in the doorway to *my* building. And I'm not the pantiless one here."

Okay he had a point. Two points actually. I *could* have stopped him. Damn him and his talent for turning me into an orgasmic puddle of mush.

He clenched his jaw and rested his forehead on mine. "I really should get going."

"Okay." I nodded, wishing I had the courage to ask him to stay the night.

He kissed me tenderly before stepping back. "I'll watch until you get inside."

I smiled at this supposed *evil* man and the way he was so damned overprotective of me. "Thank you."

I turned and began to walk away but his voice stopped me again. "Oh and...maybe I'll stop by tomorrow. You know, to check you're okay."

I didn't speak nor turn around. I just smiled to myself.

He called out again. "And...hey, I'm sorry, okay? I keep fucking up around you and I *hate* myself for that."

At those words I turned and walked back to him, cupped his face in my hands and kissed him sweetly on the lips. The familiar tickle of his beard against my skin made me ache for more. But he needed to leave and I *had* to understand that.

I pulled away and smoothed my thumbs over his cheeks. "I'm sorry too. I hurt you and that was something I shouldn't have done. I think... I think it's safe to say we both have our issues. But maybe that's a *good* thing. Maybe that's why we're drawn to each other."

I smiled and began to turn away again but he grabbed my wrist. "Oh and just so you know... In case it wasn't *blatantly* obvious a few minutes ago, I *do* want you. More than I should and you don't deserve to be caught up my fucking shit. But then again I'm a selfish bastard. I like to get what I want." A sexy smile graced his luscious lips and he shrugged as if his admission was any old meaningless statement. But it wasn't. Not to me. I could see something in his eyes.

Something...*deeper*.

My heart melted. He let go of my arm and I turned once more, heading for the keypad with the biggest, dumbest grin on my face. As I allowed the main entrance to click closed I peered out through the glass door and watched as he walked back to the bike, pulled on his helmet and sped away.

CHAPTER TWENTY

Chloe

I think I floated up the stairs to my door with a cheesy smile stretching my face but I didn't care. My bizarre day had turned out great. Since arriving at the club after ten that morning, so much had happened. It had been a *very* long day but good. And in spite of the arguments and the upset I somehow understood him more. I *understood* his motives for protecting me and I knew deep in my heart that he wasn't evil like he thought he was. What's more, I knew that he *did* want me.

Once I was inside my apartment, I threw my keys on the coffee table and went to take a shower. I stripped out of my clothes and removed what was left of my lace thong panties and dropped them in the trash with a smile. As the water cascaded down my back I thought back to the conversations we'd had throughout the day. The deep concern he harbored for my well-being was touching, even though it maybe should have stifled me. But no one had cared so fervently for me before and it felt good.

Images of him in just his black boxers, all tattooed and masculine, replayed over and over as I reluctantly washed the smell of him from my skin. I remembered how he had held me and how we had connected so intimately. The intensity in his eyes as he had fucked me. My nipples tingled as the memories of the passion he ignited in me rolled around my mind. I grinned and shook my head.

Gosh, Chloe you really have got it bad.

I stood under the water until it became too cold to be in there any longer. Once I was dry, I pulled on clean...and *whole*...panties, yoga pants and a T-shirt. By the time I got back through to the living room dusk had fallen so I closed the curtains before slumping on to the couch contemplating how tired I was. It had been an emotionally—and physically—tiring day and my muscles ached—but in a *very* good way.

As I was sitting there trying to decide what to make for dinner someone began banging on the door and I jumped. Surely it wasn't Six? Although maybe it *was* and he couldn't stand the thought of leaving me for the night either.

I excitedly skipped to the door and flung it open. Before I knew what the hell was going on a loud crack broke the silence in the still air of the building and I was knocked off my feet. I felt my head collide with the floor and I cried out just before everything went black.

———

I blinked my eyes open but a searing pain in my head almost made me throw up. I was lying on the floor completely disoriented. *What the hell?* The familiar smell lingering in the air was reminiscent of one of my scented candles and as I blinked I recognized the ceiling light. *Okay...so I'm at home...* I tried to move but as soon as I turned my head the room began to spin and I retched as my stomach roiled. A deep, dark laugh reverberated across the room and dread traveled in goosebumps down my spine.

Oh. Fuck.

"Ahh, so the little prick tease is awake, huh?" Brett's familiar, throaty voice caused nausea to spring anew up my gullet and I had to swallow fast and breathe deep to stop the onslaught of bile.

I lifted my hand to my head in a bid to stop the whooshing sensation. "What the hell are you doing here?" My voice was weak and wavered with fear and I cursed myself for not being stronger.

"Oh I think you know, sweet-cheeks. You *owe* me."

Grasping at the carpet beside me, I managed, with difficulty, to push myself to a sitting position. "I owe you *nothing.* Why don't you just leave and I'll forget you came, huh? No police. Just go, okay?" I could hear the desperate plea in my voice and I closed my eyes trying to fend off the threatening tears.

Seeming to take delight in my distress, he laughed again. "Oh, baby, I think we both know that ain't gonna happen."

He appeared in my line of sight and I was greeted with the sunken, empty eyes of someone I considered to be half man, half demon. He had changed and now resembled a monster. In fact, he had all the facial characteristics of someone addicted to heroin. Pale, almost translucent skin with visible veins, sunken cheeks, bloodshot eyes and a couple missing teeth. *What the hell did my mom see in him? And oh my god is she okay? If he's here where is she?*

I inhaled, hoping to calm my nerves. "H-how did you find me?"

"Let's just say I'm in league with the devil." He chuckled and looked pleased with himself at his apparent inside joke.

"Tell me something I *don't* know," I muttered loud enough for him to hear.

"Oooh feisty as ever huh? Jagger was right." I had no clue what he was talking about which must have been evident in my expression as he decided to clarify. "He's the guy from Loki's Legion who you flirted with at the whore house you work in. And just like the fucking tease you are when he tried to take what you were offering you got your meat head boyfriend to beat him up. Unlucky for you, Jagger happens to be a pal of mine."

Oh. My. God.

Brett is in cahoots with Loki's Legion?

My stomach plummeted like I was on the steep descent of the world's highest roller coaster. "W-what do you want, Brett? Is it money? Because I don't have any so if it is you're wasting your time here. Just tell me what you want and then leave."

He crouched down and reached out to touch the side of my head and I flinched first and then winced as he touched the place where he had struck me. He moved his hand back toward his face and I gasped at his blood soaked fingers. He sucked them into his mouth and the nausea I was fighting came back with a vengeance. I retched again and threw up on the carpet beside me.

Brett's shoulders shuddered and his eerily raspy laughter

filled the room. "Whoops. I think you made a mess of your pretty carpet there, little prick tease."

Tears began to sting at my eyes. "Brett, I need to get to a hospital. I may have a concussion, *please*."

In a mocking voice he replied, "Awww, does the little princess feel shitty, huh?" I glanced up at him to find a stupid pout on his face but it was soon replaced with an evil sneer. "Too fucking bad, bitch. Maybe you should've thought about that before ruining your step-daddy's life then, dontcha think? And anyways you won't have concussion for long. If you get my drift?"

I gritted my teeth and willed my lip to stop trembling as I tried desperately to ignore the fact he just insinuated he was going to *kill* me.

With as much venom as I could muster I shouted at him, "You are *not* my step-daddy! You're a lecherous bastard and nothing else!" I hoped that someone else in the building would hear and come to my rescue.

But a loud thwack resonated throughout my body as he struck me again, causing my head to be flung sideways. Blood spattered onto the floor from the fresh cut on my lip and I began to sob.

I couldn't help it.

Hope was no longer just slipping away from me. I had none left. This was it. I was going to die at the hands of this vile *animal*.

Here I was, injured with someone who had thought it was okay to make a pass at his girlfriend's *teenage* daughter. Someone who had assaulted me. Someone who had apparently even *lower* morals now than when I last saw him. I had been terrified of what he was capable of back then but now...*now* he was involved with Loki's Legion and he was sinking to depths of depravity even *I* had never expected.

He rubbed his chin and licked his bottom lip. "Well if you *don't* have money I can think of *other* ways you can pay me what you owe me. And what you owe Jagger for that matter. Maybe I'll call him to come around and join in our fun."

"I don't owe you *or* him anything you sick fucker!" I bellowed once more in the hope someone would hear and call the cops. Lashing out at him I decided I couldn't just *give up* regardless of how hopeless my situation seemed. *If only Six would return. Rescue me again.* But I had watched him ride away. He'd be back at the club house by now. If I could just get to my phone...

Brett leaned in close and the stench of alcohol on his breath turned my stomach again. I tried to turn away but he gripped my chin hard and forced me to face him. "I think you're forgetting the money you stole from me. And the *fuck* you promised me."

"I promised you no such thing," I growled. "I spent my time trying to *avoid* you, you pervert. Now I suggest you leave before my boyfriend gets back. If he finds you here, he'll kill you and I mean that *very* literally. Jagger knows what he's like. He's huge."

With an angry growl he pushed me back onto the floor as I swung out at him and tried my best to kick him in the balls but he was too strong for me, especially in my dazed state. All too soon I was restrained by his hand which encased both my wrists in a vice like grip and he pushed my thighs apart with his knees, pinning my legs down with his. His weight was crushing me into the floor and try as I might I couldn't move.

My shins burned with excruciating pain from being pressed on and my fingers began to go numb.

He stared down at me with a lascivious grin and moved a hand to his fly. He was fumbling with the zipper and even though I struggled I was no match for him. I started to scream but he slapped my face again.

Much harder this time.

My ears rang and I closed my eyes as tears spilled over, leaving cold wet trails back into to my hair. I waited for my fate to play out, helpless and fragile, just the opposite of the image I had tried to portray to Six.

As I lay there I tried to remember what it had been like before Brett came into our lives. Before he tainted my relationship with my mom. Before I'd run away to escape from him. I opened my eyes again, turned my head to the side and spotted my large pot vase on the floor just out of reach. He must have knocked it over one of the times he had hit me. As he fumbled around with one hand struggling with the zipper on his grubby jeans and one hand holding my wrists, I somehow managed to slip one arm free. He was too busy concentrating on trying to undo his jeans to realize, and I stretched my fingers further and further.

Please let me reach it, please, please let me stop him.

I heard a grunt and glanced toward him to find he had his T-shirt stuck in the teeth of the zip. *Dumb-ass.* He cursed and forgot himself for a moment as he released the grip on my other wrist to use both hands on the trapped fabric as he swore in vile language and sprayed saliva everywhere like some kind of rabid dog.

Seeing my chance, I stretched that little bit farther but a shooting pain stabbed at my shoulder as it momentarily dislocated. Dizziness and nausea washed over me in equal measures but I knew I had to act fast and to stay silent. My fingers touched the smooth edge of pot and I held my breath, praying silently that I could grip it enough to pull it toward me.

Everything seemed to move in slow motion and my fingers slipped into the rim of the vase. It rolled slightly closer making it easier to grip but it was almost like a lead weight. I began to fear that my efforts would be in vain but with a strength I never knew I possessed I began to lift the vase with one hand.

There must have been some serious adrenaline coursing through my veins as a guttural, banshee-like scream erupted from my chest and I swung with all my might. I followed the trajectory of the soap stone vase and met the shocked expression of my assailant just as the empty vessel collided with his skull.

There was a loud crunch and he lurched sideways, hitting his head on the door frame that led into the kitchen. I let go of the vase and it landed on the floor with a resounding thud but then everything went silent just before I blacked out yet again.

CHAPTER TWENTY-ONE

CHLOE

When I awoke again, the room was dark and very still. A heavy odor of bad breath, alcohol and a kind if metallic stench that I didn't recognize hung in the air. My legs were weighted to the ground and as I tried to move I realized that they were being pinned down by something stretched across both of them. With a pounding in my head, I scrambled to a sitting position and managed to pull my legs free. I tried to stand, but thanks to the whooshing sensation that came over me, I only made it to my hands and knees.

I had no clue what time it was. The curtains were closed and I vaguely remembered drawing them together when I had gotten out of the shower. I crawled across the room and pulled myself up by the window sill and yanked the curtains open.

The sudden illumination of bright daylight made my eyes sting and the glare temporarily blinded me. I had to blink over and over for a few moments to give them time to adjust.

When I turned around again I inhaled sharply as the events of the previous, horrific evening came back to me.

Brett was slumped in a heap against the kitchen doorway with his head at an unnatural angle and it became clear that the unfamiliar odor was fresh blood as it oozed from his badly fractured head.

"Oh shit no. What have I done? Oh fuck. Oh God." I crawled over to him and listened intently but couldn't hear him breathing. I tentatively reached out with a shaking hand to press my fingers against his neck in search of a pulse. His skin was cold and I was now covered in his blood but there was no sign of life.

I tried his wrist.

Nothing.

Panic began to wash over me and I backed away and slumped by the couch with my head in my hands. I began to rock back and forth as tears streamed freely down my face. My first instinct was to call the police. It was what I *should* have done. But something inside of me stopped me reaching for the land line phone.

Instead I reached for my cell.

After a couple of seconds the ringing at the other end stopped. "Chloe? Hey, you okay?" Six's voice was strained and I wondered if I had made a mistake contacting him.

"Umm...n-no... No I'm not okay. Something's happened. S-something awful." My voice was weak and I knew immediately he'd be terrified at my words.

"Awww fuck. Stay where you are. Don't move, okay? I'll be right there." The airspace went dead and I pulled the phone away from my head. I stared at the blank screen for what felt like hours but can have only been minutes. Every time I turned my head to where Brett's lifeless body lay slumped, my stomach roiled and fresh tears began to spill over.

I managed to pull myself onto the couch and sat there, frozen on the seat as far away from Brett as I could get, until eventually the front door was flung open. I didn't have the energy to turn and check who had entered. By that time, I had become numb, staring at one spot on the carpet where I had knocked over some red wine months before and had never completely gotten the stain out.

I heard a sharp intake of breath before a familiar voice...Six's voice exclaimed, "Oh my fucking... Oh shit, baby no." Suddenly I was scooped up into strong arms and a familiar masculine scent enveloped me. I closed my eyes and let out a long pained, guttural moan. I had no tears left. Nothing but pain and fear.

"Shhh...come on baby it's all right. You're going to be fine. We'll deal with this, okay?"

I heaved anguished dry sobs on him and he just let me. He held me tight to his chest and rocked me back and forth...back and forth as he stroked my hair.

Eventually he pulled me away from his body and cupped my face in his huge, calloused hands. His eyes were bloodshot and he looked really pale. "Now, listen to me, okay? I want you to tell me *exactly* what happened here. *Every* detail, all right?"

I nodded and in a whispered, hoarse voice I began to recount what happened from the moment Brett pushed his way into my apartment. How he knocked me out and about his fumbled—and thankfully failed—attempt to sexually assault me. Once I started to speak I closed my eyes. I couldn't bear the look of horror in Six's expression or the way his jaw clenched and his nostrils flared.

But the anger radiating from him was so very palpable. Like an entity in its own right.

My whole body shuddered and I wasn't sure if it was shock or the fact that the room was cold. But Six must have noticed as he wrapped the throw blanket from my couch around my shoulders and pulled me into his lap.

My favorite place to be.

My safe place.

"And...and he said he knew Jagger from Loki's Legion...the guy from the *Hub* who attacked me...and that's how he found me."

He slammed his fist into the couch and my eyes sprang open.

His breaths were loud and heavy like he'd been running. "I fucking *knew* it. I knew *they'd* be involved somehow. *Fuck!*"

I tentatively raised my gaze to find his locked on me. His jaw was still clenching and unclenching and I absently found myself thinking it must ache.

He tucked my hair behind my ears. "I'm so, *so* sorry, Chloe."

I shook my head, confused at his apology. "F-for what?"

"I should've known something like this would happen. I'm a dumb fucker. I should've come in with you when I brought you home. Or, at least I should've come right back here once I'd heard what had happened with Cain... God...I...I just can't believe what the fuck is happening right now."

The despondent tone of his voice worried me in spite of what had happened in my own life. "W-what happened with Cain?"

He swallowed and closed his eyes. Whatever it was it was clearly causing him pain. "No, no don't worry about that. Let's just...let's just sort this bastard out." He nodded his head toward the slumped corpse by the kitchen.

Panic washed over me anew. "I...I need to call the police."

Six gripped my upper arms tightly. "No. They'll arrest you, Chloe. There are no witnesses and the Legion are involved. No police okay? *I* can deal with it. We just need to wait until nightfall. But..."

His hesitation worried me. "But what?"

He stroked my cheek tenderly and a crease appeared between his eyebrows. Sadness washed over him and he closed his eyes briefly. "I'm afraid you're going to have to get away, Chloe."

I shook my head. "Get away? What do you mean?"

His expression turned grave. "You need to go find your mom. Make sure she's okay and then get far away. Just leave. Leave the state. Leave the country if you can. Just get the hell away from here."

"Six, I'm already terrified of what's happened here, of what...of what I've *done*. I don't think I can cope with cryptic answers just be straight with me please."

He took a deep breath and exhaled slowly. "Melody is dead. Cain found her at the house they were going to rent together. Their...their baby died with her. Colt reckons that the Legion killed her. He wants Rosa and Cain to get away after the funeral because he thinks they'll be the next target. And I'm worried that *you* will be too. Especially if this prick doesn't go back with your body in tow. It's like a fucking all-out war. All over nothing. It's so fucking dumb but I still can't even begin to understand it all. I've just about had enough."

"So come with me," I blurted the words out before thinking.

He sighed and closed his eyes briefly. "I can't. You need to get far away from *me*, baby. I want to save you from all this fucking shit. You don't need this."

My lip began to tremble and my heart ached. "But I don't *want* to leave. What if something happens to *you*?"

He shrugged. "I can handle myself. But I can't sit around shit scared they'll get to you and finish what they started. I...I need you gone as much as you need to go."

His words were like a direct hit to my stomach and I sobbed. I don't know where the tears came from but they were streaming down my face at the thought of leaving him. Of what had happened. Of the culmination of what had been a very stressful few weeks.

"Hey." He lifted my chin. "Look, this is not what I want, okay? It's what we both *need*. You can't stay here. It's not safe. But it doesn't change anything. It doesn't change how much I want you. Don't *ever* think that."

———

Six took sheets from my closet and wrapped Brett's body as I sat there like a mannequin. A dumb stupid, useless mannequin. He dragged the body over to the door and then collected cleaning products from my kitchen. It was then that I seemed to snap out of my zombified trance.

I jumped up and snatched the cloth and bottle of disinfectant from his hands. "No! Six, let me clean up. This is *my* mess."

He grabbed them back. "It's fine. Go sit. I can *do* this. I've done it before." As soon as the admission fell from his lips he clamped them shut, closed his eyes and dropped his chin to his chest.

I swallowed the bile that had risen up from my stomach. "You've...you've cleaned up after a..."

As if I had been in some kind of daze I suddenly widened my eyes and clutched my chest. "I *killed* him...I'm a... I'm a *murderer*...Oh my God, Six I *murdered* him." The shaking returned with a vengeance only this time I knew it was shock. Shock and realisation of what *I* had become.

Six dropped the cleaning products and gripped my face hard in his hands. The pain snapped my focus back to him.

His eyes were wide and determined. "You did NOT murder him, Chloe. It was self-defense. The bastard was going to... Look, you did *nothing* wrong. *Nothing*. You hear me?" I heard but I couldn't believe him. It wouldn't sink in. "Hey! If I had been here *I* would have killed the bastard and it wouldn't have been a fucking accident. *You* did nothing wrong. And you tell *no one* about any of this, okay? You do *not* breathe a single word of *any* of this to *any*one. You hearing me?"

I nodded as his features became blurred through my tears but I wasn't sure how I would be able to live with myself.

Not after this.

He stood, lifted me into his arms and carried me over to the couch. As he placed me down he told me, "I want you to lie here and rest, okay? I'm gonna clean up and once it gets dark I'll get rid of the... I'll get rid of that." I got the impression he was trying not to say certain words so he didn't freak me out more than I already was. I closed my eyes and tried not to picture the events of the last couple days. The events had drained and terrified me and in spite of what had happened I drifted off to sleep.

———

"Hey...Chloe, baby, wake up." My eyes sprang open and I gasped. But soothing hands were stroking my hair. "It's okay, it's me, Six. Everything's dealt with. And I've packed your clothes and some of the things I think are special to you. Now...it's dark out and I need to take you out of town to the bus station. I have my car downstairs ready. You need to get as far away as possible okay?"

"But...but my job...Ellie...I..."

He handed me a wad of cash and I stared at it open mouthed. There must have been *thousands*.

He squeezed my hands around the money. "I want you to wait until you get as far as you can go by bus. Then I want you to buy a car. Change your clothes, change your hair color, whatever you can okay? Contact Ellie once you're out of the state and tell her you decided to go home to your mom's as she'd contacted you and told you that Brett had left her and she needed you. Whatever you need to say, okay?"

I nodded. "Okay."

He stood and held out his hand to me. "Come on, we have to go now."

CHAPTER TWENTY-TWO

CHLOE

We drove for about an hour in complete silence until we reached the Greyhound bus depot that I'd coincidentally arrived at when I first came here. I think I was in some kind of denial. My brain was struggling to process everything that had happened. The fact that I was being encouraged to run away went against everything I believed. But then I reminded myself I was already—to all intents and purposes—a criminal, seeing as I had stolen from my own mother. I mean who *does* that, but a killer? That was a whole other ball game. And one I had no interest in playing.

Six was right though. I *had* acted in self-defense. He *would* have raped me and then maybe killed me—he'd insinuated as much when he had me pinned to the floor. And I had done what I'd had to do. But would the police understand that? I doubted it. Considering the fact that I was an *exotic* dancer they would no doubt presume I was a hooker too, as so many were, and that *he* was a client I was trying to rob.

Would I wind up in jail for defending myself? It happened. I knew for a fact I wouldn't hack jail and so maybe Six *was* right. Maybe running *was* the best way to deal with it. Maybe I could wait a while and return. Yeah, 'cause *that* was going to happen.

Six pulled his car into the parking lot just as a bus parked and people began to get off. I watched as sleepy looking folks carried huge bags to waiting cabs. Who knew that traveling at this ridiculous hour was so popular?

My heart began to pound at the thought of leaving and I swivelled in my seat to face him. "Six, I...I don't want to *do* this. I *can't*. It's not right. I want to go to the police." I feared the panic in my voice made me sound pathetic and weak.

He unclipped his seat belt and turned toward me. He reached over and took hold of my hands. "You have to *promise* me that you won't, okay? I'm sorry to have to say this but you'll land us *both* in shit if you do. And there's no point. It's all dealt with so you have to keep quiet. Can you *do* that? For me? For both of us?"

Good question. *Could* I? Or would guilt get the better of me eventually? Eating away at me until I couldn't stand it any longer and until I did something stupid. But in the dimly lit car interior, I could make out the sparkle of his caramel eyes and the concern for my welfare that radiated from him and right then I would have done *any*thing for him.

After all, *he*'d done so much for me.

With my resolve strengthened I nodded and he reached up to cup my cheek. "Like I said, baby, it's all dealt with. You have *nothing* to worry about apart from getting away from this place for a while."

It didn't matter that I hadn't known him for long. He knew more about me than anyone. And I guessed I knew more about him than he had ever intended. We had formed a bizarre but special bond in our short time together. Was it *love*? If it wasn't it was something pretty damn close, and letting go of something that *could have been* was going to hurt like hell.

He got out of the car and came around to my door. He paused before opening it and I peered at him through the window. His head was back and his eyes were closed. It was clear that he was fighting an internal battle as I watched his chest rise and fall with every deep breath. Eventually, he opened my door and held out his hand. I slipped mine into his and he ran his thumb over my skin.

It was such a tender gesture that my eyes began to sting and my lip trembled.

I don't want to say goodbye.

I climbed out of the vehicle and was immediately pulled into his arms. His masculine scent infiltrated my nostrils and I tried hard to memorize it and the feeling of his arms around me holding me close and keeping me safe. How could I leave...and how could he let me go?

He stroked his hands down my back causing shivers to follow in his wake. "I want you to take care okay? But...don't contact me for a while. Just...lay low...disappear okay?"

My stomach dropped. Was this his way of letting me down easy? "Oh...okay."

"I know it's shitty but it really is for the best. If they know you're still involved with me they'll come after you to hurt me and I would *never* forgive myself if that happened."

I nuzzled his chest and relished the familiar feeling of his hard body against mine. "But what if someone comes looking for me? What if the police—"

He kissed my head and tilted my chin back forcing me to connect with him. "I promise you that *won't* happen."

"But how can you be sure?"

Dragging his thumb across my bottom lip he gazed into my eyes and a crease appeared between his eyebrows. "Remember I told you what my crew are like. I told you we're not to be messed with. We *deal* with shit. Just like we'll *deal* with Loki's Legion and make sure they *never* cause harm to one of our own again. We...*have* people. On the *inside* if you know what I mean. We're left to serve up our own justice to a certain extent. But...the trouble is...what I *can't* do is win this damn war *and* protect you at the same time. But *believe* me, I hate that this is the only way."

I gazed up at the man who had become my lover and my hero in a very short space of time and my stomach knotted. This whole situation was the last thing I wanted. But he was leaving me no other choice. The fact that he wanted to keep me safe didn't ease the pain inside of me.

I was reluctant to board the bus. That would mean this was over. And I so didn't want it to be over.

"What will you tell people...if they ask about me? You know, Delilah and...well...*any*one." I was playing for time. It was unlikely anyone would even notice I'd gone. A sad fact in itself.

He sighed heavily. "At the moment they're going to have to deal with Melody's funeral and I'm pretty sure Colt will want Cain to get away too. Before he does something crazy and this whole thing gets worse before it gets better. And because Loki's Legion are clearly gunning for him. But once the dust settles, I'll just tell people we...we stopped seeing each other and you left to go home. It's not forever, babe."

He rested his forehead on mine and his breath heated my skin. And even though he added those few words to the end of his sentence it still *felt* like goodbye. A *permanent* goodbye. After what had happened I wasn't sure that I would want to return once I had left. And although Six was a huge draw to me, it wasn't like we were officially a *couple*. In the back of my mind, a little voice was telling me this was a *good* thing. That leaving here was the right action to take. And that realistically Six and I would never have amounted to anything.

Damn that little voice.

My stomach lurched as the unwelcome thoughts rattled around my mind.

Six took my hand and led me toward the bus. The sign on the front said *Denver, Colorado*. We stopped at the side of the huge silver beast of a vehicle and he gazed down at me.

"I'm so sorry about all of this, sweetheart. About you getting involved in my problems. And about...well *every*thing." Sadness was evident in his eyes and I wondered if this was hurting him as much as it was hurting me.

"Me too." A lump lodged in my throat as I clung to his hands reluctant to let go. He was all dressed in black and it felt appropriate in light of the events of the past twenty-four hours. "You should go. Cain needs you." I hated to say the words but they were true. Cain was his best friend.

"Yeah... Poor bastard. I don't know how he'll get through this."

My heart ached for his loss and selfishly for my own. "It's going to be a hard road for him." And that was an understatement. He had lost his woman *and* his child in one fell swoop. It's crazy to think it after such a short time, but I had wanted Six and I to become *something* like Cain and Melody had been. But you can't always get what you want. That was something I had learned from a very young age.

"You boarding Ma'am?" A voice from behind me called.

"She'll be right with you," Six replied to the driver. Then his eyes locked on mine once more. "You are one fucking beautiful woman, you know that? You're a fighter, CD. Don't let what happened back there hang around in your mind. *He* doesn't deserve to have *any* effect on you anymore. You're worth a million of him. Don't *ever* forget that."

I turned away as my lip began to tremble all over again. He didn't need to see me cry. I'd shed enough tears on him to last a lifetime. Instead I chewed the inside of my lip and began to ascend the stairs onto the bus.

As I reached the top, I faced him once again, "I'll call you from wherever I end up. Look after yourself...and Cain."

He closed his eyes and lowered his head for a moment. For some reason I *knew* what his next words were going to be and I really didn't want to be right.

When he lifted his face again some kind of mask had descended and it was like he'd somehow become a different man. His expression had hardened and my heart began to pound. I wanted to run back down the steps and kiss him. Remind him of what we'd *almost* had. But I stood stock still and waited. Holding my breath and hoping my instincts were wrong.

Sadly they weren't.

He stared up at me. "I don't *want* to hear from you. I don't *want* to know where you end up. Okay? And when I said this wasn't forever...well...maybe it is. Goodbye, Chloe dancer. It was fun while it lasted, huh?"

His words were like a stab to my heart and I exhaled the air from my lungs as I gripped the handrail in case my legs crumpled beneath me. The driver closed the doors and began to pull away from the stop before I even had a chance to sit. I watched Six turn and walk away.

Out of my life for good.

CHAPTER TWENTY-THREE

Six

Watching Chloe board that bus was one of the hardest things I've *ever* had to do. And my final blow to her wasn't something I'd planned. I felt like a total bastard. But in reality, it was for the best. I had known all along that I wasn't worthy of her. But seeing her leave caused an ache deep inside me like nothing I've ever experienced. I'd never been in love so I didn't know what the hell it felt like, but if *this* was anything close then I didn't fucking want any part of it.

———

Thankfully Melody's funeral happened peacefully. Loki's Legion showed some respect, at least for the day. It was the most heart-breaking scene. Bikers from CoSMiC's neighboring state charters attended and took part in the funeral cortège. "Set Fire to the Third Bar" by Snow Patrol, Melody's

favorite band, was played inside the church and I had to hold
Cain up to stop him from collapsing with grief. The haunting
words stuck in my head and in my selfish moments I could
relate them to my own situation.

But this wasn't about me.

Rosa tried hard to console her big brother, but Cain was
changed irrevocably by Melody's death. He became so
bitter...understandably. I really felt for the poor kid and
stepped into the role of big brother again temporarily when
she needed me. She cried on me many times and my heart
broke for her. It was like she wasn't only grieving for Melody
but for Cain too.

After the service, he spent hours sitting at Mel's graveside
drinking himself unconscious and talking to her. He was
walking a fine line between sanity and the abyss and try as I
might I couldn't seem to ease his pain. Colt had tried to get me
to convince him to leave town, just as I'd convinced Chloe,
but no matter *what* I said to Cain he wouldn't co-operate. He
insisted that he was staying put and that vengeance was at the
top of his list of priorities. He was planning all manner of
gruesome retaliations and both Colt and I knew he was dumb
enough to carry them out. He didn't care if he lived or died.
But thankfully the club did.

Only a matter of days after the funeral, both Cain and
Rosa were taken by Loki's Legion. Cain was beaten to within
an inch of his life and when we managed to locate them we
were lucky that they both weren't dead. Rosa was so trauma-
tized after what she had witnessed the bastards doing to Cain
that everyone was worried *she'd* have a fucking breakdown.

Loki's Legion had made it clear that the 'war' wasn't over
and this had been a taste of what was to come and so Colt had

made some very difficult decisions. I won't bore you with the details right now but suffice it to say that shit got a helluva lot worse before it even *began* to get better.

For weeks I played "Chloe Dancer/Crown of Thorns" over and over on repeat until I just about drove the whole club insane. And yes, looking back I *was* acting like a fucking love-sick teenager. In the end I resorted to an iPod so they'd all quit their moaning and I'd sit there in the bar surrounded by people but feeling about as alone as any man possibly could.

But such was my life. I'd made it that way.

At one point I had even tried to step down from my role as VP of CoSMiC, but Colt had somehow managed to convince me that I was needed. That I was an essential link in the chain or some other fucking dumb-ass metaphorical cliché bullshit.

Club girls were constantly trying to turn me on by walking around the damn place half naked. Rubbing their tits in my face and always dropping stuff on the floor in front of me so they had to bend and pick them up. Oh yeah, I had lots of asses and tits in my face. But they weren't the ass or tits that I wanted. For some stupid reason Dee had a chrome pole installed in the bar area of the place. For parties so she told me. She seemed to think that my avoidance of *The Fox Hub* was connected to the Loki's Legion situation, but she was *so* wrong.

On the first of the so called party nights—that were a feeble attempt to take our minds of the real hell that was going on—I got so drunk I could hardly stand. One of the girls, Selena, got up and started to cavort around the damn pole...*badly*. Her bleach blonde hair was like straw and her tits were fake. And to top it off she couldn't fucking dance a step. After putting up with the continuous encouragement from the guys to get 'Nina' out of my system and fuck some other women, I snapped.

Shoving off the advances of yet *another* bitch who promised to rock my world and make me feel sooo good, I stood and threw my beer bottle at the wall causing it to shatter into tiny fragments just like my damn patience. "Would you *all* just butt the *fuck* out of my life." The music stopped and the whole room fell silent. I pointed at the poor Nina substitute. "*She* is nothing like her. You hear me? Nothing! Chloe is fucking *gone*, okay?" I smacked myself in the head a little too hard. "I mean *Nina*. *Nina* is gone. Aww shit. She's fucking gone and none of these bitches will *ever* take her place, you hearing me? Now leave me the fuck alone."

I staggered up the stairs to the end room and virtually dragged Weasel and his two sluts out of there—how the hell the ugly fucker got so many women I just don't know—before slamming the door and collapsing onto the bed.

My dreams were plagued with visions of Chloe beneath me, and the way her soft body yielded to me as her chocolate brown irises locked on mine. My own mind was intent on torturing me to the point where I awoke on more than one occasion with the taste of her on my tongue.

I visited Hank's coffee shop and discovered that the redhead I'd seen leaving Chloe's apartment worked there. *She* was Ellie. On my third visit I decided to bite the bullet and ask where Chloe had ended up, and if she was okay. Understandably Ellie wasn't forthcoming with any information. Couldn't blame her, but I wasn't happy about it. It served me right. After all I had told Chloe not to contact me. That I didn't want to know where she was.

Idiot.

She was my first waking thought and my last before I slept.

I was obsessed.

And it was a very unhealthy obsession that showed no sign of abating.

CHAPTER TWENTY-FOUR

CHLOE

In the time that had passed since I left Rose Acres, so much had changed. I had returned to my home state of Nebraska. Thanks to an old family friend, I had managed to locate my mom in Trenton, a small village in Hitchcock County and she and I had managed to work things out. She was dealing with a lot of guilt connected to Brett and I. It was good that I had returned home when I had. It turned out she had left Brett several times, once I had gone, when he'd gotten violent through drinking. He always managed to guilt her into returning, but the final straw came when she found him in bed with another woman in her house. The creepy thing was that apparently the woman had looked *just* like *me*. She said all he talked about was me and when he got drunk he used to smack her around and blame *her* for driving me away.

Go figure.

I never told my mom the truth about what happened at

my apartment that awful night. But from what *she* told me it sounded like he'd gotten involved in some very dark stuff since I left. Heroin and cocaine played a major part in him getting involved with Loki's Legion. He'd begun running drugs for them. My mom had realized there was something seriously wrong when his appearance began to drastically change and he lost weight. She had moved from my home town of Dalton to Trenton, a few miles east to get away from him. She said she could never go back to our old house after what had happened. Especially knowing that I had left because she hadn't believed me.

It took a hell of a lot of tears and fights for us to get through it, but we were working things out and it was good to have a mom again. Albeit one *I* had to care for and not the other way around.

––––––––

Unfortunately, Six was constantly on my mind, but it was over. It was something I'd had to deal with. I'd contacted Ellie by text message as I was on the bus to Colorado just to let her know I was okay but needed to get my head straight and then a few months after I moved away I made contact again. This time by phone...

"My *God* Chloe I thought that ass-hat biker had murdered you or something. So much shit has happened since you left. I'm so relieved that you're okay. It's been awful not hearing from you."

"No, I'm fine, Ellie. Just had to get away. So...what's been going on?"

"Oh. My. God, Chloe. A girl, Rosa I think her name was,

went missing out of the blue. She was related to the Company of Sinners bikers...anyway, it happened after a funeral for the wife of one of the Sinners. The wife was found dead in an empty house. That alone was awful but then the guy who lost his wife lost his *sister* too! Rosa who disappeared was *his* *sister*. No trace. Just gone. And then, the poor *guy,* the brother and husband, disappeared too! Seriously I just don't *get* this place. There were so many rumors flying around you had to dodge them in the damn street. Honestly, it's been like crazy town."

Frick, she must mean Cain and his sister were the ones *who went missing.* I didn't bother to correct her that Melody and Cain weren't married. It seemed less important as the conversation went on. Shit. I'd gone to the same school as Rosa when I'd finished off my high school diploma. She was a lot younger than me but I remember her as being a quiet, solitary girl.

Clearly Loki's Legion had been hard at work trying to ruin the lives of the CoSMiC crew. Then the thought hit me that Six might have come to some harm and my heart stuttered, falling over itself causing palpitations in my chest.

With a knot in my stomach I dared to ask, "So... H-have you seen Six around at all?" There was a long pause down the line and a chill traveled my spine.

She sighed as if reluctant to tell me. "Umm...yeah. He's been *around*. He came in to Hank's a while ago and asked me if I'd heard from you at all. Asked where you were and if you were okay. But I told him nothing, Chloe. You don't *need* that guy in your life. The shit those motorcycle gangs have caused is un...believable. They're a law unto themselves. No one *wants* them here...well actually...things have calmed down now. The Sinners ran Loki's Legion out of the area and so things aren't so bad around here but there are rumors of a reprisal so who the hell knows what'll happen. You're so much better out of the way, honey, really you are. But I would love to come visit you. You should tell me where you're staying. Are you back home in Nebraska?"

I was listening but not really *hearing* her. I had lost concentration after she had told me that Six had asked her about me. He must have gone out of his way to find her seeing as he had only seen her leaving my apartment and had no clue who she was or where she worked. Unless he'd followed her, true to his instinctual stalking tendencies. Some things never changed. I smiled to myself as I remembered him trying to explain to *me* how he knew where I lived.

I was completely pre-occupied now. "How did he seem?"

"That *Six* guy? Oh I don't know. Like the weight of the world was on his shoulders. He wasn't so happy when I told him he could forget getting any information out of me. I thought he was going to cry. But of course I was imagining *that*. I mean guys like him don't have any emotions right? Heartless bastards." Her ire rang clearly down the line and I imagined my huge, dirty-blonde haired biker feeling some kind of *grief* at losing me. But like Ellie had pointed out, those guys were too *hard* to feel such things.

At least that's what I kept telling myself for the next eleven months.

———

I'd moved in with my mom in the house she was renting and things had settled down into a kind of routine. I had bought an old car just as Six had wanted and had even changed my appearance, deciding to go back to my own chocolate brown hair color. I'd gotten myself a job in the local library in a little town called Hallowed Springs. It was a great little place close to where I lived with my mom when I was a kid. I found that I loved the peace and quiet of the library. Being surrounded by books filled with alternate lives and dreams was a stark but happy contrast to being surrounded by lecherous, drooling patrons. In fact, it was the complete antithesis of the club I had worked in before and dancing scantily clad around a pole as licentious men ogled my curves was becoming a distant memory. Thankfully.

The one thing that wasn't a distant memory was Six.

———

I'd been on a couple dates with a nice guy I had met at night school where I had been doing a literature course. His name was Dean and he was really sweet. Handsome in a normal, no tattoos, cropped short hair, straight-laced kind if way. But he didn't get my motor running like Six had. We hadn't had sex yet and I could tell it was becoming an issue.

The only orgasms I had were with the help of my vibrator and my imagination and they *all* involved a man who was the complete opposite of Dean. A man whose beard scratched my inner thighs as he went down on me. A man who could make me come so easily because he knew my body so well...knew *me* so well. Yes, Six was a *regular* player in my fantasies.

Every time Dean and I got close to heavy petting I broke free, made excuses about not being ready and went home to fantasize about Six's tongue on my clit and his fingers working me into a frenzy.

Way to go on the moving on thing, Chloe.

———

Months passed by and life was okay. The Six shaped hole inside me was still there and I often wondered about what would have become of us if Jagger had never assaulted me at *The Fox Hub*. Would Six and I have even met? But I vowed that I would *never* return to Rose Acres. I knew time was a great healer and that *some* day I would be able to look back and feel nothing. It was going to take a while but thankfully I had no reason to *ever* see him again and I knew that because he had no idea where I was therefore there was no risk of him showing up.

It was a double edged sword that only gave me *some* relief.

Thursdays were always a busy day at the library and on this particular day I had been rushed off my feet until two in the afternoon when I had finally managed to catch a break.

I was sitting out back at one of the picnic tables flicking through one of the Librarian's Monthly magazines when an ad caught my eye. It was for a Certification Training Program in Library Science. I had become an avid reader again since moving back with my mom and was totally caught up in the language and stories of British literature. The thought of training as a Library Technician *officially* got me intrigued and I was wondering if my boss would be willing to put me forward for the scheme. The course that was being advertised included an element of work place-ment and if I could convince my boss Robert to fight in my corner, perhaps *this* could be the career move I'd always hoped for.

———

Sitting in Robert's office, I nervously knotted my fingers in my lap as he talked to his superiors on the phone. The tone of the conversation wasn't filling me with a great deal of confidence thanks to the number of times Rob had said, "Oh that's a shame," and his expression had gotten sadder as the call went on.

Eventually he hung up and laced his fingers together on the desk. "Gosh, Chloe, I hate to break this to you but they won't allow you to be put forward by me. There are no available course places in the state of Nebraska. It's already full to capacity here. I'm so sorry. You're such a good worker and you really do have a natural aptitude for the work but..." He paused and rubbed his chin frowning as if he was unwilling to impart the next snippet of information. "At the moment there are only places available in Colorado and Utah. And Colorado is on the verge of being at capacity too. It looks like you may have to wait a year or so."

I wanted to cry. I'd been so excited about the prospect of doing something with my life at last that I hadn't considered the possibility of it *not* being able to go ahead.

I nodded as I let the news sink in. "Okay...What if I were to apply for the course in Utah?"

"Well, I would be very sad to see you leave but the guy I was just speaking with *did* say that he would be willing to consider an application to transfer."

I perked up a little and smiled. "Okay, so I'll look into it."

He shook his head. "I'm afraid there's only one location partaking in the work placement portion in Utah. And you would need to decide very quickly."

I nodded. Okay so Utah wouldn't be so bad. I'd lived in the state before. "Okay. And where is that?"

"It's a small town called Rose Acres."

CHAPTER TWENTY-FIVE

Six

I've said it before, so excuse me for sounding like a broken record, but loneliness is the shittiest thing to feel. Especially when you're surrounded by people but they just don't *get* you. That was me. Melody's death had been the catalyst for so much change. And most of it was unwelcome. Especially the fact that Cain had been gone for months and so had Rosa.

And of course Chloe was gone too.

Once the issues with Loki's Legion were supposedly resolved, I wanted to make another attempt to contact Chloe. Just to say sorry for the shit I had put her through. And for my treatment of her as she left. But once again her friend had refused to tell me anything and I still couldn't blame her. Rose Acres had seen plenty of suffering and pain on account of the Sinners and the Legion. It was no wonder that Ellie had been reluctant for me to contact her friend and risk involving her in it all again. She *had* escaped after all which is exactly what I wanted...except it turns out it was the last damn thing I wanted. What I *did* want was Chloe.

I think a part of me always kept one eye on the road just in case she turned up again.

But of course she didn't.

————

Life is fucking hard, man. Months and months after Cain was gone folks were saying he was most likely *dead*. I knew what had happened to him up to a point, but I'd expected him to turn up again. When he hadn't after so long I was beginning to wonder if the rumors were true. With no word from him there was little else to think. He'd been my best buddy and having to make him disappear had been fucking *heart* wrenching. Especially so soon after Chloe had gone too. But it had been the only way to save him from the bastards who were intent on ruining his life and come to think of it to save him from himself too.

I'd decided to take off for a while, out of state, to have a change of scene and clear my head. Most things were prepared, but I went into Rose Acres to grab a few things I needed for the trip. While I was there I called in to get a take-out coffee from Hank's, but Ellie wasn't in so I couldn't bombard her with questions about Chloe. Instead, I set off walking back home to set my travel plans into motion. Colt was back to his usual happy self and all felt right with the world. Well maybe not *exactly* right, but somehow calmer. I was heading back to my apartment to pick up my back pack and then I was going to take off eastern to Colorado. It was the destination of the bus that I had put Chloe on and although I had no clue if she had even stayed there. I felt compelled to go. The stupid thing is that Colorado is not some little ass town. It's a huge damn state. The chances of me bumping into her were slim to none even if she *was* there. But I needed to get away and so Colorado seemed as good a place as any for my road trip.

As I walked along the main street toward my building I sipped on my coffee and glanced around at the folks passing me by. Most stepped out of my way like I was some kind of leper. Others actually crossed the damn street to avoid me. Very few said hello or even smiled. Instead I was greeted with scowls, head shaking or out and out fear. Talk about judgmental. It was pretty damn sad too, that's for sure, seeing as none of them knew what I was really about.

As I passed the library, a poster for a rock night caught my eye and I stopped to take a look. As I was reading the list of bands and thinking I wouldn't fucking bother, a woman appeared inside the window taking old posters out.

My heart almost stopped dead and the take-out cup slipped from my grasp spilling its contents all over the sidewalk.

Her head shot up and a pair of familiar, beautiful brown eyes peered back at me. Her mouth fell open and her hand came up to cover it.

What the fuck?

I mean seriously what in the actual fuck?

I almost ran for the door and yanked it so hard I wouldn't have been surprised if it had come off in my hand. I made my way toward her and almost tripped over my own stupid feet before coming to a halt only a few steps away.

I ran my hands through my hair to stop myself from grabbing her and pulling her into my arms. "When...when did you come back? Why didn't you come find me? *Why* did you come back? What the hell, Chloe?"

Her lip trembled and the color drained from her face. "Jeez, what's with the interrogation?"

I closed my eyes briefly and shook my head but when I opened them she was still there. This wasn't a cruel dream. And she looked even more beautiful than I remembered. Her hair was now chocolate brown and all pulled around to the side so it fell in waves over her left breast. It really, *really* suited her. I was shocked at how different her whole demeanor was. Shit, if I'd thought she was too good for me back when she was a dancer she was *so far* out of my league now she might as well have been the queen of the goddamn universe. She wore black slacks and a white blouse that showed off her slim waist. All grown up, official looking and demure, and as always my cock appreciated the sight just as much as I did.

Stunning.

I realized I'd been staring so I shook my head again to shake some sense into there. "Yeah, yeah I'm sorry for bombarding you like that...I just...I can't believe..." Me lost for words...that was a first.

She linked her fingers together in front of her and chewed her lip for a moment as if she was afraid to speak. "I've...I've been back around a month." *A month?! How the hell am I only seeing you now?* Her tongue came out and swept across her lips. "A training opportunity came up here in town that wasn't available anywhere else and I took it. Believe me if it had been available *any*where else I wouldn't *be* here." *Oh...okay that hurt.* She broke eye contact for a moment. "I...I didn't come and find you because your last words to me were that it was *'nice while it lasted'* and so I was pretty sure you wouldn't *want* to see me. And to be honest *I* didn't really want to see *you*. It's been so long after all. I knew it would happen eventually, I mean it *is* a small town." When she lifted her face again her eyes were glassy and something inside of me squeezed and knotted.

I stepped toward her. "How could you think I wouldn't want to *see* you? I've been worried *sick* about you. In fact, I was on the verge of getting on my bike to come find you."

She stepped back and scrunched her face. "*You* were the one who sent *me* away remember? And that's a pretty good reason for me not to come running to you, Jeez, Six. *You* said our goodbye was permanent when you put me on that damn bus." She had a very valid point and I felt kind of foolish. She folded her arms defensively over her chest. "And you don't have to worry about me any more seeing as you know where I am now. But, hey, don't let me stop you from your travels. I have to get on with my job so you had better leave anyway, unless you've developed a taste for reading in my absence?" The way she raised her eyebrows told me that her rhetorical question was meant to be bitchy as fuck. Shit, she really *had* changed. Turning around she made to walk away from me.

What the fuck? I reached out and grabbed her arm causing her to swing around to face me again. I glanced around to check if anyone was watching but thankfully they weren't. "So that's *it*? That's all you're going to say?"

She tugged her arm free. "There's nothing else *to* say, Six. I'm here for *work*. *Not* for you."

Her words and the sentiment behind them were like a knife to my gut. "So... you didn't come back to be with *me*?"

She snorted derisively. "Why the hell would you think *that*? You made it very clear when I left that we were over. And I'm seeing someone, anyhow." She gave a little 'fuck you' kind of half smile and then gritted her teeth and leaned toward me. "And don't worry, our dirty little secret is *still* safe. So if you're here to try and bed me so I won't tell then you don't need to worry. I'm learning to live with it eating away at me."

Okay so if I thought her earlier comments were like a knife this whole rant was a bullet to my fucking heart. She thought I wanted to get in her panties to keep her *quiet*? Like I'd fucking *do* that to her? She clearly didn't know me half as well as I thought she did and that alone hurt like a mother. But I wasn't about to show her my pain. *No* fucking way. So I did what I do best. I let my hard mask descend.

Laughing darkly, I rubbed my bearded chin. "Well that's good to know. My work here is done. I've got a long list of bitches lining the fuck up for my cock, baby, so *you* won't be missed. And so long as we're both clear you keep out of my way and I'll keep out of yours and it's all good." Leaning a little closer to make one final stab I whispered into her ear, "Oh and I hope your new boyfriend knows how to make you come so hard you fucking scream. 'Coz we both know I do, right?" And with those final crude comments I stomped to the door, slammed both fists on it to push it open and walked the hell away.

CHAPTER TWENTY-SIX

CHLOE

A whole month I'd been back in Rose Acres. A whole damn fricking *month* and I'd managed to avoid him. How stupid I was in thinking that maybe it could go on forever. That I could live here and he would never know. And I was supposed to be an intelligent woman. I was grateful for the fact that Ellie was now working for her parents in their hotel because at least that meant Six could no longer hound her at the café. And after my encounter with him at the library, it was evident that all he'd been worried about was me going to the police about Brett. Well if nothing else I'd put his mind at rest and maybe now he'd leave me alone.

Dean and I had broken up before I left, but I wasn't about to tell Six I was single. He was already well known for throwing pity sex in my direction. No, I would meet someone sweet here and things would be fine.

I would get over him.

I would.

Standing there before him in the library had been more painful than I could have ever imagined. He looked just how I remembered him. Gorgeous, tall, broad and muscular. Faded black jeans and a Slipknot T-shirt that clung to his chest and biceps under his leather CoSMiC cut. And when he stepped closer to me to deliver his excruciating final words I was greeted by that oh-so-familiar masculine scent that I'd *never* been able to forget. I would have been back under his spell had he not stabbed me directly in the heart with cruel words just before he left.

Once he was out of sight I rushed through to the ladies staff only rest room and locked the door. I hurriedly turned on the faucet and splashed my face with cold water just as the tears came. *Bastard. Bastard. Bastard.* I repeated the words in a pain filled whisper over and over as I leaned on the sink. My stomach knotted and an ache deep in my heart set in. How this could *be* after such a fleeting relationship I had no clue. But it was an agonising reality that I would have to deal with if I was going to stay here and make something of my life. At least some days I was at college and wouldn't have to even be in the town. That was one saving grace.

———

At the end of what seemed to be the longest day ever I left the library and headed back to my apartment. Thankfully I'd been able to secure one far away from the one I had rented before and it was closer to where Ellie lived with her family. As I walked away from the library I fired a quick text to my friend.

El, I need you. He's been here.

C x

In true Ellie style the response was immediate.

Kk babe. Meet me at Flaherty's.

E <3

Flaherty's was a pub on the outskirts of town where we were safe from the CoSMiC crew. It wasn't their *kind* of venue, thanks to the lack of scantily clad women, and so it was a perfect place to spend an evening of tears and alcohol. I knew there'd be lots of the former, but the promise of the latter would ease the pain. Or so I hoped.

I pushed through the door of the pub and ordered a couple white wine spritzers at the bar. Once I had our drinks in hand I slipped into one of the booths and watched the door. Five minutes later Ellie breezed in and waved.

As she approached I stood and let her pull me into a warm hug. "Oh sweetie, how are you holding up?"

Tears welled in my eyes and I cursed myself for allowing that shit head to get to me so much. "I'm okay...I guess."

She pulled away and peered into my blurry eyes. "Yeah, I can *see* that. *Totally* fine huh? Come on, let's get drinking. You can tell me all about what the dick-weed said to you and we can berate him."

We sat opposite each other in the green leather seats and I began to recount how things had happened at the library. She listened intently and managed to refrain from saying anything even though her facial expressions of horror and disgust told me she was itching to slate him.

When I'd finished recounting the whole sorry situation she heaved a sigh and sat back in her seat. "Wow. I think we need stronger drinks." And with that she got up and headed for the bar returning a few minutes later with glasses filled with amber liquid. Whiskey. Great. The drink Six brought to me on the night I found out about the Legion girl's death.

"Something wrong?" I glanced up to meet the scrunched, concerned features of my friend.

I shook my head. "No, it's fine."

"Okay, so what's the plan? How are you going to deal with all of this? How are you going to avoid seeing him?"

I sighed and swirled the liquid around my glass. "Honestly? I have no idea. It's a small town and he's hard to miss."

Ellie giggled. "Yeah you got that right. He's pretty damn *huge*." She pursed her lips and it was clear she was trying to stifle either a grin or another comment.

"What is it, El?"

With a wicked glint in her eyes she leaned toward me across the table. "Is he *all* huge? You know...*all* of him?"

Heat rose in my cheeks and I gasped with incredulity at her question. "Ellie, God! I'm *not* going to answer *that!*"

She laughed harder. "Okay, I'll take that as a *yes*. But the question I should've asked is did he know what to *do* with *it?*"

I opened and closed my mouth as images of Six writhing on top of me sprang to mind. My body began to tingle at the mere thought of what he could do to me. The immense pleasure he gave me. The earth moving orgasms I had experienced and the connection we'd had on levels *additional* to the physical.

I nodded my head and smiled. "Yeah...yeah he *really* did."

She huffed and pursed her lips. "Aww shit. See, if he'd been useless in the sack you could've moved on easily. But damn, girl you're going to struggle to find a guy like that again, huh?"

I scrunched my nose. "Gee *thanks*, Ellie. I *really* needed to hear that, *friend*."

Ellie decided a change of subject was in order and she proceeded to tell me all about a guy she'd been dating. Rick was a mechanic at the garage in the town and she was pretty smitten. We drank more whiskey but this time it was diluted with Coke which made it a little more palatable for me.

I was feeling a little light headed and woozy with the drink when my cell phone began to vibrate on the table. My mom's name came up as the caller ID and I rolled my eyes. "Sheesh she's calling to check up on me again. I'm going outside to take the call."

Ellie nodded. "I'll go get more drinks!" She clapped her hands together like a giddy school kid and I stood to make my way to the door. The bar was crowded and an Irish folk band were rocking out in the far corner meaning that taking a call inside was a *huge* no-no.

As soon as the fresh air hit me, my head began to swim. "Yeah, hi, Mom. Whassup?"

"I called your place but got worried when you didn't answer. It's after ten, honey."

"Yeah, yeah it's okay. I'm at the bar with Ellie."

"But you're okay?"

"Yesss, Mom, I'm fine, quit worrying. I'm a big girl." My words slurred and I giggled and hiccupped at the same time.

"Good grief, Chloe, be careful okay? You sound so *drunk*. Call me when you get home. Two rings so I know you're safe." It was a routine we'd set up since I came back to Utah.

"Two rings. Yep. Got it."

"Okay now go on back to your friend. And stay safe."

"Y'okay. Love you, Mom."

"Love you too, honey."

I hit end call and leaned against the wall to get my balance. The stars were out in force against the black backdrop of the Utah night sky and I stared up at it in wonder. I had no clue about astronomy but the tiny flecks of light looked so pretty from the ground.

"That there is the big dipper." A gruff male voice to my right informed me.

I glanced to my side to see dark haired man smiling up at the sky.

"Oh...I had no idea. Kind of looks like a *pan*." I giggled.

"Yeah I suppose it does. I'm Zak." He held his hand out to me.

I smiled and shook his hand. "I'm a little drunk...also known as Chloe."

"Great to meet you, Chloe. I don't remember seeing you around here before." His hair was short and tidy and he wore a short sleeved shirt and jeans.

Very clean cut. Nice. "I've only been here a month. I work at the library." I pointed in the direction of the building as only a drunk person would do.

He smiled and dimples appeared at either side of his mouth. "Yeah, thought you must be new in town. I kinda think I would've remembered you if I'd seen you before. So you get to read all the great books when they first come in, huh?"

I pointed at him and winked. I frickin' *winked*. Jeez. "Library Technician's prerogative." *Not easy to say after several whiskeys.*

He nodded, still smiling. "Can I escort you back inside? I'm guessing you're here with your boyfriend?"

I scrunched my face in what must have been such an attractive way...*not*. "Ahhh no."

"Oh...okay sorry to have bothered you. Nice to meet you though." He turned to walk away.

"Nonononono. I mean no I'm *not* here with my boyfriend seeing as I don't have one right now. And *yes* you *can* escort me back inslide."

He chuckled. "Back in*slide* huh? Is that what happens when you've had a little too much to drink?"

I smacked my head. "Oh gosh, inside...I meant inside." My cheeks heated almost to the point of spontaneous combustion and I was glad it was dark out.

He held out his elbow. "Come on then *also known as Chloe*. I think maybe you need coffee."

CHAPTER TWENTY-SEVEN

Six

I watched from the shadow of the alleyway across the street as the smart dressed guy I didn't recognize held out his arm and Chloe slipped hers through it. *So that's the lucky bastard, huh?* I wished I could get closer to eavesdrop on their conversation but my vantage point wouldn't allow it. My jaw ached from clenching so hard and I berated myself for not going over there when I first saw her come outside.

I hated the fact that she looked so damned happy with the bastard. And that I had been taking a piss when the fucker turned up. Although seeing her kiss him hello would have no doubt hurt like a bitch, I wanted to assess how deep her feelings were for him. Knowing how passionately she had kissed me, I guessed that it was a surefire way of discovering how tough my competition was.

And he *was* competition.

Because little did he know what he'd let himself in for.

Regardless of her words *and* mine, there was still *something* between us. I just had to figure out a way to make her realize it too. And no fucking preppy looking dude was going to change that. Seriously he was like the antithesis of me in *every single way*.

From where I was standing it was clear there was no visible ink. He was so clean shaven he looked almost teenage. And his clothes made him look like someone's dad. Jeez she was really all out to *not* be with someone like me.

But I had to change her mind.

I just didn't know how.

―――――

The next day I got up early and took a shower. It was peaceful being back in my own apartment. I'd gotten sick of all the drama at the club. And of the women throwing themselves at me now that Cain was out of the picture. The fucks I'd had since Chloe had been quick and simply a way to get some relief from the case of blue balls I had going on. But *none* of them could hold a candle to her. They had all been purely physical. *Nothing* else.

I watched TV while I ate a bagel and tried to figure out what the hell to do about winning her back. In the end I decided maybe I could go to the library and get a book to read. Maybe she could recommend something. Okay so it was a lame ass, high school kind of approach, but what the hell *else* could I do? Give up?

An hour later I pushed through the door of the library and scanned the place looking for the brown haired beauty. She was helping some old guy in the history section and I watched from afar until she was free. Today she wore a navy blue fitted dress with short sleeves. It hugged her curves but not in an obvious way. The neck line showed no cleavage whatsoever. But then again she was working in a *library*. Her chocolate brown waves were loose today and she wore glasses. And my god if they didn't make her even *hotter*.

Finally, the old timer had what he needed and she walked back behind the counter so I took a deep breath and began to walk toward her when another guy appeared in my line of sight.

Fuck a fucking fucker!

I dodged behind a shelf where I had a clear view of them both and realized she'd had a very good point way back about my stalker tendencies. Pushing the thought aside, I continued my stake out.

"Hi, Chloe? I don't know if you remember me from last night? I'm—"

"Zak, yeah, hi." Her cheeks colored beet red and she tucked her hair behind her ear. "I do remember you. Gosh I must have looked such an idiot last night. I don't normally drink so much and to be honest it won't be happening again any time soon. I'm suffering today." She laughed and raised her hand to her head.

"Nah, you looked cute. In fact, you've kind of answered my question. I...I was going to ask if I could take you for a drink after work, but I'm guessing the answer is no, huh?"

Her beautiful chocolate eyes widened and she hesitated. *Say no. Say fucking no.* My telepathy skills were clearly as good as my apologizing skills because she eventually replied, "Oh wow...well...I could go for coffee." *Shit.*

His whole demeanor changed and she'd obviously made the dick's day.

"Really? Great. Okay so I'll meet you after work and we can...we can go to Hank's maybe?"

She nodded. "Sounds great. I get off at five."

He nodded eagerly like an excited puppy but unlike a puppy I could've happily sucker-punched the dude.

"Okay, five it is. Bye, Chloe."

"Bye, Zak." She lifted her hand to wave as he walked away.

Okay, so he *wasn't* her boyfriend. That means she had *lied* to me. She wouldn't be going on a date if she had a boyfriend. *Now* I was pissed.

I discreetly left the building without her seeing me and went back to the bike. The douche was walking toward the end of town and I was in two minds whether to follow him. I wanted to be suspicious of him. To have some reason to warn her off him but I had nothing. He was one of those decent kind of guys that moms love. Any shred of hope I had left was fraying rapidly.

When I got back to my apartment I pulled on my leathers and grabbed my helmet. I needed to go for a ride. It was the best way for me to clear my mind and focus. Once the bike was fired up and my helmet was fastened, I set off toward Rockport State Park. It was a fairly long ride but it was early and I had all day to kill. I planned on sitting on a rock and listening to my iPod for a few hours surrounded by some of the best mountainous vistas the state had to offer.

———

At around four-thirty in the afternoon I was on my way back home. I was riding into town and I spotted the guy who was taking Chloe for coffee. He had his back to me but I recognized the clothes he'd been wearing earlier that day. As I passed I could see him gesturing wildly at someone but I couldn't see *who*. He seemed kinda pissed but I couldn't hear what was going on over the roar of my bike's engine. I resolved to keep an eye on him regardless of how clean cut he appeared. Something in the back of my mind niggled at me, telling me I was just jealous and even though I knew that to be true I ignored the voice and carried on toward home.

I pushed through the doors of Hank's coffee shop at a quarter-after-five and sure enough there was Chloe with her clean cut new friend. She was still in her work clothes but she was smiling across at him where he had his back to me. I had to quell the unreasonable urge to walk over and smash his face into the table.

Okay so I may have been just a *tad* jealous.

I ordered a flat white coffee and sat at a table by the door where I could watch them and after only a few minutes she glanced over and spotted me. The smile fell from her face and she suddenly excused herself from her companion and made her way to the back in the direction of the rest rooms. And yes, like the dumb-ass I was becoming—or already *was*—I followed.

When I pushed through the door into the back corridor she was standing there, arms folded glaring at me. "I *knew* you'd follow me. Old habits die hard, huh, Mister S*talkerson*?" There wasn't a shred of humor to her rhetorical question in spite of the comical nickname. "Why can't you just leave me alone?"

I stepped toward her and she backed up against the wall. I trapped her in the cage of my arms. "I think you know the answer."

She growled at me. "You are *so* frustrating. One minute you want to protect me and the next you send me away. Then you show up at my work and act like you've missed me. Then you make some crass comment about fucking other women. Then you show up at my work and hide. I mean *come on,* you're six-four, you dumb fucking *idiot*. How could I *not* see you? And how could you think you'd suddenly become invisible? You're driving me *nuts*. I can't keep *up* with you, Six. And I don't *want* to. *Not* anymore. *Please* just leave. Me. *Alone*."

I stepped closer still, rested my forehead on hers and watched her chest as it rose and fell rapidly and her nipples stood to attention.

Her familiar scent infiltrated my brain and I inhaled deeply pulling it all the way in and memorizing it for later. "Stop *cussing* at me, Chloe. You know I *hate* that. And I just wanna talk to you. That's *all*," I whispered in her ear and watched as the skin of her neck flushed and prickled. It was a relief to see I still affected her.

She sighed and her hot breath tickled my neck. "No... you just want what you can't *have*, Six. It's an age old problem." Her voice had fallen to a defeated whisper and I guessed she too had suffered this fate.

I stared at her mouth as she spoke and my cock hardened. It had been far too long since I'd felt her body envelop mine. Without thinking I slipped my hand into her hair and crushed my mouth to hers. My other hand slid slowly down her body to her tit and I squeezed at her erect nipple through the fabric of her dress. I was overstepping the mark and I *knew* it, but she didn't stop me. I pushed open the ladies bathroom door and pulled her inside, locking it behind us.

"Six, what are you *doing*? I can't *do* this. Zak is out there waiting for me and *you* don't want me. You're just jealous. And...and I...I don't want *you*." From the weakness in her voice I knew she was trying to convince *herself* of that and it spurred me on.

I pushed her up against the full length mirror just inside the door and hovered my mouth by her ear again. "If you don't want me then make me stop. One word. That's all it'll take. Go ahead and say it."

I moved my mouth to hers and waited for her to answer me. To reject me. When she didn't I crushed my lips to hers once more, desperate to taste her again and her arms came around my neck where she gripped and tugged hard at my hair. I let my hand travel further down her body until I found the hem of her dress. Our tongues collided and fought for power over each other as my fingers trailed up the soft skin of her inner thigh. Cupping her pussy, I groaned into her mouth when I found her panties were already damp. I pushed aside the thin sliver of fabric so that I could slide two fingers into her tight body. Her sharp intake of breath pulled my attention back to her eyes as they locked on mine.

My thumb found her clit and I began to rub as her pussy tightened around my fingers. As I dragged my thumb over and over her tightened flesh, I thrust my fingers in and out of her wetness with increasing speed and her breathing accelerated.

"Unh...unh...Six...Six I'm gonna come..."

"I *want* you to come, baby. I want you to remember what it's like between us. I want you to know that *no man* can fuck you like I can. *No man* can make you feel like *I* make you feel. Come for me, Chloe. Imagine my cock inside you right now. I'm fucking you hard, baby. Just how you like it."

She began to cry out and I covered her mouth to stifle the noise as her muscles spasmed around my fingers. I pressed my cock into her hip trying to get some relief for myself but it was nothing compared to being inside her. Watching her fight to keep her eyes on me as her orgasm ripped through her body in strong waves that squeezed at my fingers, I was ready to blow my fucking load.

But as if realization had just hit her like a lightning bolt she shoved me hard in the chest and I staggered backward. "What the *hell*, Chloe?"

"You can't *do* this, Six. You can't *mess* with me like this. It's not *fair*. You're playing with my feelings and that just makes you a callous bastard. Don't do it again. Just leave me alone. *Please*." She adjusted her clothing as she hissed at me and before I could say a word she unlocked the door and almost ran out of there.

I slammed my fist into the wall. "*Fuck!*" Lurching for the door I began to call out, "Chl—" But I stopped the word before it left my mouth and instead slid down the wall until my ass hit the floor.

CHAPTER TWENTY-EIGHT

Chloe

After the crazy encounter in the bathroom I returned to the table to find Zak sitting there on his cell phone.

He glanced up and sighed. "Oh *there* you are. I was beginning to worry that you were sick."

He had given me the perfect get out. "Actually, I'm *not* feeling too great. I...I think I'm coming down with something. Would you mind if I took a raincheck on this evening?"

He stood and frowned as he reached out to squeeze my arm. "Sure, sure. No problem at all, Chloe. Can I walk you home? Make sure you get there okay?"

"No, no it's fine really. The fresh air will do me good, and besides I don't think I'd be very good company right now. I'm so sorry. I think it may be the start of a migraine."

"Ah, yeah they can be nasty. You go home and rest. I'll text you tomorrow. Take care, okay?" He leaned toward me and kissed my cheek just as Six walked past us. You've heard the saying 'If looks could kill' right? Well let's just say if they could, Zak would have dropped dead on the spot.

We had exchanged numbers when I had first arrived to meet him and I wondered if he would throw mine away after this poor excuse for a date. The poor guy must have thought I was a flake. And I could easily have agreed with him after what I'd allowed to happen in the bathroom. What the hell was *wrong* with me? How many times was I going to let my attraction to Six overpower me like that?

Once I was home, and the door to my apartment was locked, I changed into yoga pants and a T-shirt, deciding I was going to ignore the phone and read. I needed to escape into someone *else's* love life and forget my own...or lack thereof.

My cell pinged and I checked the screen. *Ellie.*

You coming out again tonight or is your head sore? ;-)

E x

There was *no way* I was going out again. I needed to stay in and stay away from people. *All* people. Especially those who were members of a certain MC.

I hit reply,

Sorry, El, head sore. Night from Hades :-/ Early night for me :-)

C x

She replied with a sad face icon and the usual 'You know where I am if you need me' stuff. I didn't answer but turned the cell off before throwing it onto the couch and grabbing my romance novel from the side table.

————

I was restless the whole night. First it was nightmares of blood soaked, dead bodies with blank staring eyes but then...and only *slightly* better...it was dreams of familiar, sensual fingers touching me in my most intimate places, a deep husky voice whispering dirty words in my ear as a beard scratched at my skin and my nails dragging down a toned, tattooed chest. These conjured scenarios alternately plagued me all night long. I awoke to an intense orgasm at one point during an amazing dream involving the latter and had to go get a drink of water to try and calm my breathing. *Great. He even stalks me in my frickin' dreams.*

But even after a night of broken sleep I awoke the next morning feeling a little better until I remembered the bathroom incident at Hank's. And as I showered, the torturous images of his eyes boring into me as his fingers penetrated my body played over and over in my mind and I couldn't seem to switch them off.

When I was out and dried off, I checked my phone and was heartened to see that Zak had messaged to wish me well. Hopefully my drinking and complaint of a migraine—which he will have translated as *hangover*—hadn't put him off me.

He was the kind of guy I needed.

Not Six.

Work was a little quiet and I was happy for the fact. No one liked working Saturdays and it was something I had hoped I'd left behind at *The Fox Hub*, but sadly people liked to borrow books on weekends too. I spotted Six driving past the library in the direction of the MC. He cast a glance my way as he passed, and a twinge of regret niggled at me. But was it regret at what had happened or regret that it *wouldn't* likely happen again? Who knew. If *I* couldn't even figure myself out there was no hope for anyone else.

Deciding that work would actually be a great distraction from my chaotic mind, I began filing some cards away and was lost in concentration when someone cleared their throat and I looked up.

I was greeted by strangely familiar eyes but the rest of the man's appearance was completely *un*familiar. "Oh, hi, sir. Can I help you?"

He looked a little lost and a line appeared between his eyebrows which confirmed my thought. "Hi, okay, so I need to look at some old newspapers. Do you have those?"

I nodded as my brain tried desperately to place where I *knew* him from. "Um... *sure*. We have microfiche if that's any good? We haven't moved with the times, really. It's the best I can do." I cringed.

Something about his demeanor made me nervous and I couldn't quite put my finger on it. He smiled and his face changed completely. He was handsome in an unkempt kind of way. A little like a certain biker I knew.

He nodded. "Okay. Can you show me how to look through it? I haven't used it before."

I smiled in return and came from behind the counter. "Absolutely. Follow me."

I left the guy to go through the microfiche and went about my work once again. I was sitting there until five thirty waiting for him to finish but he was still engrossed in whatever he was looking for. I didn't want to bother him but I had no choice. I had to close.

Once I had apologized for having to ask him to leave, I was still racking my brain trying to think why he seemed so familiar. But my brain just wasn't helping. When I asked him if he was from the area he seemed reluctant to tell me and a shiver down my spine told me it was maybe best if I dropped the matter. The most I managed to glean was that his name was Cameron and he was originally from around the area, but hadn't been around for a long while.

Something felt strange, however, and I couldn't quite put my finger on it.

Six

My heart hammered in my chest as I rode at speed to get to the MC to tell Colt what had happened. I was so fucking *relieved* that the rumors about Cain being dead were wrong but even so, the fact he couldn't remember the shit that had happened made me feel so damn guilty.

I was so intent on getting to Colt before Loki's Legion got to Cain that I only cast a brief glance in the direction of the library. I knew Chloe would be in there but I had to make sure that my best buddy was safe now that he was back. I was pretty damn sure that Loki's Legion would want to stir the shit pot again if they found out he was still alive and back in town. Especially seeing as we'd perpetuated the rumors about him and Rosa being dead to hide what had *really* happened.

Colt was sitting at the bar with paperwork strewn all around him. Delilah was cussing about the mess he was making and he was chuckling to himself as she chuntered. They both glanced up as I rushed over to them.

"Who the fuck rattled your cage, Six? You look like you've seen a ghost." Colt laughed. I was struggling to get used to seeing the guy smiling. But it had been happening more often lately.

"Yeah well that's maybe 'coz I think I *have*."

The smile dropped from his face and he stood. He stepped up to me and in a low voice said, "Are you getting at what I *think* you're getting at?"

I let my eyes flick toward Dee who stood there clutching a bar towel to her chest. Her eyes were wide and she chewed nervously on her lip. *Fuck. Maybe I could've handled this thing with a little more subtlety. Especially where Delilah's concerned.*

"Well?" Colt urged.

"Maybe we should head on up to chapel, Prez."

Without saying another word, he turned and headed for the stairs. I turned to face Delilah who opened her mouth the speak but I held up my hand. "Don't, Dee. Okay? Not now. I can't talk to you right now."

"But...just tell me he's okay. *Is* he? Come on, Six. Just let me have that much."

I reluctantly nodded and headed off to follow Colt. As I glanced back over my shoulder my heart squeezed. Delilah was leaning on the bar, head down, shoulders shuddering.

Poor bitch. Unrequited love is the worst fucking kind.

I'd rather have none at all.

CHAPTER TWENTY-NINE

Six

After meeting with Colt it was decided that it would be best to get Cain back under the protection of the club temporarily. But we both knew he couldn't stay. Knowing I'd no doubt have to lose my best buddy all *over* again didn't sit well with me. But I *did* know it was going to be for the best.

The following day I arrived at Hank's coffee shop to find Cain sitting there twisting a full mug around in his hands. I made my way over to him and he stood. I have to say I was filled with relief that he hadn't bolted in all the fucking confusion.

I pulled him into a bear hug and slapped his back. "Fuck, dude, I'm so glad you're still here. It's good to see you, man."

He shrugged. "Where was I gonna go?"

Okay, so he had a point. Considering he told me his memory was sketchy, I doubted he'd have a clue where to start. "Oh, I wondered if you might get spooked and jump a flight out of Dodge."

He shook his head as he peered at me and scrunched his brow. A look of suspicion if I ever saw one. "Nah. I have too many questions that need answering."

Shit, where the hell should I start? "Sure... sure you do. So... what've you been doing today?"

He informed me that I had an admirer and I instantly had an inkling he meant Chloe. But I guessed he'd got it wrong about her feelings for me. Considering the recent encounters we'd had, I suspected she was filled with anything *but* admiration.

But when I questioned him he insisted. "Nope. She went all doe-eyed when she found out I knew you."

"You're talking about *sweet Chloe*? Chloe with the big brown eyes and chocolate colored hair? The one who used to pole dance over at *The Fox Hub*?"

His eyes widened with shock. "Wait, *what*? She used to do *what*?"

I couldn't help laughing at his reaction. "That's where we first met her. You *must* remember her, dude. She was the best fucking dancer they had. But then... well, something happened, I don't know what, and she left. Disappeared for a while. When she came back, she got a job in the library, and I haven't seen her much since." Okay so *some* of it was true. Cain didn't need to know all the gory-ass details and *I* wasn't prepared to tell him, regardless of how much she probably hated me for what I'd put her through. What had happened was between her and I...no one else.

I showed him a video on my phone of Chloe as Nina,

strutting her sexy stuff to one of my favorite songs in the hope it might jog his memory. It certainly jogged mine.

He asked about the track. The goddamn *track* of all things. "You're kidding me, right? I'm showing you your little sassy library assistant cavorting, and all you can think about is the *song*? Queens of the Stone Age would be proud. It's *their* track 'I Appear Missing'." I laughed again, bewildered. "Fuck, man, you must have it bad for someone if you're not looking at her tits." As soon as the words fell from my mouth a twinge of guilt tugged at my insides. I hated that I'd just spoken about her that way. But again, Cain didn't need to know the extent of my feelings when I didn't fully understand them myself.

He shook his head and a crease appeared between his eyebrows. "Come on, man. She seems really nice. Don't you think you're being disrespectful?"

Fuck, did he read my mind? I felt the heat of a furnace rise in my face and I hit the stop button on the video. Jeez it came to something when the two baddest asses in town were getting pissy with each other over treating some *woman* like meat.

"I was just trying to prove a point." I couldn't hide the sulkiness in my voice.

Thankfully he smiled. "Yeah, well, now you *have*. She really seems to like you."

I wished he was right. "I doubt it. Let's just say that I'm not exactly the kind of guy someone like *her* goes for. Well not her *now* anyway. She wasn't working at the club long. I don't think she was right for the place. She was too... I guess... *nice*."

He slapped my shoulder. "Sounds like *you* might like *her* too."

We needed to get off the fucking subject.

———

I took Cain back to the Club on the back of my bike and when
we got there he was greeted with a very warm welcome from
Delilah. After I managed to drag her off of him I took him up
to see Colt. Watching Cain's reaction as Colt filled in the gaps
in his memory was gut wrenching. And once it was over, all I
could think about was Chloe. The guilt at how I'd talked
about her still twinged in my chest when I remembered. But
along with the guilt, a little spark of hope had sprung to life at
hearing Cain say she *obviously liked me too*. Maybe she and I
had a chance after all? But how the hell could I make her see
that I was willing to change? Not *completely*, obviously. I
mean once you're involved in club life it's hard to go back to
being some normal dude with a regular job and all that shit.
But I was hoping that maybe she could learn to accept me and
all my baggage as a package deal.

If Cain was right.

God please let him be right.

———

Colt arranged a big shin-dig on account of Cain being back in
the fold. All the other CoSMiC charters from around the
state were invited, and some from out of state. The idea was
that we were supposed to drink a few beers, eat a few burgers
and come up with a plan of action. A way to safeguard *all* of
us and to stop the rival club war that was still brewing
beneath the surface.

Toward the end of the night I was bored out of my head. I
had encouraged Cain to go upstairs with Delilah and I was

getting tired of watching half dressed women cavort around badly to my favorite music, ruining it completely for me. I'd purposefully thrown away every drink I'd been handed, knowing full well I was going to leave at some point and head to see Chloe.

But would she let me in?

I rode across town at speed, the cool early morning air hitting my face and awakening all my senses. As I kicked up a gear, eager to get to her apartment, I was trying to figure out what the hell I could say to make her realize that she *did* still like me. That I'd been an asshole of epic proportions and that I'd had a severe case of male pride.

It was one in the morning when I reached her building and the door was locked. *Fuck it.* I walked around to the side and peered up at her bedroom window. *No light. Great.* But what the hell did I expect really at this time of day? A disheartening sinking sensation knotted my stomach but as if fate had wanted to intervene a light suddenly came on in her room. I did the only thing I could think of and picked up some pieces of gravel ready to throw but I caught sight of *two* silhouettes in the window.

He was there with her.

Zak.

CHAPTER THIRTY

Six

Okay so maybe Cain *had* gotten it completely wrong when he'd said that Chloe liked me. I stood there at the side of her building as if in a trance while the silhouettes in her window moved together like they were kissing. My constricted stomach muscles knotted tighter still.

Bastard, she's fucking mine.

My fists clenched around the small chunks of stone that I'd picked up ready to throw to get her attention, but the silhouettes disappeared from sight which was worse. My mind raced as it tortured me with concocted images of them in bed together and I was on the verge of finding a huge fucking rock to smash the window with. *Yeah that'll get her fucking attention alright.* But a few minutes later in the silence of the early hours, I heard the main door of the building open. Tiptoeing as quietly as I could, I made my way around to the entrance, making sure to stay in the shadows and I watched as the prick left. *Okay so maybe they didn't have sex...unless that happened* before *I arrived.* Thankfully the door was slow to close and I managed to jam my foot in and open it. Slipping inside before he glanced back over his shoulder. In the street lights I saw a smug grin on his face and immediately wanted to smack it off.

Well, I was in a whole *new* category of stalker now. There I was on the verge of breaking and entering. Something I hadn't done for *many* years. And certainly *never* because of a woman.

Once on Chloe's floor, I tapped lightly on the door of her apartment. She was smiling as she opened it—I guess expecting her new beau to be there—and there was a pink glow to her cheeks until she realized it was me and the color disappeared.

"What the hell are *you* doing here?" she growled through her clenched teeth.

I rubbed the back of my neck under my pony tail as I fumbled around my brain for the right words. "I...I *had* to see you. We need to talk, Chloe."

She tried to close the door but I wedged my foot in the space. She put all her weight behind it. "We have *nothing* to talk about, Six. *Nothing.* Just *leave.*"

The pain in my foot was excruciating even though I was wearing heavy boots and my eyes began to water. "You're gonna break my fucking bones. Just let me in, *please.* I promise I'll keep my hands to myself. I just...I need to say some things to you and *you* need to listen." My own jaw was clenched and she suddenly widened her eyes as if realizing she really *was* hurting me.

"Shit, I'm sorry, I didn't mean...just come in." Her eyes closed, defeated and she stepped aside for me to pass her.

I limped over to the couch and sat down heavily, reaching to rub at my foot. She followed me and sat in the chair opposite. I trailed my gaze up her lean, bare legs to her white shorts and on up to her braless chest under the pale blue tank top. Her nipples poked through the flimsy fabric and my tongue came out to wet my lips. Her hair was bunched up on the top of her head and she was free of make-up, like she had been getting ready for bed.

"Is your foot okay?" she whispered.

"I saw Zak leave. Did you...did you *fuck* him, Chloe?" I hadn't meant to say the words out loud and I maybe could've used better ones, but *shit* they were out there and I couldn't take them back.

She gasped and crossed her arms over her chest, pushing her breasts up but covering her protruding nipples. "That's none of your damn business. And if *that's* why you're here then I suggest you fuck off and go home *right* now."

Anger and arousal spiked deep within me as I stared at her. "No...that's *not* why I came here. I *hate* it when you cuss, Chloe, you *know* that."

"Oh yes. I forgot you're the *king* of double standards." Sarcasm dripped from her voice.

Trying my best to ignore it, I continued as if she hadn't spoken. "And I'm sorry. I know it has nothing to do with me but... *Did* you? Did you *fuck* him?" *What the hell, Six?* It was like words were coming out of my mouth of their own volition and I was powerless to stop them.

She straightened her back. "What if I *did*?"

I closed my eyes and dropped my head forward. The

thought of another man on top of her, sliding his cock into her pussy—a pussy that belonged to *me*—made my blood boil. "Chloe, just tell me the fucking truth, okay?"

She laughed derisively. "Why? So you can get angry and beat the shit out of Zak? Would that make you feel like the *big man*, huh? Jealousy is a *shit* color on you by the way. And it's funny how you don't want me until someone else *does*." I lifted my face to find her glaring at me. A fire burning in her eyes. "I wouldn't tell you the truth if my life depended on it. You don't *own* me. You have *no right* to come here and ask such personal questions. We were over long ago. Or did you forget that you sent me away and told me not to *bother* contacting you?" Her rant continued and I just sat there, listening for a few moments.

Old fucking ground.

What was the point of going over that shit again and again? I stood and walked over to crouch before her where she sat. I placed my hands on her thighs, squeezing lightly and her breath caught as she sank farther into her seat. I came up onto my knees and bent forward so that my mouth hovered over hers, dangerously close. The smell of coconut body lotion infiltrated my senses and I inhaled deeply, breathing her in. Her chest began to rise and fall quickly and initially I wasn't sure if I was scaring her. I contemplated backing off but as I watched, her pupils dilated and she pulled her bottom lip between her teeth. She moved her arms and arched her back so that her tits pushed forward.

My nostrils flared and my dick hardened. "Did. You. Fuck. Him, Chloe? Did *he* make you come?"

With her gaze locked on mine she shook her head slowly from side to side. Relief flooded my veins and without thinking further I crushed my mouth to hers. Her thighs parted and I reached down to grab her ass and pull her against my erection where it pushed at the front of my jeans. Her hands came about my neck and gripped the straggly strands of hair that had escaped from the band that was holding it back.

Fuck I *needed* to be inside her.

I was at desperation point.

I swallowed hard and pulled my mouth away. "What the *fuck* are you doing to me? I can't stop thinking about you, Chloe. And the thought of some other guy kissing you...touching you and being inside you makes me want to take fucking lives. I...I *need* you. Don't you *get* that?"

Without answering she reached for the hem of her tank top and swiped it over her head baring her pert tits to me. I immediately bowed my head and sucked a stiffened peak into my mouth causing her to moan and tug at my hair again. Fuck she tasted so damn good.

Pushing me away once more, she shimmied out of her shorts and spread her thighs. I gazed down at her pussy and could smell her sweet arousal. She reached up and pulled the band from her hair allowing it to fall free, cascading around her tits.

She took a ragged breath. "Fuck me, Six. You say you need me, so *show* me how much."

I hesitated for a split second, wondering what the *hell* was going on in that head of hers and why she had changed her mind so damn fast. But after a brief contemplation, I stripped out of my clothes as fast as I could. Once I was naked and sheathed I pulled her ass toward me, pushing my cock into her tight, wet body. A groan left my chest as the sensation of her tightness accepting me in, deep, rippled through every single nerve ending. I slipped my hands under her ass and lifted her. My mouth found hers and her nails scratched at my back as I carried her over to the door that lead to the bedroom. Finding it was closed, I pressed her up against it and withdrew my cock slowly, torturing both of us.

Her legs tightened around me, pulling me back in. "Harder, Six. I want you deep and hard. Now!"

I'd *never* known her to be like this. Vocalising a desperation that matched mine as I thrust my hips forward, driving myself as deep as I could with a throaty growl. I withdrew again but rammed myself in harder this time.

Her eyes closed and her head rolled back. "*Yes*, that's it, Six, right there. Fuck me. Fuck me harder!"

My nails dug into the soft flesh of her ass at her command and my groin tightened. I loved hearing her tell me what she needed from me. I loved that she gasped and writhed against the base of my cock searching for friction, her pussy leaving my skin glistening with her arousal. She reached down between our slick bodies and rubbed at her clit. It was the most erotic thing I had *ever* witnessed and I focussed my attention on her fingers as I pounded into her body.

Leaning forward I sucked hard at the skin of her shoulder as the pleasure became even more intense and my cock throbbed inside of her. I was on the verge of release but I wasn't ready for this to be over.

When I pulled away there was a red bite mark that stood out as a stark contrast on her alabaster skin. "Tell me Chloe, baby. Tell me what you *need*. What you *want* me to do to you."

I breathed heavily as she moaned, "I need to you own my body *right now*, fill me and make me remember you forever. I don't *ever* want to forget this. *Mark* me again, Six. Make me come hard."

Her sexual commands were such a turn on but this wasn't *like* her and fear niggled at the back of my mind at her choice of words... *Make her remember? Why?*

I pushed the worry aside, deciding I was over-thinking and I concentrated on watching her work her fingers harder and faster. "Fuck, you look so damn good, Chloe dancer. So fuckin' hot. So beautiful. You're *mine*, do you hear me? Your pussy is *mine*." Suddenly overcome with a deep, unfamiliar feeling that welled up from my soul I cried out, "I fuckin' *love* you, Chloe! I *love* you!" The words spilled from my mouth in a rush of adrenaline and emotion just as she cried out. Her pussy tightening around my cock as incoherent, hoarse, plea-sure-filled moans left her throat.

Following her into the abyss, the most mind-melting orgasm tore through my body. Wave after wave washed over me as my heart almost burst from my chest. I locked my gaze on her beautiful face once more and began to pepper her cheeks and neck with kisses. Every place I could reach was touched by my lips as my thrusting began to calm and she eventually opened her eyes. But the small flame of hope that had manifested inside me was suddenly doused by the tears trailing from the corners of her eyes.

I released her ass and allowed her feet to touch the floor as I withdrew from her body and cupped her face. "Hey, what's wrong, baby?" I wiped the tears away with the pads of my thumbs and crumpled my brow as I stooped to connect with her eye to eye. Dread began to creep over my skin like cold fingers as I watched her lip tremble.

She reached up and tenderly touched my cheek. "Six, you

need to know that *this*..." She gestured between our naked bodies. "It will *never* happen again. This *has* to stop. We're not good for each other. We're a toxic mix you and I. Poisonous. You confuse the hell out of me and I lose sight of who I am when I'm around you and *yes* I do have feelings for you but I'm trying to move on with my life. I *have* to make a fresh start. I can't be who you *need* anymore and I don't think I ever really was." More tears spilled over and her voice cracked as she spoke. "I'm plain old Chloe, the Library Technician. Your life is so complicated with so much going on. You want to protect me but you can't. I have to deal with what I've done but I don't need to add to the drama. I don't *want* it. I need someone uncomplicated...like Zak... So this...this is goodbye, Six. It *has* to be goodbye."

Her words were like a direct strike. The pain was real and I staggered back as if she'd shot me in the heart, scrunching my face and clutching at my chest with one hand. "Did you not *hear* what I just *said* to you? What I just fucking *admitted* to you? My fucking feelings? Are they worth *shit* to you?"

She sniffed as she swiped the dampness from her face. "I *heard* you, Six. And you've no idea how much I *wish* it was true... But you were on the verge of *coming*. And I think we *both* know that our emotions get caught up in such an intense moment. Things get...misconstrued. We *both* know that deep down."

What the fuck? Who the hell is she trying to convince?

Feeling utterly foolish I stared at her in speechless disbelief. *How could she even think that way? Fuck!* I wanted to punch a fucking hole in the wall.

But like the dumb-ass 'tough guy' I was, my misplaced male pride kicked right on in as it always did and I sneered at her, letting my mask fall into place. I wasn't prepared to let her see how much she'd hurt me with her rejection.

I gave a humorless laugh. "Yeah. Yeah you're right. You *got* me. I guess a guy like me is incapable of such deep feelings. And you always *were* a good little fuck. I guess your pussy and those fine tits of yours mess with my mind, huh?" I spat the venomous words at her and turned away unable to look her in the eyes any more. I began to gather my clothes, yanking them onto my body as fast as I could.

I had to get out of there.

I *had* to leave.

CHAPTER THIRTY-ONE

Chloe

He slammed the door hard as he left. In the empty silence of my apartment, I crumpled to the floor in a sobbing heap. *Why* had he said he loved me? That was so *very* cruel. I'd felt that way about him for such a long time but had pushed the feelings aside, afraid to voice them in case he bolted. Especially considering the way our intense but strange relationship had occurred and fizzled, and all the drama that had happened during the short time we were seeing each other. Yet when he'd said the words to me that I'd longed to hear, I'd gotten scared. Scared and filled with crushing doubt all over again.

My mom had always told me *never* to trust a man who tells you he loves you as he's about to come. It's the oldest cliché in the book, *she* said. But I had desperately wanted to believe that he *could* love me. Or that I could love him enough for both of us. But when the chips were down he couldn't fight for me. Instead he did what I had expected and pierced my heart with his hurtful words. But after what I had said in response to his confession maybe I deserved his venom.

It was almost three in the morning and my body was so tired in spite of the barrage of emotion whirring around my head. I needed to give in and sleep.

———

I awoke to the sound of my cell ringing. In my foggy, sleep mussed state, I picked it up and answered without checking the caller ID.

"Yeah?"

"Hey sugar lips, it's me...Zak."

I sat bolt upright and guilt niggled at me. "Oh...hey...hi, Zak. What's up?"

"Well if you remember, I said I'd take you out for lunch today. You said you had a day off? Have you...have you changed your mind?"

"Oh gosh, I'd completely forgotten. But...No that would be lovely." I glanced at my clock and realized it was almost eleven in the morning. *Shit!* "Um...I need to shower and get ready so where should I meet you?"

"Well... I hope you don't mind but I've taken the liberty of packing a picnic and I thought we could take a ride out of town to a beautiful little spot I know."

I sighed deeply. "Look...Zak...I should be honest with you. I'm... I'm kind of getting over someone and I—"

"Chloe, are you *dumping* me before we even get started?" The disappointment in his voice tugged at my insides.

"No...not *exactly*...but... Look this is hard for me to say and so I'll just say it. My... my ex turned up after you'd gone last night... and we..."

A deep, disappointed sigh resonated across the airwaves. "Shit, you slept with him after I'd gone?"

I cringed and felt the heat of shame rise in my cheeks. "God, Zak, I must sound like a total slut and I'm so—"

"Look, Chloe. I really like you. I mean *really* like you. I think you know that. So...just tell me if you still want to be with him and I'll step aside."

Yes...yes I really do. "N-no. We're not right for each other. It's so complicated. I—"

"So was last night the last time you'll *be* with him?"

Huh? Why is he not dumping my ass? "Yes. The last time."

"Are you absolutely sure?"

I nodded fervently even though he couldn't see me. "I'm sure, Zak."

"Okay. Then let's go for lunch and talk. I want to spend time with you Chloe. And I think you like me too. So let's just see where this goes, okay? I'm not going to pressure you but...I won't be your second best either. If you'd rather be with *him* you should just tell me now."

My resolve strengthened. "No. No, let's go for lunch."

"Great. I'll pick you up in an hour."

———

Right on time, there was a knock on my door and I gave my appearance one last check in the mirror. I'd worn my floaty pale blue skirt and white tank with jewelled flip-flops. The sun was shining and I wanted to look good.

I opened the door and was greeted by a wide, handsome smile. "Hey beautiful. Look at *you*." He whistled and I obliged with a twirl, giggling like a school girl.

Suddenly embarrassed, I felt my cheeks heat. "Do I look okay for wherever you're taking me?"

"Oh you look *better* than okay, honey. You look stunning. As always."

I locked the door behind us and he took my hand as we walked to his car. I had been expecting things to be awkward in light of our recent phone conversation, but thankfully he was being very mature about everything. I was relieved to say the very least. He could've judged me. Dropped me like a hot rock. But he hadn't and it felt so good to be with someone who exceeded my expectations in a *positive* way for once.

He opened the passenger door of his little blue Volvo and I climbed in. I glanced around, taking in the clean interior of the *normal* car and breathed a sigh of relief. *Normal is good. Normal is better than good...right?* On the back seat was a wicker basket with the lid fastened down. *Wow, this guy goes all out.* Once he was behind the wheel he turned toward me.

Reaching out he took my hand. "Before we go I just want to say that I've *been* where you are, Chloe. I've tried *hard* to get over someone who just won't let go. Someone who likes to keep me hanging on and use me when *they* see fit. But there comes a point when...you have to just *let go*. You have to choose *yourself* and your *own* happiness. It's difficult for a while. But... it *does* get easier. And I can be patient. We haven't known each other that long and so I don't want to pressure you. But I really do like you. And if you like me too...like I *think* you do...well then I think we can give us a try."

He had surmised my situation from very little information but most of what he said was right. Why the hell was he being so great about this? I just didn't get it.

"Thank you, Zak. I... I can't quite believe how accepting you're being of what I've done. I... I kind of...*cheated* on you." I cringed as the words fell from my lips.

He shook his head, a solemn look in his eyes. "No. I don't look at it that way. You and I weren't *official*. I mean, come on, a couple of dates doesn't make us serious does it?"

I scrunched my brow. "I guess not..."

He leaned closer and slipped a hand into my hair. "But I'd like to think we can get there. Some day."

His blue eyes sparkled as he spoke and for a moment Six disappeared from my thoughts. "I'd like that too."

He kissed my forehead and turned to start the car.

———

After driving for around an hour, we pulled down a picturesque trail surrounded by trees and drove until we arrived at a clearing. It was beautiful and so very peaceful. A little abandoned, tumble down, wooden shack sat a way off in the distance and I absently thought how wonderful it would be to wake up to such amazing views every day. Isolated, yes, but beautiful.

He stopped the car and opened his door. "Wait there, gorgeous." He dashed around opened my door and held out his hand. I took it and climbed out breathing the warm air into my lungs. He collected the picnic basket and a rug from the back of the car and walked over to a shaded area and I followed.

As we laid out the rug he kept smiling up at me. I was beginning to get self-conscious that he was laughing at me. "What?" I asked nervously tucking my hair behind my ears.

He shook his head, still smiling like a goof. "You're just so damned beautiful." He shrugged. "You make me smile. That's all."

Six

After watching the bastard pick her up in his cute little fucking family car, I'd had just about enough. I'd *seen* enough. And I'd sure as hell *felt* enough. For the first time in a hell of a long time I was going back to the club to drink myself into oblivion.

Sitting there at the bar with Cain beside me, I gulped down shot after shot. Colt had announced that we were taking a trip upstate in a couple days to take Cain to see his sister Rosa, where she'd been holed up in a safe house and he was happy as a pig in shit. But he was desperate to just go and Colt was wanting to wait until he could be sure things were safe.

My best friend slapped my back. "So come on, buddy. If I remember right you and I used to tell each other stuff. So *who* is she and why do you look like you lost a hundred and found a dollar?"

Cain's words filtered through my alcohol fogged mind and I chuckled. "She's *nobody*. Not anymore." My stupid sing song voice sounded ridiculous and Cain punched my arm lightly. What was it with the guy and physical contact?

He shook his head. "Nuh-uh. Not taking your bull. I know you got stuff going on in your head. I can tell. Spill it douche. For no other reason than to take my mind off my *own* crap."

I knocked back another shot of tequila and hissed in through my teeth as the alcohol burned its way down my insides. "You know that sweet, doe eyed library girl?"

"Chloe? Yeah, sure, man. You got it bad for her huh?"

I shook my head. "*Had* it bad. Past tense." I pointed in his face. "Passssst."

He laughed at me again and rolled his eyes. "Whatever dude. You're hooked. So what's the problem? It was clear to me she had a major crush on you."

I laughed without a single ounce of humor. "Again, *passsst* tense."

"You guys had a lovers' tiff?"

"Let's just say I fuckin' ruined it all. Like I always do. I stalked her. Got obsessed. Fell fuckin' *hard* and then got kicked in the 'nads. She fucked me and dumped me all in the same night, bro. How's *that* for bad romance?"

He cringed. "Whoa. Ouch, that's bad, Six. I'm sorry, bro. No chance of you two getting back together?"

I shrugged so hard I wobbled on my bar stool. "Nope. She's off with some fucking prissy guy called Zak. All clean cut and shit. *Total* opposite of me."

His eyes widened and he gripped my shoulder. "No way? Wow. It seems you and I have suffered a similar fate my friend. Women huh?"

"Yup. Can't live with 'em...can't fuckin' get 'em out of your damn head."

He leaned toward me and glanced around conspiratorially. "Do you think it was *love*?" His voice was low as if he was afraid to ask.

I suddenly felt sober at his question and an unwelcome clarity descended over me. "Yeah. No doubt about it."

CHAPTER THIRTY-TWO

CHLOE

Learning all about Zak and his family on our picnic had been lovely. Refreshing even. For the most part he'd had a pretty normal, happy upbringing with his younger brother, Tyler who was into rock music and was apparently quite the opposite of Zak. Their father had passed away when he was a teenager and so our lack of a father figure was something we, sadly, had in common. He had stepped in and been the man of the family when his mom had returned to work following the tragedy that had befallen them, but he said he wouldn't have changed a single thing about looking after his brother. My heart swelled as I listened to him talk about their holidays together. And the way he spoke so fondly about his dad made tears well in my eyes for his loss. I wished I could miss my dad the same way but you can't really miss what you never really knew.

Zak was such a sweet, kind hearted guy. And I was lucky

he was giving me a second chance. I was determined I wouldn't be messing it up *any* time soon.

He pulled up the car outside my building and turned to face me again. "Well I've had a wonderful afternoon, Chloe. And I hope we can do it again real soon."

I smiled warmly. "Would you like to come up for coffee?" I wasn't quite ready to let him go yet.

He nodded and his mouth widened into a handsome grin. "I'd love to, thank you."

The memory of our late night a couple days earlier sprang to mind. We'd talked and talked about *my* family and *my* life and so today had made a nice change. The other night he had only kissed me right before he left, and while his kiss didn't melt my underwear, it was sweet. And I was looking forward to trying it again.

Maybe the more I kissed him the more I'd like it? The more I would forget Six?

As we walked toward my building he took my hand and squeezed it. I smiled shyly across at him, but the thought that maybe I should tell him about my past life as an exotic dancer sprang to mind. I dismissed it deciding it was too soon. He *liked* Chloe the library technician and so did I for that matter.

Nina, and all the shit that happened to *her* was becoming a distant memory. Well almost.

Once inside my home I dropped my keys onto the coffee table and turned to Zak. "Coffee?"

His hands were bunched in the pockets of his beige pants. "Sounds good."

I made my way into the kitchen and he followed. Suddenly his arms came around my waist and his lips were on my neck. Shivers traveled my spine, but not for the reasons I wanted. I wanted to be excited by *Zak's* touch and *not* by the memory of the same situation happening with Six.

Sadly, Six won out.

Feeling awkward at my realization, I turned around to face him and nervously chewed on my lip. I wanted to explain what was going on in my head, but how the hell could I make sense of my feelings to him without everything sounding wrong?

He must have noticed the concern in my expression as he stepped back and cringed. "Too soon?"

I briefly closed my eyes and exhaled. When I opened them again I decided to dive right in. "No...not too soon. I just... I wanted to turn around so I could..."

He scrunched his brow but smiled. "So you could what?"

I nervously cleared my throat. "K-kiss you," I lied.

Without needing further encouragement, he stepped up to me again and slipped his arms around my waist before touching his lips to mine. I placed my hands around his shoulders and began to kiss him back. It was...*different*. His tongue slid along my bottom lip, encouraging me to open for him and I obliged. The kiss was soft and undemanding. But warm and sweet all the same. *Too* sweet. There were no sparks inside of me. My clit didn't ache for his touch and my panties didn't dampen.

I felt his arms move from my waist and his fingertips trail up the bare skin of my arms until they traced the shape of my collarbone. But then one hand came around the back of my head and cradled me as the other grazed down my tank top and cupped my breast. I gasped at his bold moves as his kiss gained fervor. It seemed so out of character for him. He began to toy with my nipple through the fabric of my top and bra and a groan escaped his mouth. The hand that had been teasing me slipped down my body until I felt his fingers trailing up my inner thigh. My mind was racing with images of Six that were impossible to shake off. He cupped my pussy, pressing his palm into my clit as he nuzzled my neck at the same time, sucking and nibbling at the sensitive flesh there. Then his fingers slipped inside my panties and into my body.

I gasped and pushed at his chest but he continued sliding his fingers in and out as his thumb began to rub my sensitive flesh. Shame washed over me and I wanted him to stop. I pushed at him again and he stepped back, releasing me.

"Zak...you're...*this* is going too fast. Can we just...can we slow it down?" My breathing was heavy and I felt my cheeks flush.

He shrugged. "You seemed to be enjoying it, babe. I just thought we could kick things up a notch."

As I peered into his eyes he seemed like a completely different person. Gone was the sweet guy I had been enjoying getting to know and in place of the kind blue irises I had gazed into before were dilated, lust filled, hooded eyes that undressed me as he stepped forward and caged me in with his arms.

"I...I th-think maybe you should go. It's getting late," I stuttered knowing full well that it wasn't but unable to think of any other plausible reason for asking him to leave. Apart from telling him he had crossed a line. But I had encouraged him to kiss me so how much of a tease would I seem?

He shook his head, took several steps away from me and was suddenly back to what I had considered *normal*. "Shit, I'm so sorry about that, Chloe. I guess I read the situation all wrong." He ran his hands through his short, neat hair. "God, I hope you can forgive me. I got so caught up in the moment. And you...you turn me on so much...I...*please* forgive me."

This was more like him. Worry was evident in his eyes and furrowed brow and I melted a little with pity.

I twisted my hands in front of me. "It's okay. You're forgiven. I just don't want to take this too fast. I've made that mistake before you know?"

He nodded fervently. "Oh sure, yes, yes I *totally* understand. I *should* go. May I kiss you goodnight?" I wordlessly nodded and he leaned forward placing a chaste kiss on my cheek. "I hope to see you soon."

"Me...me too," I replied, but deep down I felt that maybe I needed a few days away from men in general.

CHAPTER THIRTY-THREE

Six

I hated lock down with a damn passion.

Hated. It.

But once again, thanks to my best buddy and his determination to make every situation about *him,* that's right where we were; sitting in the club waiting for Colt to make his decision about the next fucking move.

Everything had been great. But as these things have a tendency to do, everything rapidly went to shit when Rosa disappeared. After we rescued her, we took Tyler, her boyfriend who turned out to be the little prick who had been instrumental in kidnapping her. After roughing him up a bit to teach the kid a lesson, he had been sent on his way complete with a newly shaven head and a new tattoo made up of permanent marker on his scalp, thanks to Dee, that told Loki's Legion *exactly* what they could do with their revenge attacks.

As Colt and I had abandoned the teenage douche-bag at the side of the highway, he'd made some weird comment about *big brother* still watching us that neither of us understood. I figured that once the kid arrived back at Loki's Legion, his father would insist on retaliation and it was only a matter of time before even *more* shit hit the proverbial fan.

All I could think about was Chloe and her new, clean cut boyfriend. I missed her like crazy and it was pretty clear I was driving Cain mad talking about her, but I didn't really care.

I sighed as I stared into the bottom of the glass at the dark liquid which was the same color as her eyes. "I mean...her eyes are just so—"

Cain sighed and gripped his hair with one hand in exasperation. "Aaargh! Beautiful, yeah you *said*. Jeez man can you just give it a rest, huh? Her eyes, her tits, her legs. She's fucking *gorgeous* I get it. Just *call* her, dude. Tell *her* all this shit and give *me* a fucking break, *please*." He slammed his empty glass down, grabbed the bottle he had been drinking from and disappeared up the stairs.

After he said that, I made several attempts over the next hour to contact Chloe by phone, but she'd rejected my calls. My texts then began to bounce back as undeliverable and I realized she had blocked my number. *Dammit*. She was hell bent on staying away from me, *that* much was evident. I resolved that as soon as I was able, I'd be going around to see her. I *had* to. Okay, so I was obsessed, but I couldn't fucking help it. That's what she did to me.

We were locked in the same four walls, for God only knew how long, and I was getting stir crazy. The rest of the guys were playing pool or making out with the club sluts, and for a moment I was jealous that I couldn't just go get my rocks off with some random chick.

I was relieved when Delilah came walking through to the bar from the girls bathroom grinning like the cat that got the cream. Her hair was completely different.

"Gone for a new image, huh?" My rhetorical question was more of a statement of the obvious.

She touched her hair and shrugged. "Yeah. It was time for a change."

I shook my head and rolled my eyes. *Women.* She headed for the stairs and I guessed she was off to harass my lovesick buddy again, which was a complete waste of her time seeing as he'd taken a bottle of Jack with him and would no doubt be asleep or too wrecked to talk. *When will she learn that he just isn't interested?*

Cain had been upstairs for about an hour and I was still sitting at the bar drinking yet another whiskey. Drinking wasn't something I liked resorting to. In my mind it made me weak but it was the only way I could blur the thoughts of Chloe from my mind.

I had just split up a fight between Weasel and Rapid—who had apparently been fucking the same woman and neither wanted to share—when I heard shouting coming from upstairs. Cain was seriously pissed and I guessed right away that it had something to do with Delilah. I ran up the stairs two at a time and arrived at the door to his room just as Dee shoved past me wearing only a pink robe.

I shook my head and snickered. "You lovers had a little tiff?"

Cain glared at me like I'd just killed his grandma. "This is *not* a fucking joke, man. I'm outta here, dude. This whole place is going crazy. I can't *deal*, Six." He grabbed his sweats and pulled them on followed by a shirt and he too shoved past me.

I grabbed for him but missed. "Whoa, Cain, what happened? Why are you so pissed?"

He stopped and turned around to face me. And then at the top of his voice he yelled, "Delilah broke into my room and stole the perfume I bought that reminded me of Kelly from Scotland and wore it so that she could *smell* like her. She even dyed her fucking *hair*. And then she snuck into my room sucked me off in the dark. She's *sick*. And I can't *be* here anymore."

Wow. I knew she was desperate but that was beyond the pale. Kind of made my stalking tendencies look like a nice little hobby. "Oh, man. That's some fucked-up shit." And it really was.

"Ya think?" He carried on stomping away and descended the stairs to the main room. I jogged after him in case he decided to rant at Dee again. Poor bitch didn't really need that in spite of what she'd done.

I watched as he headed for the door that led out into the compound. *Aww fuck.* I had to stop him from going out there. It wasn't safe. Before I could reach him, he was through the door and I followed, but he had already made it half way across the yard.

I called out to him, "Cain! You shouldn't be out here, man. It's not safe." He spun around and lifted his arm as the security lights came on and dazzled him.

Suddenly a loud bang sounded from outside the lot. I almost jumped out of my skin. But then I watched in horror as my best friend cried out, clutched his chest and crumpled in a heap.

"Cain! Noooooo!"

————

Six

Cain was in a bad way and I swore my heart was about to split in two. I was holding it together as best as I could. Trying to be the strong, tough guy so that Delilah and the others could fall apart on me but the vision of him laying there in the yard covered in blood as I tried to revive him made my stomach roil every time I thought about it. He was my best friend and I had already lost him once. How the hell would I cope if he *died* this time? What the hell would I do?

Loki's Legion had overstepped a major damn line and I was ready to draw blood. Anger knotted my already sore stomach and as I stood there watching Dee stroke his hair, I simultaneously clenched and unclenched my fists *and* my jaw. *The bastards. The fucking evil, scum-sucking bastards.* I wanted to finish them *all*. I wanted them all to suffer the way they had made *us* suffer. But the fact was the violence had to stop. And as much as I wanted to kick the living shit out of Deak and his puppets, I had to rein myself and my aggression in this time.

I left the hospital at around two a.m. and climbed on my bike. My teeth ached from the number of times I had squeezed my jaws together to fend off the emotion fighting for escape. I couldn't show *any* weakness. Not in front of the others. Once my helmet was secure I started up the engine and tore off at speed. I rode for what felt like hours and didn't care how much danger I was putting myself in by doing so. I just needed to ride. To try and clear my head. But for once, being on the bike wasn't helping.

There was only one thing for it.

CHAPTER THIRTY-FOUR

CHLOE

I was awoken by someone banging on my door and I was suddenly filled with fear. It was almost three in the morning. *Who the hell would be here at that time unless it was the cops or someone intent on harm?* My hands were shaking and I pulled the covers up to my chin as I stared at the bedroom door. *What the frick do I do? Shitshitshitshit.*

The banging stopped and I held my breath as I tiptoed from my bed to the door.

BANG BANG BANG!

I almost jumped out of my skin and squeaked. My hands covered my mouth and my eyes widened. Blood was whooshing in my ears as my heart battered my rib cage.

"Chloe...Chloe please."

Six? What the hell? I walked to the front door. "What do you want?"

"I just...I need to talk. I know I fucked up. But...I just need a friend right now." His voice cracked as he spoke and my heart cracked with it. "*Just* a friend."

I clicked the dead bolt and opened the door to be greeted by a lost looking, broken man. He didn't look like Six at all. His eyes were bloodshot and his skin pale. His hair was unkempt and it was clear he hadn't rested for a while.

"Please...can I just come in?"

I nodded and stepped aside for him to enter. The distasteful odor of sweat and stale alcohol wafted into my nostrils as he walked past me and over to the couch. He slumped down and immediately dropped his head forward into his hands. I closed the door and walked over to sit beside him.

Placing a hand on his back I rubbed gently. "What the hell happened, Six?"

He turned to face me. "Um... Cain's been shot... He...he may not make it, Chloe. He's...he's in a really bad way." And with that his lower lip began to tremble as tears spilled over from his red rimmed eyes.

I gasped and moved to put my arms around him but he crumpled into my lap, burying his head into my stomach and clinging to me as if his life depended on it. A pain filled sob vibrated through his body and salt water welled in my eyes too. I had *never* seen him like this. He wasn't the type to show emotion but this was clearly breaking him in two. My tough, six foot plus wall of muscle and tattoos was reduced to a little boy right before my eyes.

I stroked his hair, trying my best to comfort him but not really knowing what to do. What to say. Eventually he sat up and wiped his face roughly with his palms.

"Fuck. Sorry about that. I don't usually do that. I guess I'm just so wound up about everything. I just can't deal with all the shit that's happened over the last year."

I shook my head and reached out to squeeze his arm. "No need to apologize, Six. Look, why don't you go take a shower and I'll make you something to eat."

He chuckled and smiled. "Trying to tell me I stink?"

I cringed but couldn't help returning his smile. "A little."

His shoulders juddered as he laughed. It was a wonderful sound after what I had witnessed only moments before. He tucked his greasy hair behind his ears. "Okay, well better go get cleaned up then, huh?" He stood and shrugged out of his leather cut and jacket, dropping them onto the couch where he had been sitting.

He began to walk toward the bathroom but stopped just as he passed me. "Thanks Chloe. I know I've been a total dickweed to you and I'm truly sorry. Thanks for being a friend tonight." He squeezed my shoulder and walked through the door to the bathroom.

A *friend*. The word sounded strange when speaking about Six and I. The amazing sexual chemistry that we had always shared didn't feel the same. Perhaps he had finally given up and decided to let me move on. But could I deal with having him in my life as a friend? That was the question.

———

Around twenty minutes later he appeared in the kitchen doorway where I stood preparing him a cold cuts sandwich. I could sense him before I saw him, but when I turned around I almost swallowed my tongue. He was standing there in his jeans, no shirt, no socks. His hair wet and slicked back from his shower. The fly of his jeans was open and I could see that he wasn't wearing any underwear. I heard him laugh and I lifted my eyes to connect with him.

"Why, Chloe dancer are you *ogling* my *body*?"

His fake southern belle accent made me giggle. "Haven't heard *that* name in a while."

His smiled disappeared. "Well I don't suppose I can *call* you it any more really."

I shrugged. "Oh I don't know. I kinda liked it."

His demeanor brightened. "You did?"

I chewed my lip. "Kinda."

We shared a definite moment where the chemistry between us smouldered like a flickering ember. But he broke the spell when he cleared his throat.

He pointed to the plate on the counter top. "So, is that my sandwich?"

I turned and inhaled deeply to calm my jangling nerves and I handed him the plate.

He picked up the sandwich and took a huge bite. A groan erupted from his chest and his eyes rolled back. "Fuck me. Almost better than sex," he moaned with a mouth full of bread and ham.

"Urgh, you are truly disgusting."

He winked. "And baby you *know* it." He swallowed and gave me his panties melting grin. My heart stuttered in my chest and I covered my reaction with shake of my head and a roll of my eyes.

———

We sat in the living room as he ate his food and once he had finished he washed it down with the coffee I had made for him.

He cleared his throat. "So, how's it going with...um...*Zak*?" he asked without making eye contact.

Why the hell is he asking me? What good will it do? "Oh...fine...thanks for asking." And please let that be the end of the conversation.

"He treating you right?"

I sighed. It was *not* a topic I wanted to discuss with my *ex*. "Yes. It's all good."

He lifted his head and suddenly made intense, penetrating eye contact. "*All* good?"

I knew *exactly* what he was getting at. But he didn't need to know anything about my sexual relationship with Zak...or *lack* thereof. "Yes. *All* good," I repeated. "We have things in common you know? He has no dad..." My words trailed off as that snippet of information seemed to be all I could think of.

He nodded and pulled his lips in between his teeth. He was clearly unhappy about my response and a twinge of guilt tugged at me for lying through omission about our relationship status.

Eventually he spoke again. "I'm happy that you're happy, Chloe. I really am. You deserve to be. And you deserve someone who isn't involved in all kinds of twisted shit. So... I wish you well."

His words seemed so final and caused my insides to knot. I had to fight the growing urge to slide into his lap and hold him close to me one last time and admit the truth.

His voice dragged me from my reverie. "You know... I

used to love watching you dance. And...not because of the sexual aspect. Well not *just* because of that." I glanced over at him to see him smile sadly. "I always said you could have been... you know...like...in a show. A professional gig and all. You're more than good enough."

"That's really kind of you. Thank you, Six."

"Hey, I mean it. You're so *graceful*."

That wasn't a word I *ever* expected to fall from his lips and I suddenly felt my cheeks heating. "Really?"

His caramel eyes widened with enthusiasm. "*Really*. Chloe, you have this *air* about you. Something...*superior* but not...not in a conceited way, if you know what I mean?"

I shook my head. "No, I'm afraid I don't."

He sighed, and ran his hands through his damp hair, clearly exasperated with himself. "I mean... shit... You're too good for *The Fox Hub*. Too good for the library." He moved his face and gazed into my eyes once again. "Too good for *me*."

"Six, I—"

"Would you dance for me once more?"

Huh? I stared at him in disbelief. "What? *Here?*"

He nodded slowly, keeping his eyes focused on me. "Here. One last time." He moved closer to me and reached out for my hand. My fingers were swallowed up in his rough palm and he smoothed his thumb over my knuckles. "Look, Chloe, I *know* I've lost you. I lost you before I even *had* you. You and I are from completely different worlds. I was dumb to ever expect anything different. And...if I'm going to have to let you go *permanently*, would you dance for me one more time? *Please*? I...I don't mean in a sexual way. Nothing like that. I just... I want to see you dance again."

His eyes sparkled and at that moment my heart shattered into a million tiny pieces. He was willing to let me go and it almost broke me. I swallowed hard as I kept my focus on him, trying hard not to let my emotions run free and I nodded.

CHAPTER THIRTY-FIVE

Six

Chloe walked over and flicked on her iPod in its docking station as I dragged the coffee table out of the way. The center of her living room wasn't an ideal stage but it was all the stage we had and I needed this.

One last dance.

She wore little black sleep shorts and a black tank top. Her slender but shapely legs seemed to go on forever and as I trailed my gaze up to her tight round ass I had to remind myself I was letting her go. There was no point getting aroused by the sight of her. Not anymore. It was strictly platonic from here on in.

And that thought crushed me.

The opening bars to "Spin, Spin Sugar" by Sneaker Pimps surprised me. It was a strange choice of song and I wondered, as I listened to the opening lyrics, what she was trying to say...if anything. Or was it simply that she had danced to this at the club and that's what she *thought* I wanted. She closed her eyes and with her back to me she began to move around the small space I had created for her. But it all felt so damn *wrong*. Her moves were taken straight from a pole routine. Overtly sexual in spite of what I'd asked for. She pushed her breasts together and arched her back before bending and gripping her ankles giving me an amazing view of her ass but *this* wasn't what I had meant.

Not at all.

"Stop." The word left my mouth before I could halt it.

She did as I commanded and turned to face me, panting. "What is it?"

I stood and walked over to her iPod and hit the stop button. I rifled through the tracks and found the perfect one.

I closed my eyes to gather myself before turning to face her again. "I don't want to watch *Nina*. I want to see the *real* Chloe dancer. *My* Chloe dancer."

As the opening bars to "Anyone But You" by Hinder began to play, I gestured to the floor for her to continue and I went and took my place on the couch again. My heart was thudding at my ribs because of the song I had chosen and so I took a deep calming breath. I lifted my chin to find her standing there, staring at me. I smiled but my heart ached and I hoped it didn't show.

Suddenly she was moving again. Her eyes closed and her fingers reached out into the space between us as she expressed every single word of the song as it played out. Her chocolate brown hair fanned out as she made the tiny space feel like an auditorium. Her arms wrapped around her body as she dropped to her knees and curled up in a ball before stretching and reaching toward me again. It was *then* that I noticed the damp trails on her cheeks and I had to swallow the ball of emotion that had caught in my own throat.

Goodbye was heart-breaking.

Even for a tough, tattooed biker.

Especially when it was a word you simply didn't want to utter.

————

Chloe

He changed the track.

Such a beautiful, sad song. So appropriate for the pain I felt inside. I should've been happy that he was finally willing to move on. And that this dance was my parting gift to him. But he didn't know my deepest feelings. He presumed I was moving on because my feelings for Zak were growing. But the truth was I didn't know if I was able to do that, let feelings for someone else take over my heart.

The lyrics floated through the air and wrapped themselves around my heart. Pure, heartfelt emotion vibrated from Austin Winkler's voice as he sang of saying a final goodbye to someone he loved. The words expressed my own innermost feelings so well but I wondered... Was this truly how Six felt? Had I gotten him completely wrong after all this time? Was I making a huge mistake?

No.

No I can't think that way. I don't want the life he leads. I don't want the violence or the pain. I want peace. Normality.

Normal is good. Isn't it?

I kept my eyes closed and tried hard not to touch him as I

danced. It should have felt strange—weird even—dancing in my living room where the coffee table usually sat. But it didn't. It felt right. Dancing again made me feel almost whole. Alive. Healed. Like a part of me was returning. A part that I hadn't realized I had lost until now. I swayed and let the music fill my mind. I felt every single word as I moved and as the song ended I glanced up from the floor to see his gaze locked on me.

He was leaning back into the sofa, his hands resting on his thighs. His shirtless chest rising and falling rapidly. Jaw clenched and eyes glistening. What was he thinking? Raw, unfettered emotion emanated from him but I couldn't figure out what it was. Was is anger, lust, regret?

As I was trying to figure it out he stood and stepped toward me holding out his hand. I took it and he helped me to my feet. I wasn't quite breathless but when he pulled me into his arms I stopped breathing for a few seconds and just let him hold me. His heart was racing against my chest and I bit down on my lip to stop myself from doing or saying something I would later regret.

"That was beautiful. Thank you, Chloe dancer." He kissed the top of my head, released me and turned to walk through the door to the bathroom.

I slumped onto the chair by the window, exhaled and tried to catch my breath again. All of my energy and emotion was sapped. I didn't know what to feel any more. What to think. *Should I say something?* When he returned to the room a few moments later he was fully dressed.

"I should go. I've taken up enough of your time." He turned up the corners of his mouth but his smile was tinged with a deep sadness. "Thanks for being a friend, Chloe.

This...this has meant a lot to me." His voice was low and guarded like an unbreakable wall had appeared around his heart.

I cleared my throat and nodded, trying to pluck up the courage to speak. "You're welcome." It was lame. But it was all I could manage.

I was frozen to the spot. Unable to move for fear of running into his arms and giving in all over again. But deep inside I knew that wasn't what I needed and that it would only end in tears.

He walked to the door and wrapped his fingers around the handle. Without turning he spoke again. "Tell Zak he'd better be good to you. And that I hope he knows how damn lucky he is."

And with that he opened the door and left.

For the last time.

———

Six

Cain lay there sleeping. It was just before six in the morning and I wasn't supposed to be there. But I didn't want to be alone with my thoughts. My mind was a dark place to be at the best of times but right then... The light in my life had been completely extinguished as I'd said goodbye to the one person I'd hoped to spend it with.

Luckily I'd been able to slip the night guard a fifty. I guessed he would've let me in for free considering the terrified widening of his eyes when I appeared before the short, thin, older man. But I wasn't about to take advantage. Not anymore.

It was time to rethink everything about myself.

I sat beside the hospital bed, elbows resting on my knees as the machines around my unconscious best friend bleeped quietly. The volume presumably turned low to aid a relaxing night for the staff and other patients. The bandage on his chest was due to be changed and the red stain showing through did nothing to increase my hope of him getting through this.

But he has to.

I heard someone behind me and I turned to see Rosa, Cain's kid sister. Her eyes were rimmed with red and her skin was pallid. I stood to hug her and she crumpled into my chest, sobbing.

"I *can't* lose him again, Six. I just *can't*."

I stroked her hair as my eyes began to sting but again. I swallowed down the emotion fighting for release and kissed her head. "Hey, he'll pull through. He *has* to. Who else am I gonna annoy the heck out of?"

She gazed up at me with hope in her eyes. "You really think he *will*?"

I forced a smile and nodded. "I *know* he will, kiddo."

She lowered her face again. "I can't help feeling this is all my fault. If I hadn't met Tyler."

I cupped her pretty face, tilting it up so she had to meet my eyes and I shook my head. "Hindsight is a wonderful thing, angel."

"I just can't believe he was involved with *them*. I feel so *stupid*." She uttered the words through gritted teeth.

I shrugged. "Come on now. You weren't to know. Love blinds people to the point where we see what we want to see."

"He seemed so...*normal*. I even met his older brother, Zak. He seemed nice too. Again...so, you know, ordinary."

Alarm bells began to ring when her the name and my heart rate picked up pace. I pulled a chair up and gestured for her to sit. "Zak, huh? What did he look like?"

She didn't seem fazed by my out-of-the-blue question which I was relieved about. "Um... Blue eyes, like Tyler. Longish, shaggy hair. Goatee beard. Crooked teeth."

I calmed. He sounded nothing like the Zak Chloe was seeing. Just a coincidence, asshole. Relief flooded my veins. Shit I have to stop looking for reasons to hate the guy she's chosen. It's stupid.

Gotta let it go, Six.

"Look, I'm gonna go and get some sleep, angel. You okay to stay here alone until Colt gets in?"

I knew that security had been stepped up in light of the shooting and there was no *way* any of the Loki's Legion bastards were getting into the hospital... unless *I* put one of them in here. And *that* was a *very* tempting idea.

She gazed up at me. "Sure. I'll be fine. You do look tired. But then again I think we all are just now."

I reached out and squeezed her shoulder. Poor kid didn't need this shit. "You text me or call if there's any change in his condition, okay angel?"

She nodded and smiled sweetly. "You've always called me *angel*. I sometimes wish it was my real name."

I ruffled her blue streaked hair. "It always *will* be to me." I blew her a kiss and left.

CHAPTER THIRTY-SIX

CHLOE

Thankfully the day that followed Six's final visit to my home was a busy one at the library. My mind was filled with book recommendations, new customer applications and replacing a mountain of books back to their rightful places. I needed to be kept busy. Every time there was a lull my mind wandered back to the events of the previous evening. The look on Six's face when I caught sight of him throughout my dance. The V that formed between his brows and the sadness that emanated from his very being. An air of defeat. He'd given up and although that fact *should* have meant relief for me it had achieved anything *but*.

I was entering some new client data on to the computer when someone cleared their throat and I glanced up. "Oh, hi. W-what are you doing here?"

My visitor smiled widely. "I figured it was about time I joined this fine establishment. I think a little reading would be good for me. Don't you? I used to read when I was younger. It was mainly bedtime stories for Tyler but... Anyway, what do you need from me?"

I scrunched my brow. "I'm sorry *what*?"

He smiled again. "To join the library. What information do you need from me?"

I laughed and rolled my eyes. "Oh, of course. Duh! I need a form of picture ID and something with your address on please. And I need you to complete this form." I attached the pink sheet to a clip board and handed it over.

He took the board from me and then reached into his breast pocket. "Sure thing, beautiful. Look...I wanted to apologize again for getting out of hand the other night. I don't know what came over me. But it *won't* happen again, okay?" He handed me his drivers license and gave me a heart melting grin.

I felt my cheeks heat as I took the card from him. "It's okay. Forget about it." I glanced down at the photo on the ID. "Wow, you look so...*different*."

He sighed and ran his hands over his short, neat hair. "Sheesh, I know *right*? Urgh. What *was* I thinking? I mean, *who* has a goatee these days?"

His cheeks had colored and I found it quite endearing. "Oh I don't know. I think you rocked it actually."

That wide, handsome grin appeared again. "Aww shucks. You're too kind. But I know I looked like a dweeb."

I copied down the information I needed onto a fresh member's card and handed it back. "So, how's Tyler? Still wanting to start his own band?"

The smile left his face and he frowned for a moment but no sooner had the look appeared than it was gone. "Oh, you know what kids are like. He's a handful right now. The less said the better, if you know what I mean."

"Ah. No worries. Kids, huh?"

"Yes indeed. Anyway, what time are you done here today? I thought I could maybe bring some groceries and cook for you."

"Oh. I...I don't know."

"Look, Chloe. Excuse my language but I was an asshole last time. I won't be that way again. I got carried away." He leaned in lowered his voice to a whisper. "I find you insanely hot and you can't blame a guy for trying. But you said *no* and I respect that. I'll wait until you're ready. Cross my heart." He made the sign of the cross in the center of his chest.

I pursed my lips and contemplated his words. "So...what would you cook?"

"I was thinking something Italian maybe. Do you like pasta? I make a mean tagliatelle." He stuck out his lower lip and fluttered his eyelashes causing me to giggle.

"Okay, deal. I get off here at six. Come to my apartment at seven?"

"Sounds great. I'll even bring wine." His face was alive with enthusiasm and I was touched by how eager he was to make amends. "Now. Where do I find crime novels?"

I raised my eyebrows. "Crime novels huh? Consider yourself a regular Sherlock Holmes do you?"

"Maybe not Holmes but...well I don't like to brag but I'm an expert with a flashlight." He winked and once again I giggled like a silly school girl. *Sheesh, I'm going to have to get a handle on that habit.*

I pointed Zak in the direction of the crime novels and went back to my work. Around a half hour later he checked a couple books out and left, reminding me before he did that he would see me at seven.

————

The library manager let me leave early, seeing as we'd had such a manic day. As I was leaving the library I spotted Ellie across the street, she waved and gestured that we should go for coffee. I checked my watch and gave the thumbs up.

After jogging across to her we hugged and made our way to Hank's. Ellie pushed open the door but it disappeared from her grip, almost causing her to land flat on her face. I glanced up to find a familiar dirty-blonde haired biker holding a takeout cup with a brown paper bag dangling from his fingers in one hand and the door for us to enter in the other.

"Shit, I'm sorry about that. You okay?" he asked Ellie as she cussed him out.

"Maybe you should watch who's coming through the damn door in future." She huffed melodramatically wiping her clothing down.

He cringed at me and widened his eyes and I had to stifle a laugh. Nodding his head in mock seriousness he replied, "Yeah, sorry. You're right about that. And I will." He turned his attention back to me. "Hi, Chloe. How're you doing?"

I smiled and nodded as my cheeks heated. "I'm good thanks. You?"

"Oh, you know. Hospital visits, lack of sleep. The usual. All good." There was a note of sarcasm to his voice but I chose to ignore it.

"How's Cain?"

"I'm just on my way over there. The second surgery went

well and he's showing signs of improvement. Had a call from his sister earlier."

I sighed. "Oh that's a relief. I'm *so* glad to hear that."

"You...um...could stop by the hospital later maybe? You know, if you're free."

I cringed and spoke without really thinking. "Oh, sorry I'm having dinner with Zak later." As soon as the words left my mouth I clamped it shut.

He nodded and a crease formed between his eyebrows a look of hurt apparent in his features. "Oh yeah, sure. No problem. Enjoy. I'd better be going." He raised his hand in a kind of wave and walked away quickly as if he couldn't wait to escape my company.

"Shit, Chloe, sexual tension much?" Ellie had no clue how *off* she was with her observation.

We ordered coffees and slipped into a booth opposite each other. Her eyes were fixed on me. "Come on. Spill it. Something's going on here. What is it?"

I shrugged. "He's finally agreed to let me move on."

"Well you could look happier about it. Zak is gorgeous and so sweet. Pass him my way if you don't want him."

I hadn't told her everything about Zak. I knew that if I told her he had been a little forceful the other night she would be angry and worried about me. And seeing as I was convinced it was a one off incident she didn't need to know.

I shrugged. "Yeah, Zak is sweet. But Six...the chemistry..." I blew out through pursed lips.

"I hear you, honey. I really do. But you and I both know that the biker is no good for you. He's dangerous. You don't need the drama. And Zak is so..."

"Normal." I finished off her sentence and she nodded profusely.

Holding her hands up she pointed at me. "That's it. He's *normal*. Normal is good. Normal doesn't get you half killed."

What the hell? I scrunched my brow as my desire to defend Six fought for dominance over every other emotion. "Ellie, he never got me 'half killed'."

"Not *yet* he didn't. But look at what happens with the people who get mixed up with *those* people."

There was no arguing with her so I decided to change the subject. "Zak's cooking me Italian food later."

A wide grin spread across her pretty face. "Oh really? So, is tonight going to be *the* night?"

Rolling my eyes at my friend's insinuation, I took a sip of coffee before responding. "Ellie, not everything is about sex you know."

"Not *everything*. But I bet he's ripped under his nice, clean cut clothing, huh?"

I took another gulp of my coffee and checked my watch. "Look I should go. I want to shower before Zak comes over."

She reached over and patted my forearm. "I *bet* you do. Make sure you wear some nice lingerie. You never know your luck."

I tilted my head back in exasperation and glanced at the ceiling briefly. "See you soon, Ellie."

"You sure will. And I want to know all about those abs." She called after me as I left the coffee shop.

CHAPTER THIRTY-SEVEN

Six

Cain's vital signs were definitely improving and my confidence that he would recover was on the up. My flying visit to the hospital had simply been to pick up Cain's sister and take her home. I'd been happy to see a bit of color in the handsome bastard's face and I looked forward to the day when I could poke fun at him for shit all over again.

I handed Rosa a helmet and we climbed onto the bike. The early evening air was humid and thick and I couldn't wait to get home and shower. When I say *home* I mean to the *club* obviously. We were technically still on lockdown although things were much quieter since Cain's shooting. I was beginning to think Loki's Legion realized they'd crossed a line and had gone into hiding.

Colt had announced the decision he had made to ensure Cain and Rosa's safety once my best bud was on his feet again. The thought of him being so far away again made my insides ache. What would I do without him around? But then again, him being thousands of miles away would mean he *was* still around, as in *alive*.

And that meant far more than anything else.

As we rode toward the club Rosa clung onto me. Her arms didn't quite circle my waist and she clung onto my cut for dear life. I didn't ride too fast with my precious cargo and as we passed through Rose Acres I spotted Zak, Chloe's new boyfriend, carrying groceries in the direction of her apartment. A familiar sinking sensation occurred in my gut and I reminded myself I was moving on. She was no longer my concern. If he wanted to cook her dinner, then so be it. Nothing I could do about it. She had chosen *him*.

That was that.

Weasel opened the metal gates as I pulled the bike up to the compound. He secured them again once we were inside. Rosa climbed off and removed her helmet. A puzzled expression on her face.

"You okay, angel?" I asked after I had removed my own helmet and swung my leg over the huge hunk of metal.

"Huh? Oh yeah...yeah fine. Just tired is all."

"It's early but maybe you just need to rest. Go and grab something to eat from the kitchen and get on upstairs. Sleep will do you good." I told her like the pseudo big brother I was.

"I think I'll skip the food and go straight to bed."

I flung my arm over her shoulder and she nuzzled into my chest as we made our way inside.

Rosa slipped her slender arms around my body and hugged me tight. "Thanks for being there for me, Six. It means such a lot."

I kissed her forehead. "That's what big brothers are for,

angel," I told her. Her responding smile was warm and filled with love and I watched as she hugged Colt before making her way upstairs.

Delilah was sitting *at* the bar and so I went over to join her. "Aren't you at the wrong side, Dee?"

She glanced up from her drink of amber liquid and smiled. "Figured I'd take the night off."

I nudged her with my shoulder. "I see you changed back to being a dumb blonde."

She punched my arm. "Fuck off asshole. Nothing *dumb* about me." Her smirk told me she was kidding around.

I chuckled. "Well if it's any consolation I think you make a better blonde than a redhead. So does this mean you're letting go of the dream now?"

She turned to face me. "The *Cain and Delilah* dream?" Heaving a long sigh, she swirled the liquid around her glass. "There comes a point in your life, Six, when you just have to cut your losses. Cain won't be around much longer if Colt has anything to say about it. And I don't want to be someone's *third* best. First Melody...then Kelly... I guess I've just had enough." She shrugged.

I grabbed the glass from her hands and took a large mouthful before handing it back. "Right there with you, Dee."

She leaned on me. "Things didn't work out for you and Nina then, huh?"

"Nah. Nina's long gone. Turns out it was the *Chloe* underneath all the make-up that I wanted all along. Yeah I liked the sexy dancer but who knew I'd prefer her smart side? But like you, I want to come *first* for someone. So what do you say, baby?" I joked.

She sat up straight and regarded me with disgust. "Eeeeuw! Dude *no way*. Incest is *so* not my thing."

I guffawed loudly at her reaction. "Hey we're not *blood* related."

"Not *tech*nically but...*eeeeuw*." She shivered and slapped my arm. "Don't give me images in my head that I can't *lose*. Shit, you really are sick you know that?" She joined in with my laughter.

"Seriously though. It's a good thing neither of us are *remotely* attracted to the other. Who the fuck would we bitch and moan about the opposite sex to?"

Her shoulders shuddered as she laughed. "I'll drink to that. And you never know, maybe in a parallel universe we're married with kids."

"Ha! Maybe!" I slipped of the bar stool. "Anyway, *dear,* I'm off to retire to my bedroom."

"Goodnight, daaahling. Scrambled *heggs* for breakfast before you leave for the hoffice tomorrow?" Her fake British accent rendered me a hysterical laughing mess as I walked away shaking my head.

I stopped on the stairs. "Oh, so in a parallel universe we're from a whole other country, huh? Well tatty bye, dearest!" I replied in my best English twang...failing miserably of course.

Seeing Delilah smile again was great. Knowing that our friendship was still strong after the dumb, desperate stunt she pulled with my best friend spoke volumes. The three of us went way back and there are some friendships that just stick around.

———

Another restless night plagued with erotic dreams about a certain chocolate haired dancer meant that I was grouchy as fuck when I went down stairs at eight in the morning.

"Awww, great Scot, I forgot your heggs, daaaahling." Dee said as she handed me a mug of coffee.

I smiled but didn't reply and so she leaned on the bar in front of me. "You okay, Six? You seem...*off* this morning."

"I ran my hands roughly through my shower damp hair. "Not great to be honest. All this *letting go* crap is getting me down."

She raised her eyebrows. "Amen to *that*, bro."

I gulped at the lukewarm coffee and nodded in agreement. "So, you coming to see Cain in hospital, Dee?"

She sheepishly chewed on her lip. "I don't think he'll want to see me. Not after the whole attempted seduction débâcle. When he wakes he'll want to see you and Rosa...and *Kelly* no doubt."

"Yeah but Kelly isn't here. And *you* are. You and he go way back, Dee and he'll need his friends. You *should* go visit. You should clear the air."

She shrugged. "I'll think about it."

Rosa appeared to my right. "Hey big brother." She leaned in to kiss my cheek. Her blue streaked hair was tied back neatly in a ponytail and her eyes had regained some of their sparkle.

I pulled her in for a bear hug. "Hey, angel. Sleep well?"

She sighed and rolled her eyes. "Yeah, I *did* once I'd figured out where I'd seen that *guy* before. It was driving me *mad*."

I scrunched my brow as I swigged my coffee. "*What* guy?"

"Remember when we were on the way home from the

hospital and we saw that guy with the short hair in the pale blue shirt, carrying groceries?"

My interest was suddenly piqued. "Yeah? I saw him. What of it?"

"Well I finally remembered *where* I know him from."

Oookay... "Oh yeah? And where's that?"

"He's Zak." *Yeah, but how do* you *know him?* The confusion must have been evident in my face as she rolled her eyes again, clearly exasperated with me. "*Zak*, you know? *Tyler's* big brother? He used to have this shaggy, greasy hair and a goatee. But I'd remember those piercing eyes anywhere. He looks so much better without the chin fuzz. No offense to *you*. *Your* chin fuzz is cool. But there are clearly guys who should just *shave*. You know?" She rambled on as I tried to process what she had just told me.

Zak is Tyler's older brother. Shit.

Tyler was the son of one of Loki's Legion and he kidnapped Rosa to get back at Cain.

My heart rate increased and my palms began to sweat. I closed my eyes briefly and in my head I scrambled around for the snippets of information I could remember from my brief conversation with Chloe.

I placed my cup down, turned to face Rosa and took her hands in mine. "Angel, remember when we came to get you from the old warehouse and that guy was there claiming to be Tyler's dad?"

She shivered and I felt bad for dragging up the traumatic experience again. But she nodded. "Yeah, he *was* Ty's dad. He was at a bar that Ty took me to one night. His brother, Zak, and his dad were getting drunk and having a huge argument about *something*. I have no clue what. But things got crazy and Zak punched his dad in the face and broke his nose."

Rosa glanced down at our hands and then back up at me. The distinct look of fear in her eyes.

I too glanced down and noticed that my hands were shaking. "But...he's still alive? Tyler's dad"

Her face crumpled in confusion. "*Zak* and Ty's dad? Yeah. W-why do you ask?"

The pieces of a very unpleasant puzzle were fuzing together. Tyler was Rosa's ex. The ex who kidnapped her for Loki's Legion. Which meant that Zak had a) lied about the death of his father—one of the things he had in common with Chloe—and b) that he was connected to...

"Oh sweet mother of fuck." I immediately jumped down from the bar stool I was perched on and began to frantically search for my bike helmet.

CHAPTER THIRTY-EIGHT

CHLOE

I tried in vain to open my eyes, but a wave of nausea washed over me to accompany the thumping in my head. *Oh God...it's happened again... Why has it happened again?* Flashbacks of waking to find Brett looming over me and the stale stench of alcohol and blood rampaged around my mind and I wondered how the *hell* I had wound up in the same position for a *second* time.

I groaned.

"Zak! Bro! She's coming around!" I didn't recognize the panicked voice, but I fought to open my eyes to find out who it was. *Please let me be at the CoSMiC compound...please...* I knew my silent prayer was futile simply because my hands and feet were restrained.

The sound of heavy boots stomped closer and whatever I was laying on moved as someone sat beside me. "Chloe, baby,

open your eyes. Time to play." Zak's familiar voice encouraged in an eerie sing-song tone.

I forced my heavy lids to lift and was greeted by the some-
what manic stare of someone I *thought* I knew.

I tried to turn my head but almost threw up. "W...where
am I? What's happening?" I croaked.

I heard an evil chuckle coming from behind Zak and he
swung his head around. "Shut the *fuck* up, Ty. Go get
some water."

As I watched over Zak's shoulder a shaven haired young
man with the same eyes as Zak left the room, grinning at me
all the while. A chill crawled up my spine as the dots began to
connect.

"Zak? Please don't do this. *Please* let me go." My voice
wavered and I inwardly cursed myself for showing weakness
again.

He leaned in to kiss my mouth and I pressed my lips shut
so he gripped my chin hard. "Awww, come on now. You gotta
give it up to me *some*time if we're going to make this relationship work, babe."

"*What* relationship?" I snapped. "What the hell are you
doing this for?"

The young man Zak referred to as *Ty* returned with a
cracked glass filled with cloudy liquid.

Zak continued. "*Well* now. You see we gotta finish what
my good buddy Brett started. You remember Brett don't you?
He says he was your mom's boyfriend but that he wanted *you*
more. Dirty bastard. Anyway, he was sent to...you know...*deal*
with you. Take what he wanted and finish you off. But *I*
couldn't allow that. You see *I* wanted you for me. Been
watching you for a while. Ever since my guy Jagger met you in

that cozy little booth at *The Fox Hub*." Oh my God things were becoming scarily clear. "Anyways... I came around on the night Brett was supposed to kill you, but instead of finding you dead, I found him unconscious. You'd given him a good whack up the side of the head. I decided to finish the job and so I smashed his head in with your pretty vase." He laughed and a combination of nausea and relief that *I* hadn't actually killed someone fought for supremacy inside of me. "But our little story didn't start there. Other shit went down. I won't bore you with the ins and outs, but let's just say that your *boy*friend, the long haired bastard from the Sinners, and his chums, they kidnapped my little bro here and shaved his head. There's no need for them to do such evil stuff to my family. So we figured we'd get our own payback. So you and me are going to play a little game. It's called an eye for an eye. And even though you look mighty pretty with this long brown hair of yours, I think maybe you'd feel cooler without it. And then after *that* maybe you and I can get naked and finish what *we* started."

He laughed heartily at his repulsive suggestion and I cringed as tears welled in my eyes. Zak knew Brett and Jagger. He was connected to Loki's Legion. How had I not figured this out sooner?

Somewhere in the house a phone rang and Tyler scuttled off. A few moments later he returned and nudged Zak who was feeding the lukewarm, cloudy water to me.

"Bro...it's dad. Says it's real important."

"Can't you see I'm busy here tending to my lady?"

"Yeah, I see that but he says it's *real* important. It's about Deak. *His* words."

Zak turned to face me again. "Don't you go anywhere now

sweet lips. I'll be right back." He chuckled in that evil way once more and stood to leave the room. "You, stay here and watch her. No talking and no touching."

Tyler nodded and Zak walked through the doorway over to the right. Tyler sat on the floor about three feet away from me. He was a handsome boy. Piercing blue eyes and perfect, straight teeth. He didn't seem too bright, but he was young. Around eighteen maybe. The shaved head was severe and there were black fading marks on his head that I couldn't make out but looked liked they were once text which I found strange.

"So, your dad's *alive*?" I asked, bemused.

He scrunched his brow. "Yeah, why wouldn't he be?"

A felt a tear of betrayal slip down my cheek. "Zak told me he'd died when he was a kid and that he'd helped bring you up. That your mom had to go out to work. It was something he and I supposedly had in common."

Tyler scratched and shook his head. "Nah... Mom left us years ago. Dad has a drinking problem. *That's* why Zak looked after me. Huh, if you can *call* it that."

So their relationship isn't that great. All the fondness was a lie. "I see. Do you have any idea what Zak is planning to *do* to me?" My lip trembled as I asked the question.

He shuffled closer. "Hey, don't cry. I think he really liked you in the end."

"What do you mean *in the end*?"

"Well, he only asked you out on account of you being one of the Sinner's old ladies before. Said it was a good way to get back at them for all the shit they did to us. But he says you're damn sexy and he can't wait to...you know...seal the deal."

My stomach flipped and I retched. I'd simply been a pawn in the game to him. *What an idiot.* "Is he going to...kill me?"

I was relieved when he shook his head. "Oh no, I don't *think* so. I think he wants to have babies with you and stuff. *Really* likes you."

"But, Tyler, you do know this is *wrong* don't you? He's holding me against my will. I don't want to *be* with him. Not anymore. Not after *this*. If you care about someone you don't drug them and take them away against their will. Do you understand that?"

Tyler looked nervously over his shoulder to the door and then back to me. "I *said* that to him. I said that drugging you and stuff wasn't right. But he said you loved him but you just didn't realize it yet. That getting you away from the Sinners would be a good thing for you... That they would hurt you if he didn't do something but then I got confused when he started talking about keeping you here. But..." He shook his head and scrunched his face in a mask of confusion. "So...you *don't* love him?"

I shook my head slowly so as not to cause the thumping to worsen but more tears escaped. "No, Tyler. I'm sorry, but he lied to you too. If you love someone you don't treat them this way. And the Company of Sinners *weren't* going to hurt me. They're my friends." He nodded slowly, absorbing my words and I continued. "Tyler, have *you* ever loved a girl?"

A sadness settled into his eyes to replace the confusion. "Yeah. Zak and my dad pretty much ruined *that* for me."

My plan to get Tyler talking was working and I *had* to remain calm. "How come?"

"The girl... She was the sister of one of the Sinners.

Name's Rosa. Anyway... Zak is wanting to be VP of Loki's Legion and so he was trying to get on Deak's good side."

"Deak?"

"The Prez. Anyhow, I was dating this Sinners girl, Rosa, she was so beautiful..." *Cain...oh my God he's talking about Cain's sister.* He drifted off into a trance like state for a few moments. "We were like Romeo and Juliet... You know the forbidden love thing? But well... It all went wrong." He gritted his teeth evidently pained by the memory. "I didn't *want* to hurt her. Not physically *or* emotionally. But then..."

I needed to keep him talking. Make him realize that his brother had manipulated him *again*. "Then what?"

He snapped his focus back to me. "They *made* me take her. They said they were going to torture her to get answers or something. Or...or send her fingers back to the Sinners as a warning. Some such bullshit anyways. I was terrified. But... I didn't *want* them to hurt her. I really loved her. But because of them I lost her." He swallowed hard and stared at the floor.

Just then Zak returned and he whacked Tyler around the head. "Thought I said no talking, pussy."

I cringed for the poor kid and he glanced over at me with an apologetic look in his eyes. I smiled briefly while Zak's back was turned. I had to find a way to talk to him alone again. Maybe I could get him to help me.

CHAPTER THIRTY-NINE

Six

Without telling Colt, or any of the club what was going on, I ran out to the lot and climbed on my bike. I was all fingers and thumbs as I tried to secure the chin strap on my helmet and cursed aloud at myself. But Chloe's disappointed glare rattled around my mind, a repeat of the time I had ridden without a helmet and something inside of me insisted I put the damn thing on. I *had* to get to Chloe's place. I *had* to let her know that Zak was one of Loki's Legion. She was in danger and I *needed* to get to her.

Delilah followed me out repeatedly asking what the hell was wrong, but I ignored her pleas and shouted, "Dee, just open the goddamn gates! I need to get the fuck out of here. NOW!"

Thankfully she knew me well enough to just do it. Once they were open, I took off along the street changing up the gears as fast as the bike would let me.

"Come on, come on, come *on*." Dodging in and out of traffic and flirting with death with every maneuver, I made my way toward Chloe's apartment. Nothing else was more important than my desperate need to get to her. My heart was racing and I was so damned terrified of what I was going to find when I got there.

Please let her be okay, God, please. If you're up there and you haven't given up on me completely then please...just let her be okay. I can't make any promises of changes I'll make, but all I can say is that she doesn't deserve to be hurt. She's sweet and kind and beautiful. She never hurt anyone who didn't deserve it. Brett...well that was self-defense. Please God...I'm fucking begging you right now.

I screeched the bike to halt and threw it to the ground before I ran toward the building, ripping my helmet from my head as I stomped the pavement with my heavy boots. An old lady was exiting as I got the door.

"Hey, darlin'. You seen Chloe today, apartment four?" I asked as calmly as I could manage smiling sweetly but feeling anything *but sweet* on the inside. I was ready to commit murder.

"Oh...Chloe...*lovely* girl. Fed my cat when I went to my daughter's you know. But no dear, I haven't seen her since yesterday. She had a gentleman caller." She smiled as she replied and held the door open for me. I was on the verge of telling her off for trusting me. I could've been *anyone* wanting to get in there.

Instead I bit my tongue and smiled. "Okay, thank you, ma'am. You have a nice day now." Unwilling to continue the pleasantries, I dashed past her and took the steps two at time.

The elevator would've been far too slow and time was a commodity I didn't have.

Once outside her door, I banged on it with my balled fist. "Chloe! Chloe, honey, are you in there? Open the door. It's me, Six. I'm...I'm not angry I'm just checking up on you is all. Don't be scared, baby, okay? Just...just open the door."

Nothing.

Bang, bang, bang. "Chloe, baby. Come on. Open up, okay? I just wanna know that you're all right. I can explain why if you open up."

Nothing.

Checking the corridor for other residents and finding the area empty. I placed my helmet on the floor dropped my left shoulder, took three paces back and with as much force as I could muster I ran at the door. Much to my anger I bounced off and fell on my ass. *Fuck!* I got up and did it again. Same thing. *Please God!* Third time I rammed the door and there was a loud crack as the door flew open and hit the opposite wall with such a force it knocked a huge hole in it.

I ran inside calling out her name. There was food in grocery bags on the kitchen counter tops. I kicked my way through the door to the bedroom and bathroom. No sign of her. *Fuck it!* Was I too late? Or was she okay and out for a walk? Was I going to have some serious explaining to do when she turned up to find my stalker ways were back with a vengeance? I kind of hoped so. At least that way she would be okay.

Back in the living room I spotted two wine glasses and an open bottle. One of the glasses was almost empty and there was a lipstick mark on the rim. I lifted the glass and held it up to the light. A gritty residue floated around the bottom of the glass.

Jeez he drugged her!

Okay now things had gotten very, *very* bad. Where the fuck *was* she? What had the bastard done with her? I gripped the strands of my hair and dropped my head back as I shouted expletives at the ceiling.

———

After securing her door as best I could, I went back to the club and explained to Colt exactly what had happened.

He rubbed his eyes and shook his head groaning. "Awww fuck *no*. Just when everything seemed okay. *Fuck!* You kids are going to send me to an early grave!" He grabbed his cell from his pocket and hit dial as he walked away. "Dee, get the guy a fucking drink!" He called as he stomped toward the small office in back on the ground floor.

"Anybody'd think the dick was sixty or something," I chuntered as I watched him retreat.

Dee handed me a double whiskey. "She'll be okay, Six. Try not to worry, 'kay?"

"How the *fuck* do you know that, Dee? You've seen what those bastards are capable of! They could have killed her for all I know!" I snapped, immediately regretting my attitude toward her and hoping I was completely wrong. "Fuck, I'm sorry. I didn't mean—"

She held up her hand. "Hey. Stop. It's okay. No apology needed." She walked around and sat beside me at the bar. "I went to see Cain like you suggested."

I turned my head to look at her, aware she was changing the subject to calm me down. "You did?"

She nodded. "Told him I was sorry and that I was moving on. That I would probably always love him, but that I accepted he didn't love me."

I smiled at the poor girl. "Good for you, Dee. I think it needed to be done. What'd he say?"

"Just that he was sorry he didn't feel the same about me. And that he was sorry for the way he spoke to me."

Reaching out I squeezed her shoulder. "See, he's a good guy." I closed my eyes as I realized just how much I was missing my best friend. "I wish he was fit right now. I could use his help to find out where Chloe is. If those bastards have laid a single finger on her..." I shook my head as my mind conjured up unwelcome violent images to torture me.

"I know, Six. I know."

CHAPTER FORTY

CHLOE

I must have dozed off as I was suddenly aware of voices whispering. Keeping my eyes firmly closed to feign sleep, I listened to the hushed conversation which sounded like it was happening right outside the door to the room I was being kept in.

"You gotta let her go if you love her, Zak. That's what happens. I heard a saying... If you love someone... you gotta...um... you *don't* gotta... Aww shit... what I mean is you don't *kidnap* someone and keep them against their will, bro." Tyler's insistent tone eased my worries. I had planted a seed and it had begun to take root.

I heard muted, mocking laughter. "Oh yeah, I *heard* that saying too. Reckon it was on a fucking Hallmark card, you dick."

A loud crack occurred and Tyler protested. "Dude! What the hell was that for?"

"Because you're a dumb-ass, little brother. And for your information I *don't* love her. I just wanna fuck her."

Tyler gasped. "You told me you loved her, man. You *lied* to me. That's *so* not cool."

"Yeah? Well don't go getting any stupid ideas about letting her go, you hear me? She's mine to do with as I see fit. So you do *not* let her go. You do and I *kill* you. Capiche?"

"What are you Spanish now?"

"Seriously, Ty? You think *Capiche* is Spanish? I see it did a whole lot of good sending you to fucking college, little brother."

Someone appeared beside me but I kept my eyes closed in the hope that whomever it was would leave me alone.

No such luck.

"Hey doll face. Time to wake up. Got to put your make-up on. Got to make sure you're pretty for the photo we're sending to the Sinners."

I fluttered my eyes open and was greeted by the piercing eyes of Zak sitting a little too close for comfort. His rancid breath on my face did nothing to settle my already roiling stomach. I retched as I stared up at him, hoping that he realized how repulsive he had become to me in *every* single way.

He gripped my body and yanked me to a sitting position. "I think we can unfasten your blouse. Let's give the guys something to get excited about, huh? Ty! Bring that girlie shit in here." He reached toward me and began unfastening the buttons on my once white cotton top, but I turned my face away, unable to look him in the eyes.

Tyler appeared at the door holding a pink make-up bag. *Where the hell has that come from? It's not mine.* This thought was rapidly followed by another. *On second thoughts I don't want to know.*

"Come on little bro. You're the artistic one. You can paint her face and make it all pretty. But don't go ogling at her tits now, you hear me? She's *mine*." The sick grin on Zak's face made my stomach attempt once more to eject the minimal food it contained.

Tyler silently crouched before me and began to apply make-up to my face with an apologetic look in his eyes.

———

Six

The hours we had spent riding around the whole damned area had brought up no sign of Chloe. The longer it was taking the heavier the knot of dread became in my stomach. Our attempts to reach out to Loki's Legion had proved fruitless too. They denied all knowledge of being involved in Chloe's disappearance. But why *would* they admit it? I was dumb if I expected anything else from that set of low-life, scum-sucking bastards.

I checked her apartment again on the off chance that they had realized their mistake and brought her home. Of course that didn't happen either. Cain was still in hospital and for that I was now grateful. Knowing what he could be like in situations like this, I imagined he would have gone over to the Legion, all guns blazing—literally—to seek his own unique form of revenge. My approach was going to have to be subtler. Especially considering the information I had received about Zak from former Legion girl, Sondra.

She chewed on her nail and her eyes darted around the coffee shop as if she was waiting for someone to jump out of the shadows. "He was...I don't know...*unhinged*. One minute he would be all normal and kinda sweet. The next it was as if something had...I don't know, *possessed* him. He'd get all aggressive and shit. I had to refuse to be with him after he broke my cheekbone. In fact, it was *that* incident that made me leave the club all together. I ain't there to be anybody's punching bag." She had told me.

Every single time I thought about Chloe at the hands of this twisted son of a bitch, I wanted to rip him limb from limb. Tear his fucking heart out and hand it to him while it was still beating. I had *never* been eaten up by so much hate and that was saying something.

After another day of searching I laid in bed in the darkness of the end room upstairs at the club. Eyes closed but feeling *anything* but relaxed. Images of Chloe's last beautiful dance for me played in my mind. Her long legs and pointed toes, arched back and pert breasts pushed out toward me. I wanted to feel her against me again. Hold her. Keep her safe. But I felt that the possibilities of all that were slipping between my fingers and there wasn't a damn thing I could do about it. I rolled over and punched the mattress as hard as I could as I yelled into my pillow.

———

CHLOE

I was losing track of days. But it felt like I'd been holed up in the pigsty forever. The stench of sweaty bodies—including my own now—was enough to burn the nostril hair from anyone.

My one attempt at escape had gotten me as far as the window. Staring out at the eerily familiar location just before Zak knocked me out again was yet another blow to any hope of me finding something good in Zak. It turned out I was being held in the little tumble down shack close to the place he had brought me for a picnic. He'd clearly been planning this for a while. Knowing it wasn't something that happened on the spur of the moment terrified me even more.

My mind replayed the sick photo session I'd been subjected to. Made up like a bad transvestite with my tits on show and my hands still tethered behind me. *Creepy bastard.* I was just thankful that he hadn't attempted to assault me sexually. But I was plagued with the fear that it could happen at any given moment.

As I imagined Six, Colt and the others looking at the photos of me like *that,* my lip began to tremble and my eyes stung. What would they think of me?

I just wanted to go *home.*

I wanted to see my mom.

But most of all I wanted to see Six. To tell him I had made a huge, incredibly *stupid* mistake. To ask his forgiveness. Even if all he could accept from me was friendship after I dumped him so awfully after spending that mind blowing time with him. I just wanted to see his smile. Hear his deep rumbling laugh and watch his eyes crinkle at the corners. Feel his thick arms enveloping me, protecting me. But the chance of that ever happening again was so slim and it broke my heart thinking of what I'd done. How I had made the *one man* I truly cared for give up on me. I did that. Not Six. Me.

Tyler hadn't been in to speak to me since he had painted my face and I began to think that Zak had gotten wise to my plans to get him on side. I feared for Tyler's safety now as well as my own.

The situation was becoming more and more unbearable. And any hopes I had of getting out of this hell hole alive were dwindling fast.

I dreaded meal times. Dry bread, sometimes mouldy, and a glass of what I think *may* have been rainwater, twice a day was all that I had to sustain me. I was, in the true essence of the word, a prisoner. I was weak, making any attempts to escape completely futile. Where the hell would I go? I knew how far away from everywhere this place was. Clearly the reason Zak had chosen it. And I knew that I would simply be caught and brought back...or worse. And if there was a light at the end of the very long, dark tunnel that my life had become then I guessed someone had switched it off.

CHAPTER FORTY-ONE

Six

I sat at the bar listening to Colt tell the crew about his plans for Cain and Rosa. There would be a funeral. A fucking *funeral*. The pain in my knotted stomach worsened as I imagined standing by an empty grave to say goodbye to someone I'd loved like a brother for most of my life. And to see my little blue haired angel leave for good brought a sadness over me that weighed me down and hunched my shoulders. The *only* saving grace in all of it would be that neither of them would actually *be* in the ground. Instead, they'd be miles away from here on another continent.

My world was turning to *shit*.

The plans were being put into place within the next twenty-four hours so Loki's Legion would believe Cain and Rosa were dead. But selfishly, all I wanted to do was get out of the fucking compound and look for Chloe. It had been a week with no word. No sign. *Nothing*. I couldn't eat and it turned out that sleep was no longer my friend. The crippling emptiness inside of me wasn't only due to the lack of food though.

The MC had been patrolling the area day and night in search of anything suspicious but I was beginning to think that maybe the prick had taken Chloe *out* of Utah. He'd had plenty of time to do so and the thought sickened me. If I was *right* how the hell would I *ever* find her? Was she even still alive?

Fuck! That kind of thinking doesn't help, asshole.

———

I was laying in bed, wide awake yet again, when I heard a commotion downstairs. It sounded like furniture had been kicked over and so I jumped up from the bed and pulled on my jeans. Poking my head out of the door, I could hear whispered ranting coming from the bar area. I made my way down the hall to the stairs and peered down into the dimly lit space.

Colt had a hold of someone by the scruff of his neck and had him pinned against the wall, fist at the ready.

I ran down the stairs, my bare feet slapping against the wood as Colt's voice cut through the air. "Six, that *you*, buddy?" I arrived beside him but he didn't take his eyes of his hostage.

Slightly out of breath I replied, "Yeah, it's me. What's going on?"

"Go get the others. We have ourselves an interloper. Oh and flick on the lights while you're at it."

Obliging my Prez, I jogged over and flicked on the main lights and went banging on doors. When I returned to the main bar area I immediately recognized who Colt was pinning to the wall.

My fists clenched. "The fuck?"

A glint of terror was clear in the guy's eyes. "I'm not here to cause trouble. I swear it. I'm here to *help* you. Please...*please* listen to me." Tyler, begged in a whimper.

"Yeah? How the hell do we know *that* you little scum-sucker?" Colt spat.

I grabbed Colt's arm knowing that this may be our only hope. "Hey, let him go, dude. Let's hear what he has to say, huh?"

Colt gave the kid one last shove in the chest before stepping back and dragging him over to a chair. The other guys and their old ladies gathered around, muttering and chuntering about the Loki's Legion shit-head in our presence. Some of them baying for blood.

Colt shoved Tyler down and gripped the arm rests until his knuckles turned white. He stood and grabbed the gun from the back of his waistband and pointed it at the middle of the kid's forehead. "Okay you little prick. What you got that we could *possibly* want?"

Tyler held up his hands. "P-please...please don't shoot. It's C-Chloe...*Chloe*. I-I know where she is."

Hearing her name ripped at my heart and I slammed Colt out of the way, making him drop his gun and hurl abuse at me.

But it was *my* turn to interrogate the fucker. "If that's true you'd better prove it," I growled.

His eyes widened further and his breathing accelerated. "I...I need to reach into my pocket."

I shook my head. "Uh-uh. No you don't. *Which* pocket is it and *I'll* do the fucking reaching."

He swallowed hard and nodded down. "L-left jacket pocket. I swear I'm not armed. Like I said, I came here to *help* you."

I reached down into the left pocket of his jacket and pulled out a crumpled photograph. I stepped back to examine it and my stomach flipped. Chloe sat there with a ton of badly applied make-up on, her shirt open, legs wide, her bra pulled down beneath her tits and a deadness in her eyes.

Fuck.

A red mist descended over me and I spun around and smashed my fist into the wall with a feral cry of aggression. Everyone around me flinched. And then I was on the kid again.

I grabbed him by the throat. "I swear to *God* I will fucking *cut* you if *any*thing has happened to her."

With his hands still held up in surrender he pressed himself further into the back of the chair and yelled. "N-no! No! I swear she's okay. Scared, hungry, yes but, but *not* harmed. *Not physically* harmed, dude. I swear!"

His fear filled voice dragged me back to reality and I released his throat. "You'd better start talking *real* fast. My patience is wearing thin and I'm warning you, if you think the fucking Hulk has a bad attitude, you ain't seen nothing yet"

———

CHLOE

Zak sat beside me, brushing my hair and talking about the future we were apparently going to have. "Eventually when you realize you *do* love me, we can make it official. You *will* realize it, Chloe. I'll make *sure* of that."

I stared into space trying to extract myself from the situation as best I could. A kind of numbness had set in...almost.

I turned to face him. "I heard you telling Tyler that you *don't* love me. So how can you expect me to love you back?" My voice was small and weak but the fact that I hadn't responded to him for so long really got his attention.

He huffed. "Like I'd tell *that* little douche how I feel. He doesn't need to know *shit*."

I smiled as sweetly as I could manage, considering the contempt knotting my insides. "Well it doesn't matter anyway. I will *never...ever* love you, Zak. *You* hearing *me*?" My lip trembled and tears welled in my eyes as I used his own words back at him. "*Ne-ver*. You're a delusional asshole if you think that I will *ever* think anything good about you after what you've put me through."

His brow creased and he shook his head. "Jeez, someone's pissy this morning." He leaned in and nibbled on my earlobe. "I reckon you need a good fucking. That'd cheer you up. Relax you. Give you that sweet glow that only a good orgasm can."

I clenched my jaw. "Don't you *dare* touch me. You make me *sick*. You twisted, sleazy bastard." I pulled my head away and lurched forward, crashing my skull into his face as hard as my minimal energy would allow. The resulting cracking sound alerted me to the fact that I had broken his nose.

"Fucking bitch!" He slapped me hard across my face, making my head rip sharply to the left and adding to the pain I had caused myself.

But I turned to face him again and smiled as the metallic tang of blood filled my mouth. "Truth hurts does it?"

He snarled at me like a rabid dog complete with foam and grabbed my face in his hand. "You need putting in your place, *bitch*. I was waiting until you *begged* me to fuck you, like you know you wanna. Like the *slut* you are, with your tiny bikinis and your legs wrapped around a fucking pole. I *know* how many men you've had. But maybe it's *my* turn, huh? I think maybe I should just *take* what I want."

I snorted derisively. "Like I would *ever* beg *you* to fuck me. You conceited prick. Do you think you're so irresistible that I'd lower my standards to the *gutter*? I could *never* be that desperate." Grinning so that I could feel my face contort between his fingers I spat, "Well let me tell you *this*. You're *wrong*. You *disgust* me. And I *never* slept with the men at *The Fox Hub*. They could look but none of them were *good* enough for me. Apart from *Six*. He's a *real* man. And you can do whatever the hell you want. Kill me if you have to. But just know that *some* day...when you're least expecting it...*some*one will be waiting for you. And I think you know *who* that someone will be and what he'll do to you. And he won't make it quick and painless. He'll hurt you so bad you'll *wish* you were dead."

A growl erupted from Zak's chest and as soon as a searing pain shot through my cheek everything went black.

CHAPTER FORTY-TWO

Six

I glanced over at Colt has we rode at speed out of the town limits and toward the shack that Tyler had told us about. My stomach twisted and turned and I gripped the handlebars so hard I felt sure they'd snap right off. What would we find when we got there? Would she be okay? Tyler was behind us on Weasel's bike, hands tied to the rail at the back. I hoped to *hell* this wasn't some kind of elaborate trap.

After around an hour we pulled down a dirt track that Tyler had pointed out on a map for us and my mind wandered back to what he'd said when he came to the club in the early hours of the morning.

"He's...he's gone crazy, man. I know he's my brother but...He's acting all weird and shit. Says if he can't have her then no one will. One minute he says he doesn't love her and the next he's brushing her hair and talking about marrying her. It's freaky. He said he'd started all this to get on Deak's good side so he'd make him VP. But turns out Deak kicked him out a month ago and told him to get help. Said he needed his head looked at. Deak had nothing to do with taking Chloe. My dad tried to talk sense into Zak too but... No one can get through to him. He hadn't hurt her when I left. He'd just taken photographs of her sleeping and of her tits and stuff. Says he's going to make her fall in love with him. I've never heard him like this. It's like he's cracked up. I'm scared for him and for Chloe. But I can't go back there alone. He has a gun and a knife. See the cut on my cheek? He did that."

I clenched my already aching jaw at the thought that Zak might have hurt Chloe. And I swore an oath that if he'd harmed any part of her he'd suffer.

Colt gestured to a building off in the distance and that we should pull over. I was eager to just get down there and get her out. But I had to stop taking matters into my own hands. We were a club and I *had* to remember that.

We parked up behind a row of brush to the side of the road and climbed off our bikes with the exception of Tyler who was still tethered.

Colt removed his helmet and the rest of us followed suit. "Okay... we gotta play this carefully. Six and I will make our way down there. You guys hang back but have your guns cocked and ready. Give us a few minutes and then get the place surrounded. If he comes out, fire to *injure. Not* to kill. He needs locking up and this is the *one time* I intend to get the cops involved. He's acting as a loner now. Deak is aware of what's going down and he's not happy. He wants no part in it but says he won't stop us seeking justice and doing what needs to be done."

———

Chloe

I could hear singing when I woke. Tyler was still nowhere to be found and I wondered if Zak had hurt him. The thought terrified me. The kid was around nineteen years old and had clearly been manipulated into carrying out his brother's will. I could tell from the expression on his face whenever we were alone that he wanted *none* of this. He was a good kid deep down. I just hoped that he'd gotten away. Maybe he would call for help?

And maybe I was a stupid delusional bitch.

Zak came through to the room I was being kept in. He was shirtless and I could see the tattoos depicting hell on his body. A shiver traveled down my body at the sight of him standing there, a lascivious grin on his face. A handsome face that had now been contorted along with my opinion of him.

"Thought we could take a bath, sweet cheeks. I know how you girls like baths."

I closed my eyes and tried to calm my thumping heart. I *had* to get out of here. But how could I?

He crouched down before me. "I *said,* I thought we could take a bath, *bitch.*"

"I heard you," I whispered.

He grabbed my arms and dragged me to a standing position. He yanked my skirt and panties down my body and turned me around to untie my wrists. I rubbed at the sore red marks and gasped as he tugged my shirt from my body followed by my bra.

"I should make you dance for me," he said as he trailed his

hooded gaze down my naked body. I closed my eyes and thought back to the dance in my living room. How Six had stopped the first track and changed it to something more befitting a *lover's* dance. Tears slipped free from the corner of my eyes and I opened them again.

"Please, Zak. Please don't do this. Just let me *go*. I don't want this. I *really* don't."

For a moment his expression changed and I could have sworn I saw a hint of regret there. But it rapidly disappeared and he grabbed my arm.

"Shut up. We're going to get you clean and then have some fun."

I yelped as he tugged me forward.

———

Six

Creeping around the tumble down shack of a building, I was unnerved by how quiet everything was. The only sound I could make out was running water and splashing. What the fuck?

Colt gestured that I should peek in the window we were beneath and so I tiptoed until I could see through a gap in the dirty brown curtains. Zak was sitting there dipping his hand into the water and then flicking it up. I trailed my gaze to the corner of the room and almost lost my shit. Chloe sat there, naked with her arms hugged around her body and damp trails down her cheeks. Her eyes were closed and she was rocking back and forth.

"Aww come on, bitch. You're no fucking fun anymore. Bath time's supposed to be *sexy* time."

My jaw clenched so hard I thought my teeth would break. And I dropped to the ground, inhaling hard to stave off the dizziness as the red mist began its descent.

"She's in there. So is *he*. He's running a *bath*." I whispered over at Colt.

He scrunched his face. "A *bath*? Dude *is way* fucking weird."

"Look, I *have* to go in. I *have* to get her out of there. I kind of get the feeling that he has other plans for her and I don't like it. I *can't* let him touch her, Colt. I...I just *can't*."

He nodded his understanding. "You go around and knock on the door to distract him and I'll keep watch over the bathroom. Just be careful, okay?"

I didn't respond. My own safety wasn't my concern at that moment. The only thing I cared about was getting to Chloe.

With my gun in hand, I scrambled under every window and made my way to the front door. I banged on it and waited.

The door opened and I waited for Zak to poke his head out but he didn't. I stepped up and a fist landed on my cheek, taking me by surprise. I grabbed out and got a hold of the bastard's arm. Thankfully my lack of sustenance hadn't weakened me as much as I had thought and I managed to grab the son of a bitch and whack him around the head with the butt of my gun. He collapsed to the floor with a thud. Once I knew he was out cold I ran though the shack calling out for Chloe.

I located the bathroom and kicked open the door to find her huddled in a corner on the floor. I dropped to my knees before her and pulled her into my arms.

"It's okay, baby, you're safe now. Nothing else is going to

happen to you. I promise. Now come on, we need to get you out of here." Seeing her catatonic like this almost broke me. Water welled in my eyes and I had to rub them to clear my vision. I shrugged out of my jacket and wrapped it around the silent young woman who was barely recognizable as my Chloe dancer. She peered blankly up at me.

I cupped her cheek. "Chloe, baby it's *me*, Six. Are you okay? Has he hurt you?" I noticed the bruising and swelling to her cheek and realized it was a dumb question. Gathering her limp body in my arms I stood and made for the door.

But Zak had gone.

CHAPTER FORTY-THREE

CHLOE

The dream was *so* realistic. Like all the rest had been. Six carried me in his arms and began to jog away from the shack that had been my prison for goodness knows how long. It felt good to be in his arms again, even if it *was* all in my imagination. I found myself wondering if I was actually sleeping or finally dead. I couldn't remember it happening but I had been so numb that maybe it hadn't hurt at the end.

Voices echoed in my head. Like they were coming from a distance. *Shouting* voices I recognized...well *some* of them anyway. I glanced down at my naked body and the familiar leather jacket half wrapped around me. In the dream Six was breathing heavily as he swept me away and I nuzzled into his chest hoping that the dream would last a little longer this time.

Zak usually woke me up just as Six was about to kiss me or make love to me.

Bastard.

That familiar earthy, masculine smell encapsulated me and warmed my heart. This is what I remember of Six. And his arms. His power. His need to protect me. If only he could find me. But I knew that wouldn't happen for real seeing as Zak had confirmed where we were and how far away from civilization. I doubted that Six would know the place even existed. I sure as heck hadn't until that damned picnic. If only I'd known then what he was planning.

A little wooden shack that blended into the scenery until it was almost camouflaged miles out of town and on the way out of Utah. That and the fact that it looked abandoned from the outside. Actually, it didn't look any better on the inside. The smell of stale cigarettes and alcohol made me not want to inhale through my nose. But every time I did I almost lost my stomach contents.

The taps worked but the water was a sludgy brown color and the toilet wouldn't flush. It was the kind of place you would avoid at all costs if you had any choice in the matter. But of course I didn't.

I'd lost all track of time being out in the middle of nowhere. I think I'd actually stopped counting. What was the point? Zak hadn't hit me much, but when he had, he had said it was my fault for misbehaving. Then he would apologize and hold me. It was strange how I had forgotten how to feel.

The dream ensued and I glanced to my left and saw a group of people all wearing black waving and gesturing. They must have been the ones shouting too. Maybe I was dead after all. I couldn't make out what they were saying. But that was the frustrating thing about dreams. Things were rarely vivid and clear.

Unless they were *bad* dreams. They were always the clearest, unfortunately. Although this was probably the most vivid one I'd had. The feel of Six's hard chest beneath my cheek was painfully realistic.

A cold breeze whipped around my naked flesh and I shivered as arms tightened around me and a kiss landed on my head. I could hear someone telling me everything would be fine now. And I wished it was true. I closed my eyes and thought about the dance in my living room. The way Six's eyes had been filled with sadness. I wished I'd have told him the truth. Told him that I missed his arms around me. His mouth on mine. That he would always belong in my heart.

This dream was strangely surreal. I hadn't noticed being able to have lucid thoughts in my other dreams. I glanced up and for the first time in so long I could see Six's caramel eyes shining down at me.

"I love you, Chloe. You need to know that. You need to know that I never stopped loving you." His voice broke as he confessed his feelings to me.

Just then a loud crack rang out through the air and suddenly I was falling down...down...down. The dream was over...

———

Everything was white and too bright. My eyes stung as I tried to allow them to adjust to my surroundings. *Okay so now I'm dead.* But there was no pain, and more importantly no Zak. A serene calm washed over me and I breathed a long sigh letting my eyes drift closed once more.

———

A piercing bright light made me wince. And then a kind voice spoke, "I'm sorry dear. Just checking your vitals. I'm happy to see you're awake again."

Awake? What?

"If you feel sleepy just go with it. That'll be the meds. Your friends have been here the whole time though. I think they'll be happy you're awake.

I couldn't really process my thoughts and so when the heaviness of sleep tugged at me again, just like the kind voice had instructed, I gave in...

———

"I know we only met a couple times but...I think we *could* be friends. I think it would be cool to have a friend as tough as you. You really are kick ass you know. You survived such a shitty ordeal. I wish I had your strength of character. But I don't...I mean I already miss Cain like a part of me is gone. It hurts so bad. And even though I know I had to let him go, I don't think I can imagine a time when it *won't* hurt... Anyway, I've never really had a *girl* friend before. It's kind of hard when you're surrounded by guys who think of you as a kid sister all the time and women who think they're in competition with you. It's dumb... But that's club life for you. I hope you'll still come around...you know if... Aww look I'd better stop rambling at you. Even though you're unconscious I'm probably driving you crazy. Six always said I talked too much. It's silly but I'd give anything to hear him say all that to me again."

Once the voice stopped I groaned. My head was pounding and I felt like I'd swallowed gravel. "W-where am I?" I asked the unknown female who had woken me up.

A scraping sound like a chair on tile came from the same direction of the voice. "Shit! Hey, hey Chloe. It's Dee...um...Delilah from the Company? Company of Sinners MC that is. I don't know if you'll remember me. You've been through quite a lot. And when this happened to Cain he couldn't remember shit."

A face surrounded by a mop of bleached blonde hair appeared in my line of sight and gradually became clearer as I blinked. "Delilah...From the bar at the club? With the tattoos?"

She beamed. "Yeah! That's me! I didn't think you'd know me. I mean...I didn't know if you'd remember stuff... How are you feeling?"

"Like crap."

She laughed. "Yeah well being dropped from a height will do that to you."

"Dropped from a *height*?" I scrambled around my foggy brain to try and remember. "I fell...I remember...falling."

"Yeah... You're right. Broke your wrist quite bad too."

I glanced down and sure enough there was a cast in place. "But...how? I don't understand."

The smile disappeared from her face. "It was when he dropped you. He was carrying you away from where that crazy-ass son-of-a-bitch had been keeping you."

The vivid dream I'd had began to return to me. "Six? He was *really* there? He carried me? It wasn't a *dream*?"

She slowly shook her head and I felt her squeeze my arm.

"No, it wasn't a dream. He'd been desperate to find you. But then..." Her voice wavered.

"But then what?" I whispered.

"Then he dropped you when...when the crazy bastard shot him."

CHAPTER FORTY-FOUR

Chloe

I held Six's hand as I stared at him where he laid. His eyelids were tinged purple and his skin was pale. It was a miracle that he was alive at all and no wonder that the doctors were keeping him asleep. The bullet had fractured the right side of his skull and they'd had to shave the hair off the right side of his scalp in order to remove the fragments. Now he was bandaged across the side of his head and over his eye. They had placed him in a medically induced coma too. And he'd gone through all of this for *me*.

To save *me*.

Apparently he had been running with me in his arms when Zak fired a single shot that hit the side of Six's head just above his temple. He should have *died*. But I like to think someone was watching over him and had seen the good he'd done for me.

I just stared at him. Willing him to be okay.

Colt had encouraged the doctor to speak to *me* as Six's next of kin, which was kind of weird, but I was grateful. The doc told me that there was a strong chance he would lose his sight in his right eye and that broke my heart. I wanted more than *any*thing to turn back the clock and change the events leading to us getting here.

There was so much I needed to say to him. I wanted to tell him that I *hadn't* killed Brett. That the body he had disposed of was dead at the hands of *Zak* and not me. And that I appreciated everything he had done to protect me without question. But deep down I feared that he would resent me. Hate me for what I had put him and the others through. As I gazed at his handsome face I tried hard not to memorize the sight of him laying there helpless and unconscious. If I had lost him, I wanted to remember the cheeky glint in his eye. The way he looked when he was about to kiss me and the smile had melted my heart on so many occasions.

I decided that this would be my last visit to his room. Seeing him like this was too much. Too hard. I was so angry at myself for not letting him know my true feelings. Angry that I had chosen another man over him. And angry that I hadn't listened to my heart instead of my stupid, stupid head.

I stroked my hand down his arm and squeezed his hand as tears welled in my eyes. I would have to let him go. Because, just as I had told Tyler, that's what you do when you truly love someone. You let them go. If they come back to you then it was meant to be. I could've maybe believed that about Six and I at one point. But not anymore. Not after all of this.

"Are you ready to go back now, Chloe?" A friendly voice asked from behind me.

I wiped the tears from my cheeks and nodded. I kissed

my good hand and touched it to Six's face. Once I was back in the wheelchair, the kindly nurse took me out of the room and back to my own where Delilah and Colt were waiting for me.

"Hi, guys. How are you doing?"

Colt shook his head. "After all the shit you've gone through you're asking *us* if we're okay?"

I smiled and lowered my gaze to the cast on my arm. Delilah had created a tattoo design made up of mine and Six's names and it saddened me to know I would never get the chance to have it on my skin. I would keep the cast as a memento of what could have been if Six hadn't lost his sight on account of my stupidity.

The tattoo was so beautiful. Two intertwined wolves with hearts and stars surrounding them and our names wrapping around them. She had somehow managed to capture both of our personalities in the images. The fact that I had considered him the big bad wolf now made me smile. Hindsight can be so cruel.

So very cruel.

Colt spoke again. "Look, we need to talk to you about something." I glanced back up and watched as Dee and Colt exchanged furtive glances.

I nodded. "Okay. What's up?"

Colt took a deep breath. I'd never seen him look so nervous. "We were wondering... Tyler kind of has no one now. Zak killed his dad before he took you and now he'll be in prison for a hell of a long time. So...we were thinking..."

I smiled. "I think you should take Tyler in. Look after him. He needs family and friends. He's only nineteen after all."

Delilah whacked Colt's arm. "See, told you that's what she'd say, dumb-ass."

He shrugged at her. "Hey, I was just trying to be fair and all." Turning back to me he leaned forward. "You sure you're okay with it?"

"Absolutely. Tyler helped us all. If it hadn't been for *him* I think maybe the end of all this would have been very different."

"Great. Great. I didn't want to just go ahead. You know out of respect." Colt's cheeks flushed and I was shocked at him appearing so vulnerable.

My friend Ellie appeared in the doorway. She snorted derisively. "Respect? That's a frickin' *joke* if I ever heard one. I bet you can't even *spell* the damn word never mind know what it *means*." Her voice and choice of words caused a thickening in the atmosphere of the room and I was horrified at her attitude. "If it wasn't for you and your stupid club, Chloe wouldn't have gotten mixed up in all this shit."

I gasped, absolutely horrified at her outburst. "Eleanor Cassidy. Please *stop* with the hostility."

Delilah stood and stepped toward my friend and my heart began to race. The sneer on Dee's face told me all hell was about to break loose. Thankfully, Colt grabbed her arm and shook his head. With apparent reluctance she dropped back into her chair but kept her fierce gaze trained on Ellie.

Ellie turned her stare on me. "Chloe, I'm only speaking the *truth*. You're my best friend and I *hate* to see what you go through because of these...these *animals*."

I clenched my jaw and anger bubbled up inside of me. She had my best interests at heart but her insults were uncalled for.

Colt stood and held out his hand toward Ellie. "Miss Cassidy? Is that right? Eamon Cassidy's daughter?"

Ellie turned her stare on Colt and to my surprise she shook his hand as her cheeks colored cerise. "That's right. What of it?" She stiffened her back and tilted her chin up with an air of haughtiness.

Colt smiled and rubbed his stubbled chin. "I've spent the odd night at your father's hotel when my wife kicked me out."

With a distinct note of defiance in her voice she replied, "Sounds to *me* like your *wife* is a sensible woman."

The smile quickly faded from Colt's face and my heart squeezed. He nodded. "She *was*. Sadly Maria passed away four years ago now."

Ellie's eyes widened and she swallowed as her cheeks brightened further. "Oh...I'm...I didn't mean...I'm sorry, I—"

Colt held up his hand. "Don't sweat it, Red. You weren't to know."

In that second my anger at her dissipated, and she turned to face me once more. "Chloe...I think I'll come back later. I'm...sorry for my outburst. *Really* I am." She turned and hurried out of the room as quick as her legs would carry her.

Colt watched her retreating form with a grin. "Got yourself a real fireball for a best friend there, CD." He chuckled and I noticed a glint of amusement in his eyes.

I sighed half in relief that the atmosphere had improved and half at the *name* he had used for me. "So you're *all* calling me CD now huh?"

———

Six

It seemed that us CoSMiC guys were making some kind of habit of waking up in hospitals. It was no surprise that I had my own damn room. It should've had the CoSMiC logo on the frickin' door.

The bandage on my head was itching like crazy and I was desperate to relieve that, but a nurse had been in when I had woken and had told me to try and avoid scratching the stitches at all costs. *Can't even scratch my own goddamn head when I want. Sheesh!*

She told me that the doctor would come and explain everything which puzzled me. What did he need to explain? Some psycho bastard had shot me and I wound up in the hospital.

She must have seen the confusion in my face. She smiled warmly. "There are things he'll need to discuss with you. You've been in a medically induced coma for a while now and there have been tests carried out while you've been sleeping."

Her attempts at explaining didn't really help and I was getting more irritated by the second. The bandage covered my right eye too which was damned frustrating seeing as the vision in the left was a little blurry, apparently on account of the head trauma. I could *see* but it was like I was drunk or something. If only *that* was the damn issue. At least that way I would've had fun getting this way. I couldn't wait to get the damn bandage off and get back to normal.

Whatever *normal* was.

I think I'd been awake maybe around an hour or so when the doc had come to explain the reason for me being in there. He babbled on about comas and surgery, bullet fragments and stitches. I listened but all I could think about was Chloe.

"Can you tell me anything about the girl who was brought

in with me? Chloe Meyer... Is she okay? She was...kind of dazed. Like she wasn't really there. I just want to know she's okay. She doesn't have to come see me. I guess she won't want to but—"

"Mr. Navarro she's *fine*. She visited you a couple of times actually. Obviously, I can't discuss her case with you in detail but...I *can* tell you that she had some trauma induced confusion to begin with, but she is absolutely *fine* now. I do, however, need to speak to you about another matter. A serious, life-changing matter."

Oh great. I can tell I'm not gonna like this. "Yeah? What's that?"

He sat on the chair beside my bed. "I'm afraid that you appear to have lost the sight in your right eye." *Fuck.* My brow automatically crumpled at his words but it hurt like a bitch. The doc paused and seemed to be allowing his words to sink in.

I opened and closed my mouth several times. "For real? But...how? I don't..." The words just wouldn't come.

He steepled his fingers and rested his chin on them before he continued. "We were hoping that the surgery we carried out would have relieved the build-up of pressure and that once the swelling had subsided your sight would return. However...from further tests we've carried out that appears *not* to be the case. The damage is too grave although you were *very* fortunate in that the bullet didn't lodge inside your skull as the damage could have been far worse. Unfortunately, Mr. Navarro... you will probably *not* regain the sight in the eye which was jolted at the time of the shooting."

I nodded slowly, letting the news rattle around my sore head as my stomach tightened with anxiety.

"Do I look...does it look fucked up? Am I gonna scare kids and old ladies?"

The doc smiled. "You're healing pretty well externally. There will be some permanent scarring but I feel that is maybe the least of your worries. It may take time for you to adjust. You may need counseling."

"Hey, I'm a tough cookie. Don't worry about that shit. I got another eye right? This one's okay isn't it?" I pointed at my left, slightly blurry 'good' eye.

"Yes Mr. Navarro, your left eye will return to normal very soon. Do you have any questions about what I've told you? Do you need to speak to—"

Then panic struck. "Fuck. The *bike*? What about riding my bike?"

He seemed amused by my outburst. "You'll need to undergo thorough checking and assessment *here* while you're in hospital. And then once you're discharged we'll need to report to the DMV but, provided your assessments show that you *won't* be a danger to yourself *or* other road users, there is a *possibility* that you can still ride. Is that your main concern?"

I exhaled in a loud huff. "Fuck yeah. Jeez." I glanced down to find my hand over my heart where it had begun to race at the thought of losing my bike and my sense of freedom.

A huge wave of relief washed over me and I closed my good eye briefly. If I could still *ride* I could cope. I could *deal*. I just *had* to make sure that I passed those tests. And I had to hope and pray that Chloe would still want me if I looked like some kind of Frankenstein creation.

———

Chloe

Being allowed to walk by myself again meant that I could go home. I had fought the urge to go visit Six before I left and it had taken everything for me to walk out without seeing him, but I had to do it. I couldn't intrude. It would've broken my heart all over again if I he had asked me to leave and I just couldn't go through that.

Colt and Dee picked me up from the hospital and Ellie was at my apartment when we got back. She had brought enough Chinese food to feed an army and so Colt and Dee joined us for the meal.

As we ate we made very light small talk but I could see Ellie making furtive glances at Colt. Something was on her mind.

Eventually, she plucked up the courage to speak. "Colt...I want to apologize again for what I said about your wife at the hospital. I felt terrible when I left and it's plagued me ever since. I really should learn to think before I speak."

Colt took a swig from his beer bottle and shook his head. "Like I said, Red, don't sweat it. You didn't know. And it's a long time ago that I lost her so it's not as raw as it once was."

"Well I'm *very* sorry for your loss."

He watched her from the opposite side of the table and something unreadable seemed to pass between them. For a moment I felt like Dee and I were intruding by being present and I made a mental note to interrogate Ellie later.

Once Colt and Dee had gone, and Ellie and I had washed the dishes, we sat on my couch—me with my soda thanks to the pain meds and Ellie drinking wine.

"Okay, Ellie, what the hell was *that* back there with you and Colt?"

She snorted derisively. "What? *What* back there? I don't know what you mean."

"You shared a moment."

She scrunched her brow. "Oh *please*. Seriously? Come on, Chloe. You know me better than that. I was simply offering my condolences. The guy's *wife* died." She took a long glug of her wine.

I shrugged. "If you say so." I couldn't keep the smirk from my face.

She placed her glass down and regarded me with a stern stare. "What? You think I'm *hot* for the guy? Is *that* it?"

I pursed my lips and shrugged again as I drank from my glass.

As Shakespeare might say, the lady carried on protesting a little too much. "Well I can *tell* you one hundred percent that *old* guys are *not* my thing. Okay? And old guy *bikers* are *so* far from being my thing that I... Urgh, I can't even believe you'd think that. Jeez. You *know* my opinion on *those* people. Shit, Chloe, do you *know* me at all?"

I know you better than you apparently know yourself, Ellie...

I smiled and topped up her glass.

———

Considering I had only suffered a broken wrist in the incident, I think forcing me to be pushed around in a chair for weeks had been overkill. Being home and having my independence back was great. The appointments with the psychologist who had been assessing me for PTSD had helped me come to terms with *some* of what had happened but I had a long way to go.

Colt had told me that he had shot Zak in the leg just as the sick bastard had fired at Six, but that he hadn't shot to kill as he wanted Zak to be held accountable for what he'd done. I was relieved that no one else had died and knowing that my assailant was in prison until his trial, but that there was a very good chance he would get life imprisonment gave me a little peace back. He was a danger to the public and bail had been set so high that *no one* would be able to afford it. Add to that the fact that Loki's Legion had completely disowned him and had severed all ties to him and his actions meant he had no chance of getting out any time soon, and if for some reason he *did* get out he'd have nowhere to go.

It still weighed on my heart that I hadn't been to see Six since I had was told they had woken him from his coma. It was maybe a cowardly move but I just couldn't face him. The possibility of rejection was too much to bear. The more I thought everything through, the more all the hopes I'd had of him wanting me back were fading. And somehow it was better to never know than to have him send me away for good.

My wrist was still in a cast but I was told it was healing well. And in the two days I had been home I had figured out ways to get myself dressed without too much hassle. Colt and Dee had been keeping a regular check on me and so had Ellie. Despite my unwillingness to go see Six, Dee was updating me with how he was doing.

I was relieved to know that he handled his loss of sight so well. But the guilt at him being blinded in one eye because of me was just too much to take. I had considered leaving Utah again and moving back home to my mom, but after what had happened I knew she'd cluck around me like a mother hen in her new found matronly way. It was strange how she had been pretty darn useless as a mom when I was growing up, but now that I was an adult she was making up for lost time.

No, I needed to stay in Rose Acres and complete my course and *then* I could maybe consider leaving.

CHAPTER FORTY-FIVE

Six

Getting used to only having sight in one eye was taking some doing. And it was driving me *crazy* most of the time. But having said that, I know that if I had to do it all over again I wouldn't hesitate. Not for *one* second. Am I the only one getting a sense of deja vu here?

Anyway, the fact that Chloe had been avoiding me just fucking *hurt*. Not because I felt she *owed* me. But simply because I *wanted* her to want to see me and she clearly didn't. Dee told me that it was guilt stopping her from visiting. But she had *nothing* to feel guilty for and that's why I guessed it was *more* than that. Maybe she couldn't stand the thought of seeing me, *period*. Maybe she was sticking to the opinion that we were somehow *wrong* for each other. Hell, even if we were just *friends* it would have to be enough. It'd be *something*. I just wanted to *see* her.

I decided that once I was out of hospital, I was going around to see what the hell was wrong. When the day arrived, I wasn't up to driving yet and so Dee, being the amazing person she is, dropped me just down the block from Chloe's building. I didn't want to look *completely* useless by getting dropped at the door.

I'm a guy.

We have pride you know.

Once I had walked the short distance, I stared up at her floor and listened to the blood rushing in my ears as panic set in. What if she wouldn't open the door? Shit, what would I do *then*? Maybe she'd be *horrified* when she saw me. Or at least when saw my head and my eye patch.

I'd had Dee shave the left side of my head to match the right. Come on, I didn't want to look all odd and shit. And then she had given me a pretty fucking *awesome* Celtic wolf tattoo on the side of my noggin—the side that didn't have the stitches, obviously. The ink was a kind of throwback to Chloe's insinuation that *I* was the big bad wolf, even though I was a fucking teddy bear where she was concerned.

I thought I looked pretty cool to be honest. I'd even go so far as to say *bad-ass* with my long floppy mohawk. But I guess I wasn't everyone's cup of Joe to begin with so my new look was bound to get a strong reaction. I just hoped it was a positive one.

Joking aside, the eye patch wasn't permanent. It was just a temporary measure while my body recovered from the surgery. And I could grow my hair back in to cover the ink and the bullet scar, if it freaked Chloe out too much. I'd be willing to do whatever it took. But right then I did look like I'd been in a war zone. And I suppose in a way I *had* when you consider I'd been shot in the head as I ran away from a crazy person.

Six Navarro, you are a grown-ass man so stop acting like a fuckin' pussy. Come on. You can do this. Just walk up to her floor...or...or go in the elevator, that could work too. But just fucking do it.

Mentally pulling up my big-boy panties, I made my way over to the entrance. The same old lady who had been coming out last time I was here, was half way through the door. I expected her to run in the opposite direction when she saw me, but instead the old dear smiled.

She reached out and patted my arm. "Oh hello, young man. You'll be happy to know Chloe is in today. I hope you're feeling better now." And with that she held the door for me to walk through and wandered off down the road singing some old tune about bluebirds that I didn't recognize.

Go figure.

They say don't judge a book by its cover and I guess *that* experience right there was proof that *some* folks don't.

I hit the call button on the elevator and waited. When the doors opened I was greeted by multiples of my horrific reflection, hindered further by the harsh lighting. *Jeez. Maybe I should turn right around and go on home.* Gritting my teeth with a determination that came from God knows where, I stepped in and hit the button for Chloe's floor.

Once up there, I stood outside her door trying to figure out what the hell I could say to her. And wondering *why* I hadn't taken Dee's advice and bought her flowers or something. But here I was empty handed, bruised, scarred and battered. Handsome devil I *wasn't*. But then again I never considered myself good looking anyways. I absently wondered who had repaired the door properly for her, but guessed that Colt or Dee would have had something to do with it.

The door opened and my breath caught. Chloe stood there before me. Grey yoga pants and a baggy black sweater that slipped off one shoulder. Hair all bunched messily on top of her head and not a scrap of make-up on her beautiful face. One wrist still in a cast. And fuck me if she wasn't the best thing I'd ever seen in my sorry-ass life.

"Were you ever going to knock?" Her voice was small and her eyes glistened.

I swallowed hard unable to take my eyes off her. Unable to speak. My heart skipped and thudded at my ribs and my fingers twitched desperate to touch her.

"Are you going to speak, Six?" she asked, hugging her arms around her body and tilting her head to one side.

I exhaled a shaking, uneven breath. "I... I don't know what to say to you, Chloe. Except... I'm sorry. So goddamn sorry, *again*. For *every*thing. I...I shouldn't have come." I turned and began to walk away.

Her voice stopped me in my tracks. "Don't you *dare* fucking leave. Don't you *dare*. Not now. If you walk away from me now after all this bullshit, that's *it*, Six. We're *done...*" I closed my eyes and clenched my jaw tight. And after a moments silence she whispered, "And God knows I don't want us to be done." A sob left her chest and was my undoing.

I turned and in two steps I had her in my arms.

I crushed my mouth to hers with a ferocity that expressed my deepest emotions. Things I had no words for came out in a melding of tongues and breath. She clung to me and jumped wrapping her legs around my waist and I staggered, pushing her into the wall just inside her apartment.

I pulled away and locked my gaze on her eyes trying to read her thoughts. Trying to assess if I was about to add to her trauma. "Did he...did he *hurt* you? I mean did he...did he..." I swallowed the knot of anger down but the words just wouldn't come.

Thankfully she understood and smoothed her fingers across the shaved areas of my scalp. A small smile appeared. "Did he *rape* me? No...no he didn't. I head butted him and broke his nose before he had a chance." A wicked grin spread across her face and my respect for her increased tenfold in that moment. The *strength* of this woman. God she was incredible.

I tugged on the band that held her hair and cascades of chocolate brown waves fell around her shoulders, skimming the delicate pale skin there. Unable to get quite close enough I kicked the door behind me and slammed it shut before carrying her to the space between the coffee table and couch. The place where she had danced for me and *only* me. Dropping to my knees I maneuvered to sit against the couch and her legs instinctively wrapped around my body, her hands tugged at my hair hard enough for it to hurt where I was scarred. But I didn't care. All I cared about was being with her. Kissing her. Holding her.

My cock strained at the denim of my jeans and she rubbed herself along the thick ridge it had created. She felt amazing and I needed more of her. Releasing her for a moment, I grabbed the hem of her sweater and dragged it from her body until her bare breasts were exposed. I grabbed one roughly and bent to suck the erect peak into my mouth.

Her head rolled back and she moaned. "I need you, Six, *please*. It's been too long and I need you inside of me."

I lifted her to her feet and dragged her yoga pants down her body along with her panties and flung them aside. Her pussy was there right before my face and I needed to taste her again. Grabbing her ass, I pulled her forward and delved into her warm, wet arousal with my probing tongue. That smell, that taste.

So intoxicating.

So familiar.

So damn *good*.

"God I've missed this. I've missed *you*. I thought I'd lost you," I mumbled between long strokes up the center of her glistening flesh. She gripped at my hair and widened her stance, pulling me deeper still.

"Please, Six, *please*," she begged again and my cock began to throb.

Lifting her once more I scrambled to stand and cupped her face. I thrust my tongue into her mouth. "You taste so good, baby, so fucking good."

She pulled herself away and dropped to her knees before me. I gazed down at her where she knelt and stroked her hair as she began to unfasten my boots. One by one she removed them along with my socks and I watched in awe and she worked on my jeans zipper and button. Slipping her hands inside the waist band she slid my pants and boxers down and my cock sprang free. I yanked the T-shirt from my torso and once my clothes were discarded she lightly scratched her nails up my thighs and placed teasing kisses along my skin.

Until she reached my cock.

In one deep, wet stroke she took me in and my head rolled

back in ecstasy. Breath hitching, I reached down to feel my cock slipping in and out of her gorgeous hot mouth. Sensations of pleasure radiated from where she sucked and licked and traveled right on up to my nipple piercing. Not wanting it to end I had to bite my lip to stop from coming too soon.

CHAPTER FORTY-SIX

CHLOE

He was here.

He actually *came* to me.

My stomach had tightened as I watched him through the spy hole on my door and tears had welled in my eyes at the sight of him.

So damned beautiful even now.

His long shaggy hair was shaved at both sides but the top remained long, kind of like a mohawk but his own individual version and a tattoo of a wolf had been inked onto his scalp at the uninjured side. I had wondered if the wolf had anything to do with the conversation I vividly remembered we'd had. I hoped so. He was *my* wolf. My protector. A severe bark and bite but oh so loyal.

He had stood there staring at my door and it appeared as though he was caught between knocking and leaving. *Please don't leave.* He had a black patch covering his injured eye and fastened around his head and I had desperately wanted to kiss him there. To hold him and thank him for rescuing me from the psychopath who'd been hell bent on keeping me as some kind of pet.

After I'd watched him for a few minutes I could stand it no longer. I flung open the door.

When I spoke he lifted his face and stared at me but didn't utter a word. I had tracked a range of emotions as they'd fleetingly rested on his scarred features. Then he'd said the words I didn't want to hear. He'd said he should never have come.

No, no! My heart was breaking all over again. He couldn't leave. If he had I knew that would be the end. This was our opportunity to reconnect. To sort things out. To figure out where we stood. And I told him so.

Before I had known what was happening I was in his arms, right where I belonged.

———

I knelt before him, taking his rigid length of silky smooth skin into my desperate mouth. I gripped the tightened muscles of his ass beneath my fingers as I sucked and kissed every divine inch of him. This was the first time I'd taken him into my mouth and it was just as good as I imagined. The feel of him flinching against my tongue as he fought for control was one of immense power, knowing I could be the undoing of him if I so desired.

But I needed him inside of me. I needed to feel him deep in my core until he was a *part* of me. My clit throbbed at the thought and I stood, pushing on his chest until he dropped back on to the couch.

He gazed up at me through hooded, lust filled eyes and I could see how much he needed that connection too. He reached for me and I obliged.

I clambered onto his lap and straddled his thick, muscular thighs, watching as his huge hands slipped up my body to tease my nipples. Sensations of sheer pleasure traveled like electricity straight to my clit and I moaned, allowing my eyes to drift closed briefly. He sucked a nipple into his mouth and swirled his tongue around it before biting down and causing a spike of need in my core.

"Again," I told him breathlessly. He moved to the other nipple and repeated the swirling and biting. I convulsed with the assault of pleasure and pain and slipped my hand down to rub at the junction of my thighs, needing the friction. Desperate for release.

He grabbed my wrist and I snapped my attention on his face. "Uh-uh. No, sweetheart. Only *I* get to make you come. I want you to be mine now, baby, mind body and soul. If you'll have me I want to be yours too."

In response to his question I gripped his cock and teased my entrance with the tip, watching his mouth fall open slightly and hearing his breathing rate increase. With one slow, purposeful move I rested my hands on his shoulders and sunk my body down his length as a deep groan of pleasure erupted from his chest. Scratching my nails down his ink and flicking his nipple piercing brought more moans, the sound of which I craved, and his gaze was locked on me. Unwavering and determined.

It was hard to keep my eyes open, but I wanted to watch

him watching *me* as I slowly rose and sunk back down taking *all* of him into my pussy. He tugged at my nipples and reached up to slide his hand into my hair pulling me down so that our foreheads were touching.

"*Will* you be mine?" The intensity of his gaze penetrated my soul and my heart simultaneously as he continued with sincerity, "No more pretending we're not good for each other. No more staying away, Chloe. I *need* to know that you're mine now."

He gripped my hips and increased the pace, thrusting deep into my wet core as I began to tighten around him. His hand slipped between us and his rough, thick fingers connected with my clit where he circled me hard and fast.

"Answer me, baby. I need to know."

I threw my head back, losing all sense of control. "Oh yes! God *yes,* I'm yours. Always have been. Fuck me hard, Six, *make* me yours."

His thrusts increased and my breasts bounced with the force. I reached for my nipples and squeezed hard as my whole body spasmed around his and an intense, mind melting orgasm ripped through my body.

And the words I had been feeling for so long left my lips. "I love you, Six, I love you so much."

"Oh baby, I love you too," he growled as he came with one last powerful surge.

———

We laid there, cuddled on the couch as he drew lazy circles on my skin with a handsome smile on his face.

"What are you smiling about?" I asked, intrigued as I watched him lost in his thoughts.

"I've decided you're not *exactly* a wolf."

I scrunched my brow. "Huh? I don't understand."

His fingers trailed down my neck and between my breasts before he leaned down and kissed me. "Remember I told you that I thought you were like a wolf... Well... You're more of a kind of wolf-butterfly hybrid."

I couldn't help giggling. "Oh really? Can't imagine what one of *those* would look like. But anyway, how do you figure that?"

"You're graceful, like a butterfly. Even in the throes of orgasm there's this *elegance* about you. You're still a dancer in everything you do. But then... there's this fierce side to you still. The way you stand up for yourself. Your independence. Your *bite*." As he said that he bit down on my nipple once again and I gasped.

"*My* bite? What about *your* bite?" I replied in a breathless, needy whisper as I felt my pussy begin to tingle again.

"Oh baby you *know* you *love* my bite." He grinned and my heart melted.

He had a very good point.

I closed my eyes as his fingers began to trail down my body and I felt his erection thicken at my thigh.

I breathed, "So I'm a wolf-butterfly hybrid... I think I kind of like that. And I like your new ink too. It makes you look dangerous."

"Oh honey you don't know the half of it." He told me as he rolled me onto my front and lifted my hips so that my ass rubbed against his cock.

Sliding his finger down he found me wet and ready again.

Six

As I drove my cock deep into Chloe once more squeezing her gorgeous round ass the pleasure intensified knowing that this was no longer *just* fucking. I reached around and teased her clit and she tightened around me. Turning her face she watched me over her shoulder as I slid my length in deep and out...in deep and out. She was so beautiful when her eyes darkened with desire and it was a view I would never, *ever* tire of.

Reaching down I lifted her onto my lap so her back was pressed against my chest and my cock sank deeper. I groaned and she gasped, clenching her pussy around me. I could reach to caress her tits and her clit but more importantly I could kiss her deeply too.

"All the fucking time we wasted, Chloe dancer. Let's *never* do that again."

"Never," she gasped in agreement as I thrust into her. Connecting in the most intense and intimate way. Pleasing her. Marking her as mine.

My little wolf-butterfly.

EPILOGUE

Six

I wasn't sure who was the most anxious. Chloe or me. She was pale and her palms were sweaty as I gripped her hands and tried my best to allay her fears and calm her.

Leaning toward her I gently kissed her forehead. "Just breathe, baby. It'll all be fine."

Her eyes widened. "*Really?* That's all you've got? *Jeez!*" she snapped and I had to stifle a laugh.

Chewing the inside of my cheek I continued with my encouragement. "Just squeeze my fingers whenever you need to okay?"

"Oh don't you *worry*. I sure as hell *will*. And just remember when I *break* them that it's because of *you* that I'm here in the *first* damn place."

A bead of sweat traveled down her cheek and I leaned in again and licked it off her face.

"Eeeeuw! Six, you're *so* gross." The smile on her face belied her words and I rested my forehead on hers.

I ran my nose along her cheek as she gasped at the pain and I whispered, "Just breathe baby. Okay? In through your nose...out through your mouth."

"I *know* how to fucking *breathe*!" she shouted at me and once more I pulled my lips in to stop from laughing.

While I hated seeing her in pain I knew that it would all be worth it.

Her face scrunched as the next wave of pain hit and she gripped my fingers with such a force that I began to believe her threats about breaking them.

I was so proud of her.

After what felt like an eternity, Dee's head popped up. "All done, sweetie." She placed the gun down and sat back to admire her work. "Oh *wow*. I know I may sound conceited...and I'm a tad biased but wow. That really *is* beautiful."

Chloe sat up straight and breathed a sigh of relief. "Thank goodness that's *over* with. How the *hell* can you guys go through that over and over?"

I told her with a chuckle, "Hey, believe me, it gets addictive, baby."

She huffed. "Yeah? Well I may be the exception *that* rule."

Delilah laughed too. "We'll see, CD. We'll *see*."

"Come on, I'm dying to see it." I stood and held my hand out to Chloe to help her up.

She turned and I gasped. A lump of emotion lodged in my throat and I stared at the first ink to beautifully mark Chloe dancers alabaster shoulder.

A wolf-butterfly hybrid.
Just for me.

The End

ACKNOWLEDGMENTS

Thank you to every single reader/blog/page who continues to support me and read my stories.

A massive thank you to Tammy at The Graphics Shed for my stunning covers. Regardless of what I *think* I want you always seem to know what I *actually* want! Even before I do! You're an absolute gem.

And last but by no means least thank you to my wonderful family and friends for putting up with my incessant talk of books and publishing! I have no idea what I would do without you... probably talk to myself instead which wouldn't be half as much fun!

ABOUT THE AUTHOR

Lisa is happily married to her best friend and together she and her husband have one child and two daft dogs. Writing has always been her passion although it has only been in recent years that she has taken the plunge to try her hand at novels. Back in 2014 her debut *Bridge Over the Atlantic* (later republished by *Aria Fiction* as *A Seaside Escape*) was published by an American company and was shortlisted in the Romantic Novelists Association RONAs for their prestigious Romance Novel of the Year.

Lisa is now the proud author of both self-published *and* traditionally published titles since being signed on a four book deal to *Aria Fiction*, an imprint of award winning *Head of Zeus Publishing*.

Originally from Yorkshire, Lisa now lives in bonny Scotland, a place that features in many of her titles. And when she's not writing, reading *or* editing she can be found being taken for a walk by her energetic dogs.

ALSO BY LISA J HOBMAN

(Please note these titles are not erotic novels)

A Seaside Escape

A Year of Finding Happiness

Christmas Presence

(*A Seaside Escape Christmas Novella*)

What Becomes of the Broken Hearted

Reasons to Leave

Reasons to Stay

Duplicity

Through the Glass

The Girl Before Eve

Last Christmas

(*A TGBE Christmas Novella*)

The Worst of Me

In His Place

And coming soon:

Zara Bailey's Summer of New Beginnings

Lightning Source UK Ltd.
Milton Keynes UK
UKHW041200060219
336842UK00001B/70/P